Happily Never After

ALSO BY EMMA ROBINSON

The Undercover Mother

EMMA
ROBINSON

Happily Never After

bookouture

Published by Bookouture in 2018

An imprint of StoryFire Ltd.

Carmelite House
50 Victoria Embankment
London EC4Y 0DZ

www.bookouture.com

ISBN: 978-1-78681-481-4
eBook ISBN: 978-1-78681-480-7

For Dan
Who fixes everything

CHAPTER ONE

Everyone knows that a single woman approaching forty needs a husband.

At least, that's what Rory's mother thought.

Sheila hadn't let up since they'd arrived at the house. 'It's time you had someone, Aurora. Belle is growing up and…'

'*Christabel*, Mother. *She* was named after a suffragette, not a Disney princess. *That* joy was all mine.' Rory caught her daughter's glare at the use of her full name. *Get used to it kid; I've had thirty-eight years of that.*

'We named you after the sunrise on the day you were born, *not* Sleeping Beauty, as you well know.' Sheila wasn't about to be distracted. 'Nevertheless, Christabel will be going off to university in two years' time. Why do you need a house this big? And this…' – she wrinkled her nose – 'dusty?'

The estate agent details had alluded to the fact that the place would need some 'cosmetic work' and would suit someone wanting to 'take on a project.' But when Rory had walked in the week before, something about the light through the huge sash windows, the high ceilings and the fact that all this could belong to her and her alone, had dazzled her into making an impulsive offer. Now, seeing it through her mother's eyes, she realised the full extent of the wreck she was standing in. The walls were flaking, there were missing floor tiles and the radiators looked as if they hadn't had heat through them this side of the 1970s. They'd walked around the upstairs accompanied by a full range of creaks and groans from the floorboards, supported ably by her mother's full range of tuts and sighs.

Rory was defiant, though. It was close to school, within her budget and, due to it having been empty for the last year, they would be able to move in pretty quickly. They might even be in and have started renovations before the new academic year swallowed up all her spare time. But was she mad to take on this much work?

Sheila peered around as she walked further into the sitting room. Rory was quite enjoying watching her fastidious mother try to move around without touching anything. Shame she couldn't levitate really.

Sheila folded her arms. 'Maybe it was this ol' house that Shaky Steve was singing about all those years ago.'

Belle screwed up her face. 'Shaky who, Gran?'

Rory sighed. 'It was Shakin' Stevens, Mum. And *Belle*' – her daughter nodded approval at her preferred name – 'he was a singer a long time before you were born.' Rory strode ahead and turned slowly. There was something almost literary about the proportions of the place. The walls were patchy and calamine pink, but the cornice was beautiful – apart from the fact it was painted turquoise. 'It's got nice high ceilings. I've always wanted to live in a house with high ceilings. Makes me feel like Jane Austen or Charlotte Brontë.'

Sheila squinted at the ceiling as if it might fall on her. 'Can you actually *call* that a ceiling, Aurora? The parts you can see beyond the cobwebs, I mean.'

'Stop making that face, Mother. And stop calling me Aurora.' Rory pulled at a corner of the paisley patterned carpet, bringing with it a cloud of dust. Underneath, the floorboards looked in a decent condition. The more Sheila was critical of the place, the more Rory was glad she'd made her offer on it. It was a familiar pattern.

Sheila sneezed and rummaged in her bag for a tissue, which she placed over her nose and mouth. 'I'll stop calling you Aurora when you stop calling me Mother.'

Belle stepped in. 'I think it's got real potential, Mum – like those places on the home programmes. Let's go and look at the kitchen.'

Rory put an arm around her daughter's shoulders as they walked. It still came as a surprise to her that they were almost the same height. With Belle's long, dark ponytail and fresh face it was easy to pretend that she was still a little girl. Thank goodness Rory had been spared the rumoured teenage angst and screaming matches. Belle was sixteen now. They were home and dry.

The kitchen was a bit of a shock, even to Rory, who'd seen it before. It was large – with plenty of room for the island Rory coveted – but the cupboard doors were more grime than pine, and two doors were missing completely. There was a whiff of something greasy and the floor was sticky. Rory didn't want to know why.

She took her arm from around Belle's shoulders and thrust her fingers into her own short, dark hair, massaging her scalp. She had to be sensible. It wasn't only her and her bloody-minded will of iron who would be living in this mess. Belle had always been more dolls and dresses than hammers and hard hats. Rory closed her eyes. *Think with your head. Your heart can't be trusted. Life is not a fairy tale.*

Rory heard the squelch of Sheila's shoes enter the room. She opened one eye and looked at her mother. Sheila looked at Belle. Belle looked at Rory.

Then they all started to laugh.

'Well, if this room doesn't put you off, nothing will. I give in.' Sheila wiped her eyes. 'I know better than to try and change your mind.'

Rory kissed her mother's cheek. 'I can still retract my offer if I do have second thoughts. Let's go back into the sitting room; this smell is making me queasy.'

Belle went first and sat on the deep windowsill in the big bay window. 'We could put a window seat in here, Mum. Then we could read our books and eat apples like Jo in *Little Women*.'

Her daughter knew exactly how to play her.

Rory joined her at the window. 'Do you think you could cope with all the chaos whilst we are doing it up, though? We're going to have to do most of the work ourselves, including all the boring prep work. Stripping wallpaper, ripping up the carpets, cleaning everywhere. It'll take a while.'

Sheila turned an incredulous gaze on Rory. 'Surely you wouldn't move in while it is like this?' She swept an arm around the room: the flaking plaster, the tatty carpet and the door which hadn't seen a paintbrush since 'Shaky Steve' was in the charts.

'We'd have to, Mum. We can't afford to rent somewhere else and pay the mortgage on this place. It'll be okay.' Rory had no idea yet whether it would be anywhere near okay. But there was a roof, walls, a floor. How bad could it be?

'There must be *somewhere* you can stay? I have a spare room in my new flat at Seymour House, but I'm not sure there's room for both of you.'

Belle twisted her ponytail through her fingers. 'Dad did say we could stay with him a bit longer.'

Sheila nodded and readjusted her jacket. 'As much as Scott is not my favourite person right now, that might be a good option. You can stay where you are until this place is habitable.'

'Absolutely not.' Rory was not going to be swayed on this. 'Scott and Megan are about to have a new baby; there's no way we can stay there. It's bad enough at the moment, with him moving his stuff back in and all the baby things too.' Watching the two of them *ooh* and *aah* over their baby bath had given her murderous ideas. Scott had *not* been so interested when Rory had been scraping together the necessary supplies for Belle sixteen years ago. The New Man performance was nauseating.

'I can't believe he is just chucking you out like that, after all these years.' Sheila, almost forgetting where she was, leaned against the wall and then quickly righted herself. She crossed her arms. 'Particularly Belle. His own daughter.'

'He didn't chuck us out, Granny. Did he, Mum?' Belle was always quick to defend her dad. To be fair, when they'd broken up – nearly fifteen years ago – he'd let Rory and Belle carry on living in his house and he'd been the one to move out. Scott had been a crap husband, but he wasn't a bad dad.

'No, he didn't. They can't live in that poky little flat with a baby, Mum. The house was always his. He has every right to want to live in it and, as Belle says, he told us we could stay as long as we wanted. I just don't want to.' She rubbed Belle's back. 'But you can, Belle. He's your dad.'

Belle shook her head then put it on Rory's shoulder. 'No Mum, I want to be with you.'

Sheila sighed and patted her hair. 'You are as stubborn as your mother, Christabel. You've both got Frank's blood in your veins.'

This from the woman who had moaned that her house was far too large for one person but had taken twelve months of persuading to even look at a retirement apartment.

'Of course. *Dad* was the stubborn one, wasn't he, Mum?'

Sheila poked a damp spot on the wall with her finger then pulled her hand back as if it had bitten her. 'I just wish I hadn't sold the house already; you could have stayed there. There was plenty of room. We could have all lived there together.'

Live together? Rory loved her mother dearly, but Sheila was all coasters and regular mealtimes whereas Rory was more toast-on-the-run.

'It was too far from work and Belle's college anyway. Thanks for the offer, but we need to have our own home at long last.' Rory looked around and held out her arms. 'I'm beginning to get a feel for this place.' She smiled at Belle. 'I think we can do this, you know.'

'Of course we can. We can do anything we set our minds to. What is it you say, Granny? Nothing a bit of elbow grease won't fix.' Belle kissed Sheila on the cheek.

'Well, now you're using my own words against me I don't have a chance, do I? Next you'll be putting on one of your Disney CDs and encouraging the local wildlife to come in and help you make it spick and span.' Sheila turned to Rory. 'I don't suppose there's any point in me trying to persuade you out of this? Your dad was a builder. I know how much work is going to be involved in something like this.'

Rory shook her head. 'No, Mum. There's no point. I want a house rather than a flat, and we can't afford one that's already done up round here on my wages. This is our only option.'

'In that case, let me give you some…' Sheila trailed off at the look on Rory's face.

Rory squeezed her hand. 'Mum, I'm grateful. But I don't need your money. You should enjoy the profit from the house. Spend it on gin and Italian waiters.'

Sheila made a harrumphing sound. 'I might just do that and bring one home for you, my girl.'

Rory shook her head. 'I won't have time for *amore*; I'll be too busy painting walls and laying carpet.'

Sheila was back on her favourite subject. 'You will need to make time for it sometime, Aurora. You're not getting any younger, you know.'

Rory rolled her eyes. 'I know. I know. But if we're back to *Aurora*, it must be time to go.'

As she shuffled the two of them out of the front door, Rory looked back up the hallway and through the door to the sitting room. This place wasn't so much in need of a facelift as full reconstructive surgery. She knew how it felt. There was an awful lot of work to be done and, apart from following her dad around when she was young, she didn't actually have any DIY experience. Would she be taking on more than she could manage?

Sheila stood on the front step and it crumbled beneath her feet. 'Are you really sure about this, Aurora?'

There was a huge oval mirror hanging near the front door. Rory blew the dust from its centre and looked through the scattering motes at her reflection. With a bit of polish, it could be made to look beautiful again.

She'd make a start with that.

CHAPTER TWO

There might have been a long list of lesson planning and photocopying waiting for Rory in her classroom, but at least the place was clean, tidy and the roof wasn't in danger of falling in. 'We'll have you in in no time!' the estate agent had promised when Rory's offer had been accepted back in June. After a lot of gratuitous and expensive toing and froing between solicitors, they had eventually got the keys two weeks ago. She and Belle had almost killed themselves to make a few rooms habitable, and now it was September and she was back at work.

Ten minutes until morning briefing. Just enough time to make a quick coffee: nectar of the teaching profession. Rory took just a splash of milk from each of the two cartons which looked fullest. Raiding the fridge at work was like sneaking into your parents' drinks cabinet as a teenager: you had to make it look as if nothing had been touched.

'Morning, comrade!' Susie strode into the kitchen area of the staffroom. Blonde curls, big boobs and a beaming grin made her the exact opposite of the computer geek stereotype; no wonder so many boys opted to take Information Technology. 'Milk snaffling again?'

Rory held up her hands. 'My need is great this morning. How was your weekend?'

Susie slumped back against the counter with a dramatic groan. 'Don't ask. I had a date from hell. I'll tell you later when I can bear to talk about it. You seriously must start coming out with me; I need help to stop attracting all these weirdos.'

'I'll let you know when I'm free to perform weirdo-repelling duties. I've mastered the art. Have you seen the new deputy headteacher yet?'

Susie stood up straight and leaned in, lowering her voice. 'He's definitely no weirdo from what I've seen. I saw him go into the head's office this morning, all sharp suit and expensive aftershave. Looks about thirty-five, no wedding ring. He's going to cause a bit of a flutter, I think.'

Rory wasn't about to get excited. If you were male, below forty-five and had a pulse, Susie would give you a chance. Rory was a little choosier. Too choosy, her mother would say. 'As long as he doesn't flutter near me. I could do without it, quite frankly.'

Susie raised a perfectly shaped eyebrow. 'Apart from me, you're the one person I know who is most in need of a flutter or two. How's the house going?'

'It's not. Apparently, the whole place has to be rewired so that Belle and I don't electrocute ourselves by turning on a light switch. I'm beginning to think that buying an old wreck wasn't such a great idea.'

'Really? You think?' Susie had told Rory she was crazy to buy the house, although her main objection had been that it would give Rory less money to go out with her. 'Come on. Let's find somewhere to park; the delegation has arrived.'

First day back, everyone had turned up for briefing and the staffroom was packed. Rory and Susie looked for a spare seat amongst the threadbare collection around the coffee table, which was strewn with newspapers, magazines and old textbooks. There was also the odd confiscated item which hadn't made it down to the school office. They'd just managed to squeeze on a seat together – one cheek each – when everyone hushed for the first morning briefing of the new term.

The head gave his usual 'welcome back' speech and updated the staff on such scintillating information as the new floor in the

Sports Hall. Derek Brown – or DB, as he was known to the staff and pupils – was a kind man, but he was no public orator. Then he turned to indicate the man standing on his right. 'And I'd like to introduce our new deputy head, Nathan Finch. Nathan has a wealth of experience in using data for pupil progress, so we are hoping that he will help us to be ready, should we get our *visitors* in the next few months.' He made pretend speech marks in the air with his fingers; using the words 'OFSTED' or 'inspector' in school was akin to saying '*Macbeth*' in a theatre. 'Would you like to say anything, Nathan?'

It wasn't what Nathan Finch said that irritated Rory – that was just the usual waffle about looking forward to being part of the team, and that his door was always open. No, it was the way he said it. Touching his cufflinks like James Bond, making eye contact with each and every person in the room, smiling just enough, but not too much. It didn't help that DB was beside him, beaming like he'd just signed Ronaldo to the school football team. Rory could smell change and she didn't like it.

It got worse when he rolled out his agenda for the day. Training? On the first day back? First day of term was for sorting out class lists and books and trying to remember which kids you could trust to sit at the back and which ones you needed right under your nose. As soon as the meeting was over, Rory grabbed her things and made a run for her classroom before DB could catch her and introduce her to Mr Finch. Susie hung behind, clearly hoping for the opposite. She was insatiable.

Pushing open the door to her classroom with her elbow, whilst trying to balance her mug and the pile of papers she had excavated from her pigeon hole, Rory didn't notice Charlie Lewis until she was inside. It was surprising how small a fourteen-year-old boy could make himself, sitting in the back corner so that he couldn't be seen from the corridor. When he saw Rory, he jumped up.

'Miss, Miss. I know I'm not supposed to be in the building yet, but I couldn't find my tie this morning and Brownie is going to kill me if he sees me without it again. Do you have one I could borrow?' He took a breath and held his hands together in prayer. 'Please?'

Rory dropped her papers onto her desk. 'It's Mr Brown to you. However, I'm sure I can find you a tie in my infinite drawer of resources. I wouldn't want your death on my conscience at 8.30 in the morning.' She rummaged around and pulled one out. 'How's your mum?'

'Thanks, Miss! You're a life saver!' Charlie struggled to loop the tie around a clean but crumpled shirt. He seemed to have grown upwards in the holidays without filling out and looked like a string bean with spiky blonde hair. 'Mum's having a flare. She can't go to work and she's really tired all the time. She was sleeping when I left and I didn't want to wake her up to ask about the tie.'

Rory perched on her desk and resisted the urge to help him with the knot. 'I understand. It must be pretty tough for you both at the moment. You know that my offer of help is open if you need anything, don't you? Are you both eating? Is your mum able to cook at the moment?'

'Bits and pieces. Mum can't have much because her Crohn's is so bad. I made dinner for myself last night. Egg and beans on toast.' He practically puffed up his chest.

'Sounds delicious. The Food Tech department would be proud. Now go and run around the playground, or whatever it is you boys do before school starts. I'll catch up with you in our lesson. We're starting with creative writing and I'm looking forward to seeing what my favourite writer is going to produce.' When she had asked for Charlie's class on her timetable again this year, there'd been no argument from the head of the English department. Especially now they were starting their final exam texts: with them being the lowest-scoring class in the year group, they would need English lessons five times a week, meaning Rory would see them more than almost any other class she taught. They were an acquired taste, though.

Charlie grinned and made for the door. 'Okay. I'll see you later. Thanks again for the tie, Miss.'

Rory sat down at her desk and turned on the computer. Something about Charlie made her want to scoop him up and take him home. What would happen if his mum was admitted to hospital again? Or worse. A fourteen-year-old boy needed his mum. Even a thirty-eight-year-old woman needed her mum. Not that she'd ever admit it to Sheila.

On the screen was the usual deluge of emails about PE kits lost from last year and updates on Fire Procedures and Child Protection. Halfway down the list was one from Belle: a picture of Colin Firth with the message: *To cheer you up!* Rory smiled. Her daughter knew her well, but it might take more than a picture of Mark Darcy in a tuxedo to stop the sinking feeling that she'd bitten off more than she could chew this time.

*

During staff training sessions, the teachers were worse than the kids.

Susie flopped down next to Rory. Penny, the final member of their trio, passed her a cup of coffee; she could always be relied upon to look after them both. Tall and gangly, with dark straight hair, the gentle Religious Education teacher had been adopted by Rory and Susie after she'd discovered her fiancé of three years carrying on with the dog groomer. He'd got custody of the Lhasa Apso. 'What is this session about?'

'Marking, ironically.' Rory sipped the drink Penny had made for her. 'Although how I'm supposed to make inroads into the Everest of summer homework assignments currently on my desk when I'm sitting here listening to someone talk about it, is anyone's guess.' The electrician had been coming tonight with a quote on the rewire. If the house blew up, she was blaming Nathan Finch.

Susie wriggled in her seat. 'These chairs are so uncomfortable; I'm spilling out the sides. I wish the caretaker would put them a little further apart. Don't get me wrong, I like you. But I don't want to rub my hip against yours.'

'Aren't we supposed to be starting now?' Penny's question was answered when Nathan Finch sauntered up to the front of the hall. The room went quiet almost immediately.

'Good afternoon, colleagues.' He paused and smiled at them all. 'We've updated the school marking policy and wanted to share with you some good practise we have seen in other schools, which we are planning on implementing here.' Without turning around, he clicked the remote in his hand and his PowerPoint presentation came alive behind him.

'How did he do that?' breathed Penny, as if he'd just sawn a woman in half. She was only a few years older than Rory and Susie, but she'd started teaching in the age of overhead projectors.

'I use PowerPoint, too,' Rory shrugged.

'But he didn't even look.' Penny clamped her mouth shut and sat up straight as Mr Finch looked directly at her. Rory, on the other hand, slumped lower in her chair. Was this how the kids felt?

'Firstly, we know that marking is a very time-consuming part of your job. You'll be pleased to know that we don't want you to mark more...'

'Well, that's not physically possible,' mumbled Susie.

'...we just want you to mark *smarter*.'

'I knew there would be a catch,' Rory whispered back.

The PowerPoint changed again. Penny looked at him like he'd performed another miracle. Rory shook her head. The slide read: USE OF TRAFFIC LIGHT COLOURS IN EFFECTIVE FEEDBACK. Rory groaned inside and let her head fall back onto the seat. This was going to be a long hour.

Susie sent her a note scribbled onto the back of an agenda: *Back to yours after for wine?*

It would have to be wine. After rescheduling the electrician, Rory wouldn't dare to boil a kettle.

CHAPTER THREE

When you buy something new, particularly something that costs thousands and thousands of pounds, you feel the need to justify the money you've spent. Therefore, it was possible that Rory had romanticised the house somewhat when she'd described it to Susie and Penny. Judging by the look on Susie's face when they walked in through the door, she had completely misrepresented it.

Penny was kinder. 'It's a great size, Rory.'

'Yeah,' agreed Susie. 'But where's the butler with the bolts through his neck?'

'Very funny.' Rory opened the door to the sitting room. 'You should have seen it two weeks ago. It's taken thirty gallons of Cif and Flash to get it looking like this.'

The sitting room and kitchen were clean, at least. Rory had taken the furniture from Scott's house – apparently Megan wanted 'all new' – so there was a sofa and a couple of chairs for them to sit on. Before they got comfortable, Rory took them on a quick tour of the house, ending up in the kitchen.

'Well, I think it's got a lot of character.' Penny patted Rory on the arm. 'If anyone can do this, you can.'

'I think you're bonkers.' Susie took two red wine bottles from a bag and stood them on the kitchen counter. 'But I agree with Pen. It will look fabulous once the work is done. When do your builders start?'

Rory ducked behind the kitchen counter and hunted through unpacked boxes for wine glasses. 'I haven't got a builder.'

'What?' Susie and Penny asked in unison.

The glasses weren't in that box. Rory pushed it aside for another. 'I'm going to do it myself.'

When Susie started to laugh, Rory stood up. 'What?'

'Even for you, Little Miss Independent, that has got to be a joke.'

Penny frowned and pulled her cardigan closed. 'She's right, Rory. You need to get professional help with this.'

Rory stuck her chin out. 'I've got an electrician and I'll get a plumber. But I can do the rest of it. I'll do some classes. Read some books.'

Susie nodded exaggeratedly, her blonde curls bouncing. 'Sure, sure. Because you do have a lot of spare time on your hands. It's not like you spend all your evenings marking and planning lessons or anything.'

Susie had a fair point. But doing up the house would drag Rory away from her desk. Teaching prep could take over your life if you let it.

'I just need to organise my time. Anyway, with Nathan Finch's new "mark smart" scheme, I'm going to free up *hours* of my day.' She rolled her eyes.

Susie groaned. 'Don't remind me. My head hurts. What happened to easing us back into work gently? Did you even understand half of it?'

Penny used her fingers to help her remember the order: 'The pupils write in blue pen. We mark in red pen. We highlight something good in yellow pen and something they need to improve in pink pen. They then go back and make changes in green pen. Have I got it right?'

Rory shook her head. 'You lost me at the word *pen*. I'm lucky if my lot have got a pencil they've lifted from the pot in IKEA.'

'What about the "RAG rating"?' asked Susie. 'Aren't we supposed to tell them to use red, amber and green to show how well they have understood the lesson?'

'Oh Susie, you're so last term.' Rory was back under the kitchen unit. 'Next you'll be telling me you've gone back to last academic year and are using two stars for something good and a wish for something they can improve.'

'I liked two stars and a wish.' Penny sounded mournful. 'It was so hopeful.'

'Speaking of hopeful, what do you think of the new deputy?' Susie started to unscrew the red wine they'd picked up on the way here. 'He's pretty good-looking and clearly not married.'

Rory finally found the wine glasses she'd been looking for and pushed them towards Susie so that she could pour the wine. 'I'm not keen, to be honest.'

Susie sighed. 'You're not keen on anyone, Rory. For us normal women, he looks quite a catch. They're probably paying him a fair whack, too.'

'I'm with Rory, I'm afraid.' Penny held up a hand to stop Susie from filling her glass to the top. 'He looked quite arrogant to me.'

Susie threw her arms into the air. 'What am I going to do with you two? We don't have forever, you know. I have very little left of my thirties and, post-forty, women have more chance of being abducted by aliens than getting married.'

'Is that true?' Penny's eyes were wide. She was already past forty.

'Of course it's not bloody true, but it might as well be. In the last year, I've had three dates. Three.' Susie held three fingers up for emphasis. 'One spoke in sentences of three words or less, one was into dogging and the third one reminded me of the last puppy in the pet shop.' She looked at them intently. 'Mr Right is not going to fall into our laps, ladies. We need to work at it.'

Rory raised an eyebrow at Penny and nodded her head towards Susie, before leading the way to the sitting room.

'You can mock me,' continued Susie as she followed, 'but you know I am right. We work in a job where over seventy-five per cent of the staff are female.' She looked at Penny. 'And that one *is* a fact. If we want to meet someone before we are pensioned off, we have to put down the red pen for a night and go out and find them.' She sat down on the sofa and took a large gulp of her wine.

Rory fiddled with the radio for some background music. She should introduce Susie to her mother. The two of them had a lot in common. But maybe Susie had a point – maybe a night away from dust and rubber gloves would do her good. 'Okay,' she conceded. 'Where are you going to take us?'

Susie put down her glass. 'How about speed dating?'

'No.' There was no way Rory was doing that.

'I don't think so, thank you.' Penny dropped her eyes and sipped at her wine.

'Why not? It'll be fun.' Susie held out her hands as if she was amazed at their lack of interest. Rory loved her for her eternal enthusiasm but love only stretched so far.

'It will be ridiculous.'

'And too fast. I want to get to know someone properly this time. No philanderers.' Penny shuddered.

The front door banged and Belle appeared at the entrance to the sitting room. Sometimes her beauty made Rory gasp. Over this summer, she had lost the last of her girlish softness. Her face had become stronger, more womanly, and her body had followed. Every time Rory looked at her, Belle seemed to have changed again.

'I'm home, Mum. I did my homework at Fiona's.' Belle waved at Susie and Penny. 'I had dinner there too, so I'm just going to chill in my room for a bit.' She blew Rory a kiss and disappeared again.

'She is such a lovely girl,' Penny sighed, after Belle closed the door.

Rory nodded. 'She is. I'm very lucky.'

Susie picked up her wine glass and took another large swig. She nodded in the direction of the sitting room door. 'She'll have a boyfriend before you do.'

'Belle?' Rory smiled. 'No, she's not interested in boys yet. Other than as friends, obviously. She's got some good friends.'

'Hello? She's sixteen, woman. Of course she's interested in boys. And isn't her sixth form college co-ed?'

'She's only just turned sixteen.' Rory wasn't naïve; of course Belle was growing up – as her mother liked to keep reminding her – but Belle had always been young for her age. Maybe it was the single-sex grammar school she'd attended, maybe it was the fairy tale princess obsession, but she had just never shown much interest in real-life boys.

Susie was right, though. Starting A-levels meant that Belle would be sharing classes with boys for the first time. Come to think of it, she and Fiona had been very giggly about it on their induction day. Maybe Rory needed to prepare herself for some changes. Boy-shaped ones.

But Rory had had enough change in the last few weeks. 'Anyway, leaving Belle out of this, who says I want a boyfriend? I've just bought a house – I don't want to have to share it with anyone other than Belle.'

Susie looked around, and Rory followed her eyes. She didn't need to see the expression on Susie's face to know what her thoughts were on the place. It was shabby. Needed work. If you were feeling mean, you might describe it as run-down. Rory had hired a steam stripper and she and Belle had spent the last two weeks stripping wallpaper and cleaning the place up. Despite joking about the steam giving them a free sauna, it had been bloody hard work and they had barely scratched the surface. Literally.

'That's probably a good thing: you'd be hard pressed persuading anyone to move in here, anyway. I was thinking you could find a boyfriend who lived somewhere habitable and then move in with him? You know, cut your losses.'

Susie was joking, but the thought had crossed Rory's mind more than once in the last couple of weeks. Not the boyfriend bit, the cutting her losses. But she had never given up on anything in her life, and Belle, bless her, hadn't complained once. No, they were going to do this.

'You will be jealous when you see what a palace this place is going to turn into.' Maybe if she repeated it enough times she might begin to believe it herself.

Susie topped up their drinks, although she was the only one who'd finished. 'A palace? I didn't think you believed in fairy tales?'

Rory picked up her glass. 'I believe in the ones that I would write. The ones where the princess saves herself.'

At that moment, the lights and music turned off. There was a sudden gloom and silence.

'What happened?' squeaked Penny. 'Did you do that on purpose?'

If Rory wasn't terrified about the electrics, she would have laughed. 'No, Pen, much as I am enjoying the dramatic effect, I did not do it.'

'Mum!' Belle shouted down the stairs. 'My computer just switched off.'

'It's all right, love,' Rory called. 'It's just the electrics. Don't touch anything for a minute.'

Thankfully, she'd had the foresight to buy a couple of torches when they'd moved in, and it wasn't getting dark yet anyway. Gingerly, she opened the door to the cupboard under the stairs and scrutinised the electricity box.

'Bloody hell,' Susie was peering in behind her. 'I'm no electrician but that does *not* look good.' She patted Rory on the shoulder. 'Good luck with saving yourself from that, Princess.'

CHAPTER FOUR

'Promise me you will NEVER touch the electrics again.'

Rory should not have told her mother about the blackout. Where ordinary people might remark on the inconvenience, in Sheila's head, Rory was going to end up spread-eagled in the hallway with frazzled hair and smoke coming from her fingertips.

'Mum, you do realise I am thirty-eight years old, right?'

'Yes, and sometimes I don't think you have the sense you were born with.' Sheila shook her head in disgust. 'Electrics!'

John Lewis's soft furnishings department was predictably empty on a Thursday evening. Sheila had asked Rory to go shopping with her for some cushions for her new flat, but Rory suspected an ulterior motive. For a start, her mum already had enough scatter cushions to furnish a stately home. 'What kind of cushions are you looking for, Mum?'

Sheila waved her hands around in front of her. 'Stop rushing me, Aurora. I just want to have a look around, get some ideas. I need to modernise myself a bit. The lounge area in Seymour House hasn't a hint of a high-backed chintz chair or a lap tray. Just lots of single armchairs in different colours. It's inspired me.'

Rory sighed. 'I know, Mum, I've been there.' She felt a pang of guilt every time her mother mentioned Seymour House. It hadn't been so bad when Rory had still been living in Scott's house, because it had only had two bedrooms. But now Rory had such a large house, she couldn't shake the idea that she should at least *invite* her mum to come and live with her and Belle.

As always, telling Sheila that she already knew something didn't stop her mother from continuing. 'Yes, well. Thankfully, that modern furniture in the lounge is quite light, as we have to push them all back against the wall when we have our tai chi class.'

Rory ran her fingers over a chenille rug. She needed to at least ask the question. 'Mum, do you like it there? At Seymour House? I mean, does it feel a bit strange? Living in a flat. After the house?'

'It's fine, now I'm settled. The flat is quite small, but that means I have less to keep clean.' Sheila picked up a psychedelic pink and orange cushion. 'What do you think of this? Too much?'

Rory took it out of her hands and frisbeed it back onto the shelf. 'Way too much.'

Sheila picked the cushion up again and replaced it neatly. 'Anyway, I've got two bedrooms, so Belle can still come over and stay whenever she wants. I love our sleepovers.'

The guilt again.

Rory took a deep breath. 'Mum, I've been thinking. Now that I have the house – once it's done up, I mean – would you want to move in with Belle and me?' There. She'd said it.

There was a stony silence next to her. Rory looked at her mother. They stayed like that for about ten seconds.

Then Sheila reached out and took Rory's arm. 'That would be wonderful, Aurora.'

Rory felt sick. 'Really?'

'Oh, I've been hoping you would ask! I didn't want to presume, but…'

Rory turned back to the cushions and started to rearrange them. 'Okay. Great. So, we should…'

She turned back to Sheila as she heard her mother start to laugh raucously.

'The look on your face!'

'What?'

Sheila put her hands either side of Rory's face and kissed her cheek firmly. 'Oh, my darling girl, thanks for asking, but we both know that living in the same house would result in one or the other of us heading to an early grave.'

Rory breathed a huge sigh of relief. Then grinned. 'Thank God.'

Sheila laughed again. 'Thank God, indeed. Anyway, your place would be too dull for me these days. It's very sociable at Seymour House. You would laugh if you saw some of the other residents. Well, you've met Barb.'

'The one with the dangly earrings and the fluffy high-heeled slippers?' Barb made Bet Lynch look like a wallflower.

'That's the one. Well, since the poker night has started, a few more have come out of the woodwork. Mainly ladies – single men are VERY thin on the ground after sixty-five – but we do have Sid. Bless him, he seems a little bit frightened of us all, especially Barb, but he still turns up every week.'

'So I can stop feeling guilty?'

Sheila was refolding a woven throw that Rory had moved. 'I don't know. If I let you stop feeling guilty, will it mean that you visit me less?'

'Depends if you make me do tai chi and play poker.'

Sheila frowned. 'We wouldn't let you youngsters play. No, you don't need to feel guilty at all. It did feel strange when the house sale finalised. It's weird to think I won't be going there again. Your dad and I were there for over forty years.'

Rory swallowed down the huge lump in her throat which developed whenever Sheila mentioned their old home. Although she hadn't lived there in over sixteen years, she felt the same as her mum about its sale. *It's just a house.*

Sheila was still talking. 'I'm sure the young couple who bought it will change everything. I told them that the carpet had only been in for four years and I never allowed anyone to walk on it with their shoes on, but I don't think they were really listening.

They'll probably change it to wooden floors like those houses in magazines. Funny, isn't it? When I was a girl, wooden floors meant you were too poor for carpet. Anyway, that reminds me, there's something I want to talk to you about. I'm bored of cushions. Let's go and get a coffee.'

Whilst her mum found a seat, Rory queued for the drinks, under strict instructions not to let them put the tea bag into the pot because, 'It'll be stewed by the time I get it.' She had known the cushions story was a ruse. When did her mum ever need help to shop?

Rory slid the tray onto the table. 'Here you go. And here's your tea bag and milk in a separate jug.'

'You are a good girl. You know I only like a splash of milk.'

Rory picked up her coffee. 'So, what did you want to talk to me about?'

Sheila reached into her bag and brought out an envelope.

Rory knew what this was. She put down her mug and held up her hands. 'No, Mum. We've talked about this.'

'No, Aurora. You've talked about this. I wasn't listening. If you don't take this cheque – and pay it into your account – I will draw the money out in cash and deliver it to you in a briefcase. Then it will be on your head if the headlines read: *MAD OLD BAT GETS MUGGED CARRYING FIFTY THOUSAND POUNDS*. You are not the only stubborn woman in this family. That place is an absolute wreck. And if it hasn't even got proper electrics,' Sheila shuddered, 'I will not sleep until you've got someone in to sort that out.'

'I've contacted an electrician. I'm not stupid.'

'Good. Then you can use some of this to pay for it. I am not arguing with you, Aurora. Sometimes you have to give in and accept help from somewhere.' She sighed. 'I do wish you had a man around to help with things.'

Well, that was guaranteed to get 'Aurora's' back up.

'How would a man help? I can do this on my own.'

'It's not as easy as all that. I know you think you just need to read a book about it and learn as you go along. But you can't even knit, let alone decorate a whole house. And it isn't as if you have lots of spare time on your hands. The amount of work you bring home every night: piles and piles of marking. Belle tells me you are up until midnight sometimes, trying to get it all done.'

Rory would kill Belle when she got home. She must have known that Sheila would give her a lecture about working too hard. There was no point getting into this with her mum. She should just accept the money for now and change the subject.

'Okay, Mum, I'll take the money. But I am going to put it into an account for emergencies only. If you need it back, it'll be there.'

Sheila nodded. A compromise.

'Speaking of Belle, she's settled really well into college.' Belle was always a safe bet to distract Sheila, who was nothing if not a proud grandmother.

'I know! She popped in to see me. How lovely was that photograph of her on her ID card? She looks just like one of her princesses with those beautiful brown eyes of hers and all that hair. That's one thing she can thank her father for; he always was a good-looking boy.'

Rory nodded. Belle had looked absolutely beautiful in her picture. Unlike Rory's staff pass for St Anthony's which looked like a picture from a 'Don't Take Drugs' campaign. That's what you got for not wearing make-up to work.

Sheila was gazing into the middle distance, reminiscing. 'It doesn't seem five minutes ago that she was click-clacking around the kitchen with my shoes and shawls on. Now she's got a boyfriend.'

Rory coughed on her coffee. 'A what?'

Sheila picked up the small jug and splashed the merest suggestion of milk into her cup. 'Well, I don't know if he's her boyfriend yet, but she likes him. Hasn't she mentioned it?'

Rory shook her head. *A boy?* Belle had never shown an interest in boys before. And why hadn't she mentioned him? They told each other everything.

'We haven't really seen each other much this week. I've been busy with the first week of term and she's been at Fiona's a lot.'

'Well, there is a boy on the horizon. Things are going to change. You've had it easy with her up until now. I certainly didn't have such an easy ride mothering through *your* teenage years. You were a nightmare. Every time I told you not to do something, it would be the exact thing that you would set out to do. It didn't help that your dad indulged you so much. He was almost proud of your devil-may-care attitude. It wasn't him that had to go up to the school every time you'd broken another rule.'

Rory smiled. Her dad had let her get away with murder. She was grateful that Belle had not taken after her rebellious side. Belle had always been a good girl. Too good, sometimes. Someone could take advantage of her very easily. Rory needed to talk to her about this boy. Or should she wait for Belle to open up to her?

Sheila had changed the subject again. 'Speaking of rules, one of the women at Seymour House – Flo – is trying to get a residents' committee together so that we can make sure that everyone is behaving appropriately. I've never been one for committees myself. I learned my lesson after joining the PTA when you were at school. Endless evenings spent listening to other people prattle on about nothing. Some people have far too much time on their hands and some of them, like Flo, want to spend it telling other people what to do.'

Rory couldn't agree more. She had managed to side swerve joining any 'working groups' at St Anthony's or 'parent consultation groups' at Belle's grammar school. Maybe she and her mother weren't total opposites after all. 'Why does she think you need to keep an eye on residents' behaviour?'

Sheila leaned forward and lowered her voice. 'Well. Barb – she of the dangly earrings and fluffy slippers – has some conspiracy theory that Flo wants to curtail her "activities". Flo doesn't like it when Barb has gentlemen coming to visit her; she thinks it's dangerous for her to bring unknown men into the building. Barb thinks Flo shouldn't worry. With her cable knit cardigans, she's not in any danger from the kind of men that Barb knows.'

Rory started to laugh. She had only met Barb once, but she could just imagine the kind of men she went for. 'Hasn't she tried to fix you up, Mum?'

Sheila looked embarrassed. She picked up her insipid tea and sipped. 'Actually, Barb has been on at me to double date with her, but I don't think it's for me. I didn't really date the first time round – I met your dad at sixteen and we knew we were going to get married from the first week. It all seems a lot more complicated these days.' She sipped again and then leaned forwards. 'Barb even showed me a book she got from the library: *Sex for Seniors*. It had drawings of positions you could do "it" in and everything. I asked her if there was a picture of my favourite position: sitting in an armchair with a cup of tea and a biscuit.'

Rory chuckled. 'Oh, Mum. You're not past it yet, you know.'

'Maybe not. But I won't be around forever. Which is why I would like to see you settled down. Why can't you give it a chance, Aurora?'

Rory wasn't about to go down that path again. 'Has the vacant flat been filled yet?'

'No. Obviously, Barb is hoping for a single man, which makes Flo shake her head in disgust. With any luck, it'll be another Barb and they can go out together and leave me alone.'

'Well. Don't rule anything out, Mum.'

'Same to you, Aurora.'

But it wasn't a love interest for herself, or for her mum, that was on Rory's mind. Why hadn't Belle told her about the boy she liked?

CHAPTER FIVE

Standing in front of a display of screws and nails, Rory was at a loss. Some of the skirting board was coming away in her bedroom and she just wanted to screw it back. Why were there so many different types?

If there was one thing she hated, it was asking for help in a shop like this. Not only was there rarely anyone around to ask but, when you did, they were usually male and had a way of making you feel like an idiot. She had had enough of being made to feel stupid this week. Nathan Finch had been introducing new initiatives at school on an almost daily basis.

At this evening's staff training, he had instructed them that they would need to produce a seating plan for each of their classes. This was something they already did, but he wanted a lot more than a sketch of who sat where in the room. 'For each student, you will also need to indicate the following things. Firstly, their gender and ethnic origin. Then whether they have a Special Educational Need, are "Gifted and Talented" or receive free school meals. Lastly, their current National Curriculum level and whether they are making above, below or expected progress. We would like this colour coded as indicated and, ideally, I would like you to complete these by the end of the week.'

Although this was going to take a great deal of time and effort (and would have no impact whatsoever on the teaching of the children in her classes) at least Rory knew how to do it. Online dating, however, was a whole different ballgame. Susie had bullied her into looking at it with her over the weekend. They had scanned the websites together and had tried to work out what they needed to do.

'Who are these people?' Rory had been quite incredulous at the photographs people chose to use to promote themselves to their potential future life partners. Some of them looked like they were auditioning for the adult channel, whilst others decided that they would be most attractive atop a camel or beside a national monument. One picture looked like it had been taken in the Amazonian rainforest and the man in question was a tiny dot way in the distance. 'That's either an attempt at irony or he has got some serious self-esteem issues.'

'Maybe we shouldn't look at the photographs.' Susie kept scrolling through the list. 'Let's read their descriptions instead.'

This was worse. '"I love long walks in the countryside",' read Rory. 'That's the tenth one who says that. Maybe they should be thinking about getting a dog rather than a girlfriend?'

'What about this one?' Susie looked hopeful as she read. '"I've dated many women, but I am still searching for my soulmate."'

'Clearly wants someone to agree with everything he says.' Rory leaned over the keyboard and hit return. 'Next.'

'How about this one? "Recently divorced, I am looking for that special lady who will help to mend my broken heart."'

'Rebound. Next.'

'"Open minded, and seeking adventure, I would love to meet a woman who wants to try new things."'

'Swinger. Susie, I don't think this is going to be for me. I can't even face writing my description. Anyway, it's too risky for us. What if one of the kids from school found us online? The humiliation! We'd have to leave the county.'

'Maybe you're right. But if you won't try speed dating and we're not going to do online, you have to promise that we will start going out more. You might be happy expending your energy with a paint brush or a hammer, but I need to meet someone soon or I am going to start walking funny.'

Rory had duly promised that she would go out more but she was starting to regret it already. She had had about the same success with choosing the right man as she was having with choosing these screws. She didn't have a clue which ones she would need to buy and couldn't afford to start buying materials which turned out to be useless. Although she had the money her mum had insisted on giving her, it was safely in a separate account and she was only going to use it for emergencies. Like that damn rewiring.

Walking to the end of the aisle, she found an assistant who seemed to be idly raking through a tray of metal. May as well give him something more productive to do. 'Excuse me, could you give me some help? I need to know which screws will fix a skirting board to a wall.'

Without any particular rush, he ambled over to her before crouching forward slightly and squinting at the display. He must have just come from the warehouse because his trousers were covered in dust and his boots were splattered in different types of paint. Rory could imagine him hefting boxes around; he had the shoulders for it. Maybe this was B&Q's new marketing strategy to attract more female customers: good-looking sales assistants. This one could almost be auditioning for a builders and decorators calendar shoot. He was upright again and holding something out to her. 'They should do the job. Although you may want to glue it as well; sometimes screws aren't enough.'

She took the packet from him. His hands were paint-spattered too, but his nails were clean. 'Great, thanks.' Whilst she had his attention, she may as well get the other things on her list. 'Actually, I also need some help with plaster. I have an electrician coming tomorrow to rewire my house and apparently he is going to channel out the walls for the new cables. He told me I would have to fill them back in myself. What do I need?'

The assistant shook his head. 'I'd get a plasterer in for that if I were you. It's a tricky job.'

Rory had been expecting this ever since she'd walked into the DIY shop. In fact, she had been just waiting for someone to ask her if she was looking for her husband. 'Thanks for the advice, but I'm sure I'll be able to fill in a few holes with plaster.'

Rubbing his unshaven face, the assistant fixed a pair of bright blue eyes on her. 'Have you done it before? It's quite difficult to get a smooth finish. Plastering is a bit of an art form, actually.'

She had been asking for directions to the correct aisle, not a tutorial. 'If you could just show me where it is, I'd be grateful.'

The man shrugged and smiled. 'Okay. I think I saw it a couple of aisles down. They keep moving things, but I'm sure we'll find it. Follow me.' As Rory followed him, she wondered how much of an expert on plastering he could be when he couldn't even remember where products were kept in his own store. His long strides forced her to practically skip to keep up. When he stopped, she almost ran into him. 'Here you go. These are the fillers. A professional plasterer would use Thistle, but if you've just got thin channels to fill in, you'll probably get away with this stuff.'

Again, Rory was faced with a choice to make, as there were three different brands. Reluctant to open up the possibility of more advice, she picked the one in the middle. 'Thanks for your help.' She nodded to indicate that she didn't need him any more.

'You'll be wanting sandpaper, too. Follow me.' He walked away without giving her the chance to refuse him. Getting help in this place went from one extreme to another. Obviously, he must be on commission. At least he seemed quite confident about where the sandpaper could be found.

Again, more choices – there were even different colours and different numbers to choose from – but this time he didn't wait for her to decide. He selected a couple of types and gave them to her. But she would have to admit her ignorance. 'What do I need this for?'

'After you've used the filler. You'll need to let it dry until it's completely hard and then sand it down. Like I said, it's a tricky business. I really do think you should consider getting a professional. Did you say you were having a room rewired?'

Rory shook her head. 'Not just a room. The whole house needs new electrics, apparently. We turned on a light switch and there was a big bang. The electrician I called in spent a lot of time making tutting sounds as he looked around. I got him off the Internet, so I'm hoping he knows what he's doing.' She had been tearing her hair out about the expense of the electrical work. She would have to use Sheila's money and she hated it. 'I've taken on a bit of a project, to be honest. The estate agent wasn't entirely truthful. By the time we got the survey back and realised the extent of the work, my daughter and I had already fallen in love with it.' She didn't add that everyone, from her mother to her ex-husband, had told her that she was being completely ridiculous. They would have to admit they were wrong when she single-handedly transformed it into a show home. Belle had already made a sign for the front door: THE PALACE.

'Then you really do need to think about getting someone in. Otherwise you'll be looking at hours and hours of hard work. Hard, dusty work. You'll need a mask.' He took one from the shelf above the sandpaper and put it onto the pile of products in her arms. 'Where's your house? If you're local, I could pop back with you and take a look at it now, if you like?'

Rory was slightly alarmed at the prospect of taking a strange man back to her house. She hadn't done that in at least seventeen years, and she wasn't about to start now. 'Do you usually offer this kind of service to your customers, or is it just the inept female ones? I'm sure your boss wouldn't be too pleased with you following me home halfway through the day.'

He looked confused. 'I don't work here.'

Rory could feel a deep flush starting at the base of her neck. She started to stammer. 'I'm so sorry. I thought... Well, you know what I thought... And I was dragging you around the shop.' The flush had reached her cheeks. 'I'm so sorry. Why didn't you tell me?'

He grinned. 'Because I was taught never to ignore a damsel in distress. Look, I'm a builder. I can get one of my friends to give you a quote on the plastering if you like, then you can decide what to do. Let me give you my card.' He felt around in his back pocket, then held out a small white business card. 'With a job as big as yours sounds, you're going to need help with some of it.' As she couldn't move her full arms to reach out for it, he tucked the card into her hand, under the original bag of screws. 'Anyway, I'll leave you to it. I was supposed to be in here to get some drill bits before you tempted me away to the plastering section.' He tapped the card she was still holding in front of her, then looked her straight in the eye. 'Give me a call.'

After dropping her purchases onto the conveyor belt at the till, Rory had a closer look at the man's card: JP Building Services. Maybe he was right, maybe she would have to give in and pay someone to do the more difficult work on the house. Obviously, she hadn't planned to do the electrics or the plumbing herself, but she had hoped to do most other things. The problem was, she and Belle had to live there *now*, so they couldn't wait for months for it to be made habitable. Even if they could get a couple of the bedrooms straight, and the kitchen and bathroom, they could be more patient with the rest. Unless someone she knew could recommend someone, maybe she would give this guy a call. Looking for a contact name and number, she flipped the card over. It looked as if JP Building Services was the man's own company. His name was John Prince.

Her mum was going to love that.

CHAPTER SIX

Rory had spent so much time at work trying to get these damn seating plans done for Nathan Finch that she hadn't even begun to think about what to cook for dinner. It was probably a moot point anyway; she only had one working gas ring and the microwave would be out of action until the electrics were done. Pizza?

Sheila arrived at the house before Belle got home. Belle was spending a lot of time at Fiona's – her own house being a building site – but Rory missed having her around, and they still hadn't discussed this boy who was supposedly on the horizon.

'How was your day?' Her mum always asked this, and Rory always answered the same way.

'Fine. Busy. Yours?'

'Fun. We had our first meeting of Flo's new committee today. Barb and I sat at the back and giggled like two naughty schoolgirls.'

'She's a bad influence on you.' Rory was shuffling through a drawer for the pizza delivery menu.

Sheila grinned. 'I know. Marvellous, isn't it? Anyway, Flo wants to have a rota for checking the laundry room to make sure that no one is leaving behind oddments of their washing. Apparently, there was a Y-fronts incident.' She made pretend inverted comma marks in the air. Belle must have taught her that.

Rory grimaced. The thought of old men's baggy underwear nearly turned her off the pizza idea. 'Thanks for that, Mum.'

'She also wants each of us to organise a social event. You should have seen her face at Barb's suggestion. To be fair, I am not sure speed dating would really work, either. It takes some of the older ones more than three minutes to get out of their chair. The date would be over before they'd got a chance to shake hands.'

Rory looked up with a smile. 'I had Susie trying to persuade me to do the exact same thing. It sounds hideous. Would you do it?'

Sheila had been on her own for over fifteen years now. Although Rory hadn't thought about it at the time, her mum had only been in her early fifties when Rory's dad had died – she could have met someone else. Still could?

'I don't think so. We've only really got Sid who's on his own, and I'd rather collect the random pants from the laundry room than get romantic with him. Where's Belle? Has she spoken to you about this boy yet?'

Rory shook her head. 'No. She's at Fiona's all the time at the moment, so I've hardly seen her, and I don't want to be the one to bring it up. I'll wait for her to tell me.'

Sheila crossed her arms. 'I don't want to make you feel worse, Aurora, but that's the trouble with being such an old cynic – people don't want to talk to you about their romances, not even your own daughter.' She put her head on one side. 'It is normal for teenagers to keep secrets from their parents, though. As your mother, I know that better than anyone.'

That was what bothered Rory the most. Up until now, her relationship with her daughter hadn't been normal in the sense that Sheila was talking about. Belle had been barely a year old when Rory had found out about Scott's affairs and had asked him to leave. Since then, it had always been the two of them against the world. They had been a team. They had never had secrets. Until now.

The front door banged and Belle's breathless face peeped around the sitting room door. 'Hi, Mum. Hi, Gran. What's for dinner?'

Rory held up the menu. 'Pizza.'

'Great. I'm just going to get changed out of my uniform. I'll be down in a minute.'

'Pizza?' Sheila's nose wrinkled. 'You could have come to me if you were too tired to cook.'

'It's not that, Mum. The cooker isn't working properly.'

Sheila threw her hands in the air. 'Oh, Aurora. If that doesn't constitute a reason to crack into your so-called "emergency" fund, I don't know what does. You have to *eat*.'

'It's in hand, Mum. I've met a man.' Rory paused on purpose. She had been waiting to get her own back on her mum for pretending she wanted to move in with her. This was her chance.

Sheila nearly combusted on the spot. 'Really? Oh Aurora! How wonderful! Who is he? What is his name? Where did you meet him?'

'His name' – Rory was enjoying this – 'is John *Prince*.'

Sheila's hand fluttered to her chest. She looked like she might actually faint, so Rory decided it was time to put her out of her misery. Or false hope.

'Don't get excited, Mum. He's a builder. I might ask him to do some work on the house. No romance.' She picked up her mobile and scrolled through to find the pizza delivery app.

But Sheila was still smiling. 'We shall see. It's early days.' She paused and frowned. 'You did check he wasn't married?'

Rory looked up from the screen. 'How the hell would I know that?'

Sheila rolled her eyes. 'What woman doesn't check for a wedding ring when she talks to a man? Sometimes I wonder if you are my daughter at all.'

Rory wished she hadn't started this. 'Whether or not he is married is irrelevant, mother. As long as he does a good job and doesn't charge me too much, that's all I'm interested in.'

Her words fell on deaf ears: Sheila was lost in thought. 'A builder. Like your dad.'

'Mum. I am warning you.'

Sheila held her hands up. 'I'm not doing anything.' But she was still smiling when Belle reappeared, slipped in next to her on the sofa and gave her a kiss.

Sheila turned her attention to her granddaughter. 'How's college?'

Belle pulled her legs up under her. 'It's good. I'm really busy but I'm enjoying it. How're things at Seymour House? Any more gossip? What's Barb been up to?'

Sheila settled into the sofa, ready to launch into a story. These two loved a gossip. It was amazing how interested Belle was in her grandmother's anecdotes. They made Rory want to boil her own head.

'There has been quite a bit of excitement actually. New residents moved into the vacant two-bedroomed place on the floor below mine – a couple. Although we've only seen the man so far. Well, you can imagine, Barb was all over him like a rash. Introducing herself, telling him about all the social events we have on. He said it wasn't his sort of thing. Although I think he probably meant Barb wasn't his sort of thing. She calmed down a bit when he told her his wife was moving in later.'

Belle wriggled closer to her gran. 'I didn't understand what people meant by *man-eater* until I met her.'

Sheila smiled. 'You can't blame her, really. Decent men are a bit thin on the ground and she's been divorced for over twenty years. I think she's hoping for a bit of fun. A bit of harmless fun can do anyone the world of good.' Sheila looked pointedly at Rory. 'He's pretty good-looking, I suppose – the new resident – he looks a bit like Cary Grant. Only thinner. And with less hair. There was something a bit strange about him, though. Shifty eyes.'

Rory looked over the top of the pizza delivery menu. 'Now who's being choosy?'

'No, I'm serious.' Sheila turned back to Belle. 'He came and went a few times, bringing boxes of belongings, and then disappeared into his flat. No one has seen his wife.'

Belle was leaning forward now. Listening to every word. Rory loved how close they were. When Belle was little, Sheila would collect her from school every day and they'd have a wonderful time. Sheila would let Belle play with her make-up, which drove Rory mad. She didn't want Belle encouraged to do typically girly things. All Sheila would say at the time was, 'I'm sure even Germaine Greer wears a bit of lippy now and again.' Rory was biased, but she thought that Belle was beautiful just as she was. Although she was wearing more lipstick than usual today. And was that mascara on her lashes?

Rory was less interested in this new man and his invisible wife. 'He probably made her up to get away from Barb.'

Sheila shook her head. 'No. We saw him bring in armfuls of women's clothes on hangers. There must be a wife.'

Belle had the wild imagination of the young. 'That's so suspicious, Gran. Do you think he's keeping her prisoner? You should go and find out!'

'Hang on. Hang on.' Rory needed to put the brakes on these two. 'Don't you think you should wait and see what the situation is before you go ploughing in?'

'Of course I will.' Sheila leaned in to Belle. 'And then we'll sweep in and save her.'

Rory sighed. Here they went again. 'You two can't fix a happy ending for everyone you meet, you know.'

But Belle put up a hand. 'We know. We know. "*Life is not a fairy tale.*"' She rolled her eyes at Sheila, then winked at Rory. That was definitely mascara. 'How was your day, Mum? Was that Finch man still awful?'

Sheila's ears pricked up. '*Another* man? They're like buses around here. Nothing for sixteen years and then two at once.'

Rory groaned. 'Don't mention the "M" word around your gran, Belle. She gets overly hopeful.' She turned to Sheila to nip any potential unpalatable comments in the bud. 'He's the new deputy head at school and is an emotionless educational robot.'

'Deputy head, eh? How do you know he's really emotionless? Maybe he's just finding his feet. You know, like when you did your teacher training and they told you to start off strict and get nicer once you had them under control. What was it that you used to say? "*Don't smile until Christmas.*"'

'No, it's not that, Mum. He's actually quite unpleasant – to the staff as well as the pupils. He's clearly very ambitious, and it's never about the kids with people like that.' Everything about Nathan Finch was irritating, but the worst part was the way he spoke to the students, like they were dirt on his shoes. He'd roared at Charlie the other day for messing around in the corridor. Everyone lost their temper at times – goodness knows the kids could push you to it some days – but, if you disliked children as much as he obviously did, why start teaching in the first place?

Sheila got up and prodded Rory in the direction of the kitchen. 'Well, maybe you should give him a chance, too. What were you just saying about waiting before you plough in? Anyway, if you're going to order this pizza business I at least want a proper plate and cutlery. Do you want a hand with that washing up?' She motioned towards the sink full of the morning's breakfast things. And last night's dinner things. Rory had been busy.

The sink was the one part of the kitchen that had worked up until now. But when Sheila tried to drain the water, it didn't go anywhere. 'Rory, is there a problem with your sink?'

'I don't think so. Is there something blocking the plughole?' Rory stuck her hand into the greasy water and whirled it around. It made her feel queasy. But there was nothing blocking the water. Great. That meant something else that needed fixing.

'I can't face dealing with that tonight. We'll use the other plates and I'll think about it in the morning.' The morning, when she had already planned to be in early, to catch up on the marking she hadn't done because of those sodding seating plans. She'd like to stick Nathan Finch down this greasy plughole.

But Sheila looked almost pleased at the prospect. 'Oh well, maybe you can give your John Prince a call? I'm sure he'll be able to fix it in a trice.'

She wouldn't be giving her mother the satisfaction of calling John while she was still here. Rory wouldn't put it past her to make kissing noises in the background. Besides, John was a builder, not a handyman.

Although, maybe she could just ask him to tell her how to do it herself?

CHAPTER SEVEN

Rory sent John a text first thing in the morning but she wasn't expecting him to call her back almost immediately.

'I can pop round tonight if you like?'

'No, no. I don't need you to come round. I just thought you could tell me what to do. I can't get the sink to empty.' She sounded like a feeble woman. She didn't want him to look down the plughole, take two seconds to fix it and then leave her looking like an incompetent. Even if she was.

'It's probably just the trap. But it might be the drains that are blocked. It's no trouble.' There was a muffled sound and she heard him speak to someone else. 'Sorry, I need to go. I'll be there about five.'

She didn't want to admit it, but she was relieved. Once this week was over, she'd research some local DIY classes. Then she wouldn't need to call for help every time something went wrong. Right now, it was more pressing to get into school and cut up strips of coloured paper for a lesson.

*

'Good morning, everybody. Lacey, can you sit on a chair rather than a desk please, and can you put those crisps away, Harry?' Rory was usually at the classroom door ready to greet her class, but after cutting the paper strips, she'd had a violent altercation with the photocopier which had made her late.

A chubby-looking boy towards the back of the classroom grumbled something about breakfast under his breath and scrunched a family-sized bag of Doritos into his pocket.

'Is it going to be a fun lesson today, Miss?' Lacey swung her long legs and her not-so-long skirt under the nearest desk. The frequency with which that question was asked would lead a casual bystander to believe that every other lesson included cartwheels and rap music.

Rory pretended to think for a moment. 'It all depends on your definition of fun.'

'That means no.' Harry snuck a hand into his pocket and another Dorito into his mouth.

'We're actually going to plan some extended writing. That's going to be your assessment at the end of this half term and we need to practise.' There was a collective groan. 'I knew you'd be excited.'

'I 'ate writing,' a stringy boy at the front of the class moaned. 'Can't you read us that book again?'

There was nothing Rory would like better than to open her copy of *A Monster Calls* and read the next chapter. But even an hour of English every day wasn't enough to cajole some of these kids into writing more than a couple of paragraphs, and the book was far more effective as a bargaining tool. 'If we get forty minutes of preparation done now, and you work hard, I can read you another chapter at the end of the lesson. Does anyone know where Charlie is?'

Every time Charlie was late, Rory worried. His mum was a lovely woman, but her Crohn's Disease was debilitating at times. Some days Charlie had a lot to do before he came to school in the morning.

Just then the classroom door opened and Charlie hurried in. 'Sorry I'm late, Miss.'

'Good to see you, Charlie. Just sit yourself down and you can tell me why you were late in a minute. Harry, can you give the books out?'

Lacey jumped up and wriggled to pull the bottom of her skirt down just far enough for decency. 'I'll do it, Miss. If we wait for

Harry, it'll be break time before we start.' She had a point; Harry looked like he'd just realised someone had called his name.

'Thanks. The rest of you, I want you to try and think of someone who is really important to you. It can be anyone. A family member, a sporting hero, a best friend, but it needs to be someone who is special to you in a personal way.'

A smile spread across Harry's face. 'Kylie Jenner.'

Tactically ignoring him, Rory continued to explain. 'Our assessment this half term is going to be to write that person a letter. Today we are going to plan the three main sections, so to begin with, I am going to give you three strips of paper and I want you to write down the three most important things you would like to say to that person.'

Lacey has sat down and was now chewing the end of her pen. 'Can it be anyone?'

Rory nodded. 'Anyone you like.'

Lacey clearly had someone specific in mind. 'Can it be someone in this class?'

At the predictable reaction of 'Ooohs', Lacey stuck her middle finger up. Rory pretended not to notice. Don't sweat the small stuff. 'Yes, it can. But only if it's a positive letter: no hate mail.'

Charlie started to raise his hand as if he was going to ask her something, and then thought better of it. Rory had a pretty good idea who he was going to write to and it made her heart hurt.

Then she brought out her secret weapon: the strips of coloured paper. Non-teachers wouldn't believe how even the most reluctant writer was happy to write on coloured paper. That was something you wouldn't find on a stupid annotated seating plan.

When they had been working for a while, there was a sharp knock on the door and Nathan Finch came in. Rory could tell from the pupils' reactions that some of them had encountered him already and were none too keen. 'Sit up!' he barked at Harry. Then he took one look at Lacey and sent her down to the head of year room to remove her nail polish. 'And you can unroll the top of your skirt whilst you're down there.'

Rory sighed. They had just begun to get into the task. If she'd started attacking them for every misdemeanour, they'd still be on the opening paragraph at Christmas.

Nathan then turned his attention to Rory, changing his tone. 'Good afternoon, Ms Wilson. I was wondering if I could have a quick word with you outside.'

Giving her class a 'get on with it' look, Rory followed him through the classroom door.

When they were in the corridor, he gave her that car salesman smile again. 'Sorry to interrupt your teaching, but I wanted to ask why you haven't entered any data yet this half term? Mr Brown informs me that the deadline was last Friday.' He looked at her expectantly.

Rory tried her most surprised face. 'Oh, was it *last* Friday? Sorry, I thought it was *this* Friday. I'll get onto it straight away.' She resisted the urge to make a mock salute. Nathan Finch didn't strike her as a man with a particularly developed sense of humour. She also needed to get back to her class before Harry started selling his surplus snacks.

Nathan didn't look convinced. 'I understand that data collection has not had a strong profile at St Anthony's hitherto.' He paused for emphasis. 'You must understand that, unless I – I mean *we* – can get a clear picture of our pupils' current levels, we will not be able to put in place the interventions they need to make their expected, and above expected, levels of progress.' He stopped and smiled, as if he had just explained how he was going to solve world hunger.

Rory could have told him the current level of every pupil in her class right there and then – it was called *knowing your students*. Plus, they were more likely to make progress if she spent her time planning good lessons rather than entering numbers into a spreadsheet. 'Of course.'

Nathan leaned in towards her. He smelled of expensive after-shave. Rory hadn't had a man this close to her face in a while. It was disconcerting. 'I know change can be difficult, Ms Wilson. But I am determined to make this an outstanding school, and accurate data is a very large step in the right direction. I don't expect everybody will want to go on that journey with me – us' – he paused – 'but that is what needs to be done.'

When she got back into the classroom, Charlie looked concerned. 'Are you in trouble, Miss?'

'Of course not, Charlie. Whatever gave you that idea?'

Harry was nodding sagely. 'Cos Finchy only ever talks to people when they're in trouble.'

'Nope, all fine.' It wasn't their fault that she'd be sitting here until late tonight, inputting irrelevant data on each of her classes. But the prospect meant she wasn't in the mood for cheerleading them through their writing planning either, particularly as a sulky-looking Lacey had just rejoined them, looking more like she was ready to wield a knife than a pen. 'Shall we leave it there until tomorrow, and read a chapter?'

Harry moved out of his seat for the first time that day and gave out the copies of the book. As Rory read to them, they transformed before her eyes into a group of young children, spellbound by a story. You couldn't input that onto a spreadsheet.

By five o'clock, she wasn't even halfway through stabbing at her computer keyboard with her finger. She hadn't begun to plan tomorrow's lessons and a large pile of books glared menacingly from the corner of her desk; they would be her date for tonight. Just for a moment, she lay her head down on the desk and took a deep breath.

'All getting a bit too much, chick?'

Rory raised her head. Susie walked in and perched on the edge of her desk. 'You doing data too?'

Rory nodded. 'What is the point of all this? I spend longer on doing the assessments and marking the assessments and entering the data on the assessments than I do on actually teaching. It's bonkers.'

'It's not quite as bad for me in IT, but you're right.' Susie raised her hands and did a mock bow. 'Data is king.'

'It's got worse now that bloody man has started. I think he might have threatened me this afternoon.'

'You're not the only one. He's been paying quite a few visits this afternoon. Penny was almost in tears when I saw her earlier.'

'Penny?' Rory sat up straight. She and Susie could take it, but Penny was a sensitive soul. 'He'd better not start on her.'

Susie clapped her hands together. 'I think we all need a night off this business already – and the term has just started. How about I grab Pen and we come over to you tonight for a takeaway and a bottle of wine?'

'I can't do tonight, I've got someone coming…' Rory glanced at her watch. 'Damn! Is that the time? I have to go.' She logged out of the computer – she'd have to come in early again tomorrow to finish the data – and scooped up the pile of books.

'Where are you going in such a hurry?' Susie's heels click-clacked after her down the corridor.

'I've got someone coming to fix the sink.'

The click-clack got quicker. 'The Prince man from B&Q? Is he good-looking? Can I come?'

'Susie, I've really got to go. I'll see you in the morning.' Rory pushed open the front door with the pile of books and picked up her pace towards the car park.

'Tomorrow night, then,' Susie stood in the doorway and shouted after her. 'No excuses!'

CHAPTER EIGHT

'Crikey, that's a lot of books.' John helped her from the car with some of them after she'd apologised profusely for being late. The pile looked smaller when he held them.

'Yep, one of the many joys of a teaching career. I've got a hot date with a red pen tonight.' Rory opened the front door the only way that seemed to work: key in the lock, turn it, throw yourself against the door.

'Hey, you're going to hurt yourself.' John ran his fingers around the door frame. 'You've got some nasty swelling there. I'll get a plane out of the van and sort that out for you before I go.'

Rory dropped her pile of exercise books onto the table and John placed the ones he'd taken neatly beside them.

'Thanks for coming. I really didn't expect you to come and look at it. I thought you could just tell me what to do over the phone.' The thought of digging around in the muck below the plug hole made her retch. It had been bad enough using a saucepan to scoop up the cold and dirty water in the sink and chuck it on the garden. She would have done it though. Eventually.

'It's no problem, I knew I'd be on my way back from a job anyway and I didn't have plans tonight.' He moved his head slowly to take in the rest of the sitting room. 'This house will be beautiful when you've done it up.'

At last, someone else could see it. 'I think so. Paint, new tiles – you won't recognise the place.'

John turned to look at her. He rubbed his face, which made a scratchy noise. 'It'll take more than a bit of paint.'

Here came the hard sell. 'I know, it needs everything doing to it, but I'm not afraid of hard work.'

John pressed his lips together. 'It'll take a very long time if you do it all yourself.'

'I won't be doing it all myself. Belle is helping me.' Rory should have used past tense. Belle had helped in the last two weeks of the summer but wasn't keen to carry on now she'd started college.

John was looking up at the ornate coving. It had a few chips out of it, but Rory thought it would look better once it was painted white. John's expression suggested otherwise. 'Look, why don't you let me help you?'

Rory stiffened. Either he believed she wasn't capable of doing it, or he thought that he could make some easy money out of her. She wasn't stupid. 'Thanks. But I'm fine.'

Now John was crouched on the floor, running his finger along the skirting board. 'There are so many original features. You need to make a good job of this.'

Rory tried not to stare at his hands. 'I intend to.'

John rested back on his haunches. He had noticeably muscular thighs. 'I grew up in a house just like this. I'd enjoy working on this place. Restoring it to its former glory.'

Did she need to tell him again that she hadn't asked him to? And why was he looking up at her like that? Was he appraising her for restoration, too? 'I'm sure I'll enjoy it. However long it takes.'

'Look.' He stood up and did that scratchy face rub again. 'I've got a mate who wants to make me a website. And I need some photos of my work. Kind of a *before and after* type thing.'

Rory could see where this was leading. 'Okay.'

'And. Let's face it, you won't find many more extreme *before* photos than this place.' John grinned, then stopped, coughed and frowned up at the coving again. Clearly, it was very interesting. 'So, if I can take some pictures for my website, I'll give you a big discount on the work.'

Rory could almost hear her mother telling her not to look a gift horse in the mouth. But she wanted to do this herself. And who was this man, anyway? Anyone could drive a white van and give out business cards in B&Q. 'I'm not sure. This was supposed to be my project.'

John dragged his eyes away from the interesting coving and held up his hands. 'It will be your project – I'll just be the hired hands. I'll do the bits you don't want to.'

If he'd said the bits you *can't* do, Rory would have refused on the spot. But the enormity of the task she had taken on was beginning to dawn on her. Maybe some help would be a good thing.

'I'll think about it.'

John gave a short nod and pointed to the kitchen door. 'Shall I go and get on with it?'

'Thanks. I'm just going to run upstairs and get changed.'

It felt slightly odd to have a man in the house. Especially when she was taking her clothes off. Obviously he was only there as a handyman, and would not be bursting into her bedroom, but it was still weird.

It wasn't that she hadn't dated since Scott. They'd split up over fifteen years ago and, whatever Susie believed, Rory hadn't been a nun since then. But there had been no one special. She hadn't wanted anyone special. Sex was sex, but her real life was her and Belle, and she didn't want anyone else to spoil it.

That was a point: she should warn Belle that there was a man in the house, just in case she'd done her usual and changed into her PJs the minute she got home. She knocked on Belle's bedroom door. There was no answer. Rory peeked inside. Where was she?

She paused for a moment on the threshold. The walls of Belle's bedroom were like an insight into her teenage mind. Oddly, the pictures of princesses – which Rory had always hated – now made her feel nostalgic for that time when they weren't fighting for wall space with Justin Bieber. Since Belle had turned sixteen and started sixth form there had been a definite change in her. Of course, Rory had always wanted to raise an independent, strong-minded woman – and she'd fought a long-standing battle against the role models of Snow White, Rapunzel and their chums – but now the memories of a toothy little girl in a Cinderella costume tweaked her heart a little. *Be careful what you wish for.*

Hearing the front door open, she went downstairs to find her daughter hanging up her coat.

'Hi, Mum, sorry I'm late. I was at Fiona's house and we were talking and I just forgot the time.'

Rory kissed Belle's cool cheek, which smelled of the outdoors, and pushed her fringe out of her eyes. *Eyeshadow?* 'That's okay, I've only just got in myself. Listen, I have a stack of marking to do, so how do you feel about pizza again tonight?'

'Pizza? That sounds good,' John walked into the hallway. 'Nice to meet you.' He held out his hand. Belle shook it a little self-consciously, shaking her fringe back out from behind her ear, and then looked at her mother.

'John is here to sort out the sink for us. I couldn't get it unblocked.'

'And now you're joining us for pizza, too. Great!' Belle gave her mum an enquiring and expectant look.

John's eyes widened. 'No! I wasn't inviting myself. Er… there's nothing in the trap. I need to… uh… go out the back and check the drains.' He backed out of the hallway into the sitting room. Practically ran.

Rory flushed. She blamed her mother for Belle's desire to fix her up with any man who crossed their path.

'I did wonder what that big white van was doing here.' Belle nudged Rory. 'John seems really nice, Mum.'

Rory pointed a finger at her daughter. 'Don't you even start with that. I assumed you'd learned your lesson a long time ago, after trying to fix me up with your primary school teacher. Your *married* primary school teacher.'

'You need to start thinking about it, Mum. Gran and I were talking about this the other day. It's about time you fell in love.'

Rory was about to start on her usual rant about the illusion of romantic love, when John popped his head around the door. 'It is the drains. I'm just going to dredge them. Might stink a bit.' He disappeared again.

Rory lowered her voice to a stage whisper. 'Life is not a fairy tale, Belle.' She swiped at her daughter's legs as Belle mouthed the words along with her. 'And don't mimic your mother.'

'Gran says you make your own life story.' Belle had her hands on her hips. 'And mine is *definitely* going to be a fairy tale.' She dropped her hands and looked at Rory: more seriously now.

Rory needed to tread carefully. 'What is it?'

Belle looked down at the black and white tiles on the hallway floor, and then back up again. She lowered her voice a little. 'I wanted to talk to you about something, actually.' She paused. 'I've started seeing someone from college. A boy, I mean.'

Rory motioned with her head that they should go into the sitting room and sit down. Finally, Belle was going to tell her about the boyfriend. She should be pleased. She should be relieved. But the mention of a boyfriend made her feel strange. 'Is he nice?'

Belle blushed and nodded. 'Really nice, Mum. But I don't want to talk about him too much yet. I might jinx it.'

But Rory needed a bit more information. What was his name? Was he kind? Was he careful? What was his family like? Could she trust him? Did he know how lucky he was? Okay, she wanted a *lot* of information. But then John came back in and he was holding a... Was that a frog?

He was beaming. John. Not the frog. 'Look at this little fella!'

Belle ran to him: she had always loved any kind of animal, that girl. Rory was less keen. Particularly with regard to amphibians. 'What is that doing in my house?'

'He was sitting on the drain cover. So I brought him in to say hello.' John gave the frog to Belle. 'I'll just go and put the cover back on.' He disappeared again.

Belle took the frog to Rory and held it up to her. 'You should kiss him, Mum. Might turn into a prince.'

That girl was starting to get way too cheeky. 'Please take him back outside. I don't have time in my life for frogs. Or princes, for that matter. Speaking of which, this boyfriend of yours…'

John walked back in and started to run the tap in the kitchen. The water drained away perfectly. 'All done. Now I'll get my plane out of the car and sort that front door.'

Belle and Rory looked at each other. The boyfriend conversation would have to wait.

*

Later that evening, Rory gave Sheila a call to check in.

'Belle told me about the boyfriend tonight.'

'I'm glad. Do you feel better about it now?'

Rory wasn't sure whether she did or not. 'Maybe. She hasn't really told me very much yet. Apparently, she doesn't want to jinx it.'

'Well. You'd better get used to that. You never told me anything about your boyfriends when you were a teenager.'

This was partly why Rory was uneasy. She could remember distinctly *why* she'd never told her parents about her boyfriends, and it wasn't a good thing.

'She also mentioned that you'd had a conversation with her about me meeting someone. Thanks for that.'

Sheila tutted. 'Oh, don't be so sensitive. Belle is a romantic; she wants to see you happy. I want to see you happy.'

'I *am* happy.' Rory didn't consider whether this was actually true or not. 'Anyway, it's not just the two of you on at me. Susie and Penny are coming round tomorrow night and I think I'm going to get the same from them.'

'I like that Susie. She's got a lot of get up and go. Penny could do with a bit of backbone. You should tell them to try the singles classifieds. Barb came round last night and she'd cut some of them out of the paper. The things these people ask for!'

'Really?' Rory had never read a singles ad, but she assumed they would be tame. Companions for long country walks and a penchant for log fires and argyle sweaters, that kind of thing.

'You would be *amazed*. It's not the women, obviously. The women looking for men are generally realistic, some are even a little pessimistic. One had actually written "No time wasters" like she was selling a used car. But the men! Oh my word! Almost all of them are looking for women fifteen years younger than they are. They even have specific requirements about looks: slim, blonde, medium height. I bet they are short, fat and bald. There were a few who wrote that they wanted someone "active". I assumed that meant they liked to play sports, but Barb says it's about sex. Charming, eh?'

Rory could imagine the look on her mum's face. 'Maybe they were written by the estate agent for this house. He was rather creative with his descriptions.'

'Exactly! And if you don't understand what they mean, you could get yourself into no end of trouble. They even have letters after their names which are like a secret code. For example, GSOH means Good Sense of Humour. Barb thinks we should put an ad in and see what happens.'

'Maybe you should, Mum. Might be a laugh.'

Sheila snorted. 'What would I write, for goodness sake? Grandmother of one, sixty-five, looking to meet a tea-drinking, newspaper-reading, quiet man in his sixties.' She thought for a moment. 'AMOT.'

This was a new one on Rory. 'What's AMOT?'

'All My Own Teeth.'

*

Rory peeped in the door at Belle before she went to bed. Her daughter had fallen asleep with her phone in her hand and it took every ounce of Rory's self-control not to tap in her code and look at her messages. Belle could be trusted. Of course she could. Rory would make time this week for them to sit down and have a proper conversation about this boy. Belle was a clever girl, but she was naïve; Rory didn't want her to get hurt.

One person who wouldn't wait much longer for a boyfriend conversation was Susie. Rory was already regretting agreeing to a get-together tomorrow night. With the house, school and everything going on with Belle, she had so much to think about. The last thing she needed was one of Susie's 'Find a Man' schemes.

CHAPTER NINE

The next evening, Susie arrived at Rory's front door with two bottles of red wine. Which was good. And a large brightly-coloured book. Which was bad.

'We need a plan.'

'Can't we just have a chat and see how the evening goes?' Rory shut the front door – which closed smoothly thanks to John's work with the plane – and spoke to Susie's determined wiggle as it disappeared into the lounge.

'Not a plan for tonight. A plan for finding husbands. Hello, Pen.'

Penny gave a little wave from the sofa. 'Where are we going to look for them?'

Susie sat down on the edge of an armchair, her blonde curls straining to escape from their hair band, and she smiled as if she was about to sell them a time share. 'That's the beauty of "The Law of Attraction". We don't need to go and look; they will come to us.' She employed the tone of a yoga master.

Rory put three wine glasses on the table and groaned. 'Is this from another of your books?' Susie had a minor addiction to the self-help section of the local bookshop. In the last eighteen months, she had tried to become a goddess, make friends with fear, and feed her inner child (who seemed to seriously like cake). If she was branching out into the relationship section, they were all doomed.

Penny, ever the supportive friend, was nodding her head slowly. 'If you build it, they will come. I think I saw a film about that once.'

'I am not building a baseball pitch in my back garden.' Rory poured them all a large glass of Susie's wine. 'The neighbours already hate me for using the electric sander after nine p.m.'

Susie was not to be put off. She laid her book down onto the coffee table dramatically, as if it were a religious artefact. Rory looked at the title. '*Attracting Your Perfect Mate*,' she read aloud. 'Are you going to have us paint our bums red and flash them at passing males?'

Penny giggled and wrapped her arms around her cream polo-neck sweater. 'Can I just wear red cycling shorts? I get a bit chilly.'

'The Law of Attraction,' Susie continued, as if she hadn't heard them, 'tells us that we have to visualise what we want and then it will come to us. We just need to focus.' She pointed a red fingernail at each of them decisively. 'So that is what we are going to do. Visualise the man we would like to marry.'

Rory sighed. She'd learned from experience that it was easier to give in to Susie when she was in this mood. 'Okay, how long will it take? I was hoping we could order in some Chinese food.' She gave Susie a mock-serious face. 'I've been *visualising* it all day.'

'Very funny. Right, both of you put your wine down on the table.' Penny and Rory both took a big gulp before doing as they were told. 'Now, close your eyes.'

Rory kept one eye open. 'Is this when you take our valuables and do a runner?'

'Sshh!' Susie had both eyes firmly closed. 'You are ruining my concentration. Now, both of you, start to think about the kind of life partner you would like to have. What will he look like? What job will he do? Where will he live?' They heard a rustling as she consulted the book on the coffee table. 'What will his life goals be?'

'I'm visualising George Clooney,' Penny whispered. 'What about you, Rory?'

Rory opened one eye and looked at her. 'I'm visualising someone putting the bins out and then knocking up a spag bol.' They both collapsed into laughter.

Susie was not amused. 'You need to take this seriously. Stop laughing. Just stop.' She sighed. 'Open your eyes. You're clearly not ready for the visualising part. Let's make a list instead. Have you got pens and paper, Rory? We need three sets.'

Dutifully, Rory disappeared, and returned with a notepad and three pens. Susie tore off a sheet for each of them.

'Okay, we need to write a list.'

'This is very low-tech for you, isn't it? Don't you have Excel spreadsheets for this kind of thing in the IT department?'

'Don't talk to me about spreadsheets.' Penny slumped back into the sofa. 'Nathan Finch has been on to me this week about them. He says he is concerned about the "validity of my data".'

Rory put down her pen and paper. 'What does that even mean? Susie – translate.'

'It means he thinks she is making it up.'

'But I don't! I slave for hours over those things because I don't know the first thing about spreadsheets. I have to ask Colin in the library to help me with them.'

This time Susie put down her paper. 'Oh, really? So that's what you two whisper about over his desk.'

Penny frowned. 'Yes. We have to whisper. It's the library.'

Rory smiled. 'I think Little Miss Matchmaker here is suggesting that there might be something more interesting than spreadsheets going on between the two of you.'

'Yes, I am.' Susie tapped her nose with the pen. 'Maybe there are some other sheets the two of you might be interested in exploring together?'

Penny's eyes bulged. 'No, no, no! We are just friends.'

'He's too old for Penny, anyway.' Rory would have guessed Colin was mid-fifties; Penny was a decade younger.

'It's not that. I don't mind an older man, actually. But I've known Colin for years. And anyway, he's… I've known him for years.'

Susie crossed her arms. 'Methinks the lady doth protest too much.'

Rory shook her head. 'You stick to the IT; I'll do the Shakespeare quotes. Come on, what are we doing with these lists? I'm getting hungry.'

Susie picked up the notepad. 'So. We have to make a list of the ten qualities we most want in a life partner.' She pointed her pen at Rory. 'And if you put spag bol or bins on that list, I am going to make you write it out a hundred times.'

'You're not allowed to give lines any more.' Rory waved her own pen back at her. 'It's not a learning experience.'

Penny had already started her list. 'I'm going to put *kind* at the top.'

'Kind?' Susie pretended to be sick. 'That sounds a bit boring.'

'Actually, I think kindness is very underrated.' Penny continued to write.

'And it is *her* list,' Rory pointed out. 'What are you going to put on yours?'

'Well…' Susie flourished her pen as if she were a playwright about to commit to paper her magnum opus. 'Number one: strong arms.'

Rory choked on her mouthful of red wine. 'We're keeping it to the important things then?'

Susie looked affronted. 'That is important. I like a man who is physically strong. I want to feel protected.'

Rory put her hands up to her face. 'How on earth are we friends? Every time we talk about men – pretty much all the time at the moment – you take me back fifty years.'

Susie wasn't going to be put off. 'Number *two*: intelligence. Is that better?'

'That you don't want someone stupid? Uh, a little.' Rory looked to Penny for back-up.

Penny smoothed down her skirt and tried to help. 'Have you got anything in there which is to do with being a nice person?'

Susie looked like she'd smelled something bad. 'Nice?'

Rory opened her mouth but was interrupted by a knock on the front door. That was a surprise. No one arrived unannounced these days.

'Hi, hope I'm not interrupting anything?' John was wearing his work clothes – Rory needed to stop picturing him in that imaginary B&Q calendar – and was carrying something long and red on his shoulder.

'Er, no. It's fine.' There was no way Rory was going to invite him in. Susie might eat him alive, and there was already a shortage of builders in the area. What *was* he carrying? It had a gold fringe.

'I know you haven't got back to me yet about doing some work, but I saw some old friends earlier and they were getting rid of this rug. I thought it might do you a turn until you sort out the flooring in your sitting room?' John scratched the top of his head and moved from foot to foot. 'You don't have to have it if you don't want it.'

This was really kind of him. She couldn't just leave him out on the doorstep now. 'Thanks. Come in.'

Rory had a brief internal debate as to whether she should run on ahead and warn her friends – well, Susie – to behave themselves, but John was already strolling in front of her into the sitting room. He stopped short when he saw she had guests. Susie's eyes nearly popped out of her head.

'Sorry to interrupt your evening. I'm just dropping this off.' He knelt in the middle of the room and unrolled the rug. It was Persian and had probably been expensive when it was new. It wouldn't have been Rory's first choice, but she had torn up the rotten paisley carpet in the frenzy of her first week here, and it was a lot better than the bare floorboards which were still awaiting repair and varnish.

As John pushed out the corners of the rug to make it flat, Susie was mouthing over the top of his head and pointing at him: 'Who is *that*?'

'Susie. Penny. This is John. He might be doing some work on the house.'

Susie's next gesture bordered on obscene. She really needed to rein it in. Rory tried to avoid looking at her altogether. 'Thanks for that, John. It looks great.'

John sat back on his haunches. 'Yes. Not bad. It'll do you for now, will it?'

'Yes, thanks. It's fine I'll…' Rory stepped onto the rug just as John was moving it to straighten it. Her legs went from under her and she tripped backwards, caught by the armchair.

'You nearly sent her flying!' Susie's expression was less concern for Rory's fall and more admiration at John's strength.

John jumped up. 'Sorry, Rory! This floor is so slippery. Are you all right?'

It really hurt, but she didn't want to make him feel bad. 'I'm fine. Honestly. Always wanted a ride on a flying carpet.'

John was leaning over her in the chair. He looked really concerned. Then he righted himself and ran his hand across his head. 'I've got some anti-slip webbing in the van. I'll go and get some before it causes a real accident.'

The minute the front door closed, Susie jumped up and looked out the window. 'Who the hell is that?'

Rory was taking the opportunity of John's absence to rub her bottom. She had landed with a real bump. 'I've told you, that's John Prince. The builder I met in B&Q.'

'Yes, but you didn't tell us he looked like *that*. I assumed he was some old guy with his bottom hanging out of his trousers.'

Rory's elbow hurt too. She'd whacked it on the arm of the chair. 'Like what? Why would I tell you what he looked like?' Especially when she had been doing her best not to notice what he looked like from the first time they'd spoken.

Susie turned and wagged a finger at her. 'You've been trying to keep him to yourself, haven't you? No wonder you've been less than interested in any of my dating ideas. You've already got your sights set on…'

'I've only got a bit of this left, but…' John was speaking as he walked back into the room, but trailed off as he realised that all three women were looking at him. 'What?'

'Nothing, John. Thanks. I'll take that and do it later.' Rory was mortified. Had he heard what Susie was saying? 'I'm really grateful for the rug, but we need to get back to our school work now.'

John glanced at the notepads and pens. It would be believable that they were working – so long as he didn't read the lists.

'Of course. I'm sorry again about the… carpet and the… flying. The sending you flying.'

Rory stood up. 'Honestly, I'm fine.' She almost herded him out of the door as he raised his hand in a short wave towards the other two.

After she closed the door, she took a deep breath before subjecting herself to Susie's third degree. She was *not* interested in John romantically. But she didn't want Susie to be, either.

CHAPTER TEN

The kitchen showroom was busy that Sunday afternoon. Sleek white and modern? Traditional wood? Sparkling granite? Rory had no idea which kind of kitchen she wanted. She'd be fitting it herself, so 'easy to install' was top of her list.

Sheila had insisted that she came shopping with her. 'I don't want you just choosing the cheapest option; I know what you're like. I gave you that money so that you can make the place nice for you and Belle.'

'I'm not even sure I need a new kitchen. Maybe just an oven and a new sink would do.' The cost of these kitchens was eye-watering.

'That's what I mean. I don't want you to make do. I want you to have a nice home.' Sheila held up her finger. 'Plus, I do not want to have any more dinners out of cardboard boxes at your house, thank you very much. Now, which one do you like?'

Rory looked around her. 'I honestly don't know.'

Sheila prodded her in the back. 'Well, try one of them on.'

'Pardon?'

'Have a go in one. See how it feels.' She pushed Rory firmly towards a mahogany ensemble. *Corsica*, according to the plastic display board. 'Go on.'

Rory stood helplessly in front of the oven. 'What do you want me to do?'

Sheila waved her arm around. 'Open the oven. Pretend you're looking at a roast chicken.'

This was ridiculous. But Rory opened the oven and peered inside. 'Is this method acting? Because I really need time to get into character. Channel my inner housewife.'

Sheila shook her head. 'No. That isn't you. Too old-fashioned. Try the white one over there.' She frowned as Rory ambled over to it. 'Don't just stand there. Stick your hands into the sink. Pretend you're washing up.'

At least this was more fun than wandering around aimlessly. 'You need to give me something to work with here, Mum. Am I washing a roasting tin? Wine glasses?' Rory turned back to the sink and pretended to hold up a glass. 'The smears on this. I really should change my liquid.'

'Do you need any help, ladies?'

Rory jumped and turned around to see a man young enough that she could have taught him in the last five years. He gave them a toothpaste-ad smile.

'Yes, please.' Sheila had taken control. 'We would like to buy a kitchen.'

The young man winked at them. They probably deserved that. 'Then you're in the right place. Shall we sit down?'

As per the instructions on the showroom's website, Rory had written down the dimensions of her kitchen, marking on the doors and window. She passed these to the young man – 'Please, call me Adrian' – and he punched them into his computer before spinning the screen around to show her a 3D picture of her kitchen.

'Well, isn't that clever?' Sheila looked like Penny had when watching Nathan's PowerPoint. 'It looks just like your kitchen, Aurora. Only cleaner.'

Call Me Adrian took them through the rest of the process, moving cupboards and white goods around the room with a flick of his mouse. 'Once you have the layout, you can choose which doors and worktops you want.'

Rory leaned closer to the screen. 'And are these all quite easy to put together?'

Call Me Adrian slid an A4 glossy brochure across the desk. 'We have a full installation service available. It starts from as little as two-nine-nine-nine.'

Rory nearly choked. Three thousand pounds? 'It's okay. I'm going to do it.'

It was impossible to tell who looked more incredulous: Call Me Adrian or Sheila.

'Don't be ridiculous, Rory.' Sheila got there first. Although Call Me Adrian didn't contradict her. 'Just let the professionals do it.'

But Rory was not going to be persuaded on this one. Electrics and plumbing were beyond her, but she'd put together a variety of IKEA furniture over the years. How different could this be?

Then Sheila's eyes lit up. 'Unless you were going to ask Mr Prince to do it?'

Rory ignored her and turned back to Call Me Adrian. 'How soon can I get this delivered?'

*

Rory and Sheila were still arguing about whether or not she should pay for installation, when Rory heard her name called. 'Ms Wilson?'

She turned with a fixed smile. Bumping into pupils, or parents of pupils, was relatively common when you lived in the catchment area of your school. Often it happened when you had a large bottle of gin in your trolley, or you'd decided to dash to your local Spar without combing your hair.

But this wasn't a student or a parent. It was the deputy head. Nathan Finch.

He looked very different outside of school. In place of the sharp suit was a polo shirt and jeans. His hair wasn't quite so perfect. He was softer, somehow.

He waved a brochure in the air. 'Are you kitchen shopping too?'

'Er, yes.' Rory was conscious of Sheila floating at her shoulder. 'This is my mother, Sheila.'

'Hi.' Nathan stuck out his hand. 'Nathan Finch. I work with your daughter.'

Sheila beamed, shook his right hand, then looked directly at his left one. Oh God, she was looking for a wedding ring.

'Your daughter is a real asset to St Anthony's. Everyone speaks very highly of her. I only joined this term, but I'm already beginning to see why they are so keen on her.'

That was surprising. Praise?

'Nathan is the new deputy head, Mum.' If Rory was hoping that this information would signal to her mother that she could dial down on the 100-megawatt smile, she was sadly disappointed.

'That's a lovely thing to say. Every mother likes to hear that her daughter is doing well.' Her laugh was borderline flirtatious. Rory needed to escape. Could she fit herself inside the under-the-counter fridge behind her?

It got worse. Sheila was on the offensive. 'So, have you moved into the area? With your family?'

There was no time for the fridge. Rory should just fake a faint. Right now.

'Yes. I've got a flat near to the school. Just me, though. No family.'

Had Nathan just flicked a glance in Rory's direction? If she held her breath, could she make herself pass out?

'Well, I'm sure you've got lots to do and Mum needs to sit down, so we'll leave you to it.' Rory put a firm hand on Sheila's back and nearly catapulted her in the direction of the door.

'See you Monday!' Nathan called.

Once they were sitting down with a drink in the café next door, Sheila started. 'He seems lovely, Aurora. And not at all how you described him.'

To be fair to her mother, Nathan hadn't looked – or acted – as he usually did. It was quite unsettling to see this other side to him. Now Rory knew how the students felt when they encountered her out of school and treated her like an E-List celebrity.

'Don't be fooled, Mum. He has not been like that in school.'

Sheila was not for turning. 'Perhaps you haven't seen the real him yet. You shouldn't judge people until you have got to know them.' She brought her teacup to her lips and blew on it. 'Speaking of which. I've seen the new tenant. The wife.'

At least this would get her mum off the subject of Nathan Finch. 'Did you?'

'I bumped into her in the lift. She looks older than him, although it's difficult to tell – it really ages a woman when she doesn't dye her hair. And' – she paused for emphasis – 'she had a big bruise below her right eye.'

Rory frowned. 'Did you speak to her?'

'Well, she seemed a bit agitated, so I asked if she was okay and she shook her head. When the doors opened at the ground floor, her husband was standing there waiting for her! He looked *really* cross and took her away with him back to their flat; barely even looked at me. I felt very uncomfortable.'

Maybe Belle had been on the right track about him. 'That does sound odd, Mum. Maybe you should be suspicious.'

'That's what I thought. So, what shall I do? Go round to her flat?'

Rory drained her coffee mug. 'I don't know. You still don't know much about them.' Rory was all for helping people out, but she didn't want her mother to put herself in a vulnerable position. 'Give it a couple of days and see what he's like once they've settled in properly. If you're still worried, I'll come with you and we'll drop by and say hello.'

Sheila poured the last four drops out of her teapot into her cup. 'Thanks, love. You're right, I need to let them settle in first.'

Rory wanted to leave. She was concerned about running into Nathan again. Plus, John was at her house repairing the cornice. She'd merely asked him to loan her a large stepladder so she could reach, but he'd mumbled something about his public liability insurance and how he'd have to do it himself. Nevertheless, she really wanted to get back and help. 'Shall we go?'

Sheila put down her cup and shuffled to the end of the booth. 'Yes, let's go. It's the same with your deputy head chap, you know. You need to let him settle in before you make your mind up.'

Not this again. Rory stood and held Sheila's coat out for her. But could her mother be right? Had Rory misjudged Nathan Finch?

CHAPTER ELEVEN

By Monday morning, Nathan was back in Deputy Head Mode. He caught Rory as soon as she got into the building.

She crossed her fingers that it wasn't about data again. She had entered everything she had to and did not want to see another spreadsheet until half term. However, when she found out what it was about, she would have happily swapped it for typing numbers into small cells for the rest of the day.

'Ms Wilson, could you step into my office for a moment?'

He closed the door behind her gently. 'You have 10-G today, I believe? I just wanted to give you the heads up that Charlie won't be in your lesson. Apparently, his mother is in hospital again and he has been taken into emergency foster care. But it seems he has run away.'

Rory's heart plunged. 'Run away? Are the police looking for him?'

Nathan nodded. 'I'm afraid so. They called the head last night to ask if he had any information about his whereabouts. Apparently, it's happened before?'

Rory wanted to drop everything and go and look for him herself. If the police had called Derek Brown yesterday, that meant Charlie had been out all night. She couldn't bear the idea of him walking the streets, cold and alone. 'Yes. Last time his mum went in, he did the same thing. But he turned out to just be at the hospital with her. I presume they have already checked the hospital?'

Nathan clasped his hands and leaned forwards. 'Yes, they have. The police have asked us to keep our ears to the ground. Find out if any of the other kids know where he is.'

Charlie's mum must be beside herself, Rory thought. If she was in hospital, that might mean she needed an operation. It had been on the cards for a while. 'Of course. Of course. I'll let you know if I hear anything.'

Rory hurried towards her classroom. She was glad that Nathan had told her about Charlie. He had seemed almost caring when he spoke about the boy. Maybe there was another side to him. Right now, though, she had to focus on finding Charlie, and she knew exactly where to start.

*

As soon as the class had dragged themselves into the room, she closed the door purposefully and looked at them. 'Okay. Where is he?'

'Who?' Lacey's mock innocence wasn't going to win any Oscars.

Rory didn't have time to play nice. 'You know who. Charlie.'

'We already told Finchy.' Harry had his legs stretched out in front of him, crossed at the ankles, his pose more appropriate for a beach café than a secondary school classroom. 'We don't know where he is.'

They must think that Rory had been teacher-trained yesterday. 'So, if I check your mobile, there won't be any messages from him?'

Harry sat up quickly and crossed his arms over his chest. 'You ain't allowed to do that. That's my civil liberties.'

'And Charlie is a boy whose mum is in hospital and he has nowhere to go. I think I'll take my chances with the Human Rights Police on that one.' Rory held out her hand for Harry's mobile.

'Just tell her.' Lacey nudged Harry. 'Charlie likes her.'

Harry sighed and took another bite from the chocolate bar that Rory hadn't even noticed until that moment. 'He slept at mine last night. He's gonna go in and see his mum later. He ain't run away. He just don't want to stay with those idiots the social have put him with.'

Rory breathed again. If Charlie was in contact with his friends, he was all right. She would call the hospital at breaktime and speak with his mum. That poor woman didn't need any added stress exacerbating her condition.

Just then, there was a knock on the door. Nathan. He beckoned at her through the window. For the first time, Rory wasn't angry to see him. She held the door open but didn't go out into the corridor. 'Yes, Mr Finch?'

'Just wanted to let you know that the boy has been found. Emergency over. He turned up at the hospital. They are letting him stay there with his mother today and she has made him promise to go back to the foster carers tonight. He will be back in school tomorrow.'

'Thanks for letting me know. I appreciate it.' And she did. He probably had a lot of other important things to be getting on with. It was thoughtful of him to let her know that Charlie was okay.

Then he had to go and ruin it. 'Mark his absence as an "authorised family event" on the register. No need to damage our attendance data.' And he turned and left her with the door, and her mouth, wide open. *That's* why he'd been concerned.

*

'That man is a data machine.' Rory had come to the staffroom for coffee as soon as the students left and had bumped into Susie doing the same.

'Yes, but a nicely packaged one.' Susie winked.

This was almost as bad as her mother having scanned him for evidence of a wife. 'Eurgh. Can you stop? What is wrong with you?'

'What is wrong with me is that I haven't met a decent man in months.' She lowered her voice. 'I just had to throw away a twelve-pack of unopened condoms because they had gone out of date.'

'Do they go out of date, then?' Rory stopped stirring her coffee. She'd never scrutinised a condom box enough to notice a best before date.

Susie hit her forehead with the heel of her hand. 'That comment is why you also need to find yourself a man. And soon. Things have changed since people made acquaintance with the opposite sex whilst taking a turn around the drawing room, you know.'

'Hello, ladies.' Penny joined them in the kitchen. 'What are you whispering about?'

Rory threw her spoon into the dishwasher. 'I was moaning about Mr Finch and Susie was rutting the fridge.'

'By which she means I am making it my personal crusade to ensure Rory gets some action this side of the menopause. I'm arranging a girls' night out. Are you in?'

'Maybe.' Penny flopped down into a nearby chair. 'I'm rather more interested in the slagging off Nathan Finch conversation. He's dropping into my lessons almost every day. Always going on about the same thing. *"Consistency, Miss Phillips. Consistency."'*

Penny wasn't the most modern of teachers. She wasn't at the cutting edge of three-part lesson plans, catering for different learning styles and incorporating whatever latest technique in pupil engagement was doing the rounds on Twitter. But she was a wonderful teacher in the holistic sense of the word. Students in her lessons really got to learn something important. And they got good grades.

Rory was sick of hearing Nathan Finch's favourite word. 'What was he criticising?'

The gentle RE teacher shrugged her shoulders. 'My books weren't marked according to his new marking policy, and when he looked at my data on the system, it didn't match the data on my seating plans because I haven't had a chance to update them.

I tried to explain that I have fourteen different classes, but he didn't want to listen. He even accused me of cutting and pasting the marks from their previous assessment. Which is ironic, as I didn't even know you could do that.'

Rory knew that you could do it because she'd done it. Last Friday. Although she'd had the foresight to tweak some of them so that it didn't look obvious.

'I know why he's doing this.' Susie pressed her lips together. 'You've got a student teacher in RE, haven't you? She'll be looking for her first full-time job at the end of the year. Newly Qualified Teachers are a lot cheaper than you, with your years of experience.'

Penny's hand went to her neck. 'Surely, you don't think…'

Rory nodded. 'She could be right. Well, he's not going to get away with that. You are an excellent teacher, Penny; the kids love you. So what if your seating plans aren't perfect? And what about all the extra stuff you do – bringing in the wedding costumes, and getting in interesting guest speakers? I am so angry.' And to think she had begun to question whether she had misjudged the man. If he was going after Penny, her original view of him was spot on.

'Me too.' Penny didn't look angry. Just upset. 'But what can I do about it? Obviously I'll get my seating plans up to date this weekend but if he's really after me like Susie thinks, it'll just be something else next time.'

Rory wanted to put her arms around her. Penny was one of those people who needed someone else to fight their battles. Like Charlie.

'We need to talk about this off-site.' Susie was decisive. 'We need to make a plan to meet this head on.'

'Hold up.' Rory was most definitely on Penny's side, but she had Sheila's warnings about not assuming she knew the whole story still whispering in her ear. 'Maybe we are getting ahead of ourselves. It could just be that he wants to scare everyone into action. New broom and all that.'

'Do you think?' Penny looked hopeful. She wasn't the type to meet anything head on. She'd be more likely to be found hiding in the stationery cupboard until it was all over.

'No. We need to be ready, and we need to find somewhere we can discuss it.' Susie was being uncharacteristically militant about this. They were both protective about Penny, but Susie was very keen on discussing this off-site. Surely she didn't think the place was bugged? *Could* it be bugged?

'Be ready?' Penny's voice wavered.

'Yes. Ready. And I know just the place we can meet to talk about it. Ronnie's Bar on the High Street. This Friday night.' Susie held up a hand to silence Rory's protest. 'This is our friend's career at stake, Rory. I do not want to hear any dissent from you. There are some things which are non-negotiable.'

So that was why. And Rory had no choice. Penny was looking at them like a lost puppy. Rory couldn't tell her that she needed to stay home and pull 1960s kitchen cupboards from the wall so that she could paint it before the new stuff came. Call Me Adrian had pulled out all the stops to get the kitchen delivered during the half-term holiday.

It wouldn't be so bad if they were just meeting for a coffee to discuss Penny's problem. But Susie had a lot more in mind than work talk.

Somehow, Rory was going on a girls' night out with St Anthony's answer to Cupid.

CHAPTER TWELVE

Friday night came around far too quickly. Rory had got home from school relatively early for once and had a few hours before she needed to get ready to go out with Susie and Penny. She changed into her jeans and an old rock band T-shirt of Scott's from the 1980s that had somehow moved to the house with them. The band were called Cinderella – maybe Belle had requisitioned it for that reason.

The sitting room had a cast iron fireplace in need of a lot of love. For reasons best known to the previous occupant, it had been painted pumpkin orange. John had suggested she get it sandblasted, but Rory had done a bit of research online and found instructions for doing it herself with chemical paint stripper.

Belle was in her room doing homework, so Rory closed all the doors to the sitting room; she didn't want the acrid smell of the paint stripper travelling upstairs. Belle had come home full of a story about something Alfie – her boyfriend – had done in Maths. Now Rory knew about her boyfriend, he dominated their conversations. Rory knew Alfie's favourite colour, what he liked to eat, how hilariously funny he was. But she still hadn't met him. She'd shooed away Sheila's suggestion that she invite him over: "*It's not the Victorian age, Mum. He's not about to send a calling card.*" But she might feel less concerned if she'd seen him in the flesh.

She'd painted a section of the fireplace with the paint stripper. The instructions said to leave it as long as possible without letting it dry. This was the problem with all these DIY instructions – they were too vague. What was wrong with giving an exact time? Should she sit here and watch it? The doorbell rang.

It was John. 'Hi, I got some more of that wire wool that you need for… are you all right?'

Maybe it was the rush of fresh air after the chemical fumes of the paint stripper. Maybe it was the sight of John in a bottle green shirt and dark jeans. Maybe it was the smell of his aftershave doing something funny to her insides. Whatever it was, John swam before Rory's eyes and she had to grab hold of the arm he offered her. 'I just need a minute.'

John tilted his head backwards and smelled the air. 'What is that smell? Have you started on the fireplace? Please tell me you had all the windows and doors open when you used that stuff? It's toxic! Can I…?' He pointed at the sitting room door. Rory nodded and stood aside.

When he pushed the door open, he pulled his head back, grimacing at the smell. 'No wonder you feel strange. I'm surprised it didn't knock you out.'

He covered his nose and mouth with his hand and walked around the entire downstairs of the house, opening any windows and doors. He was right. The smell was very strong. Somehow, Rory hadn't noticed it so much whilst she'd been painting it on. Then she remembered the instructions and called out: 'You're not supposed to let the paint dry.'

He came back to the hallway. 'Is that what you've been doing? Watching paint dry?' His face broke into a grin. It was infectious.

'That's what my life has come to. It's Friday night and I'm watching paint dry!' The more Rory thought about this, the funnier it seemed. She couldn't stop the laughter.

John was watching her. 'You've got a great laugh, you know.'

Well, that stopped her. They stood in silence for a moment. Then Belle's head appeared over the bannister. 'What are you two laughing about?'

John was still looking at her. Rory coughed. 'Nothing, I was just about to make John a drink. Do you want one?'

Belle put a hand over her mouth. 'Yes, please. What is that stink? I'm going back upstairs.'

Rory held her breath through the sitting room and closed the kitchen door behind them. 'Speaking of Friday night, you look like you're on your way out.'

John looked down at his clothes as if he hadn't seen them before. 'I'm supposed to be meeting a couple of mates for a drink later, but I'm not really in the mood. I could stay and help you with the fireplace?'

'Don't be daft. I was only going to have a go at a bit of it anyway, and you'll ruin your shirt.' It was very odd to see John in his real clothes. He'd shaved too, and he smelled good. Why did she have that weird feeling when she looked at him? Maybe it was the paint fumes.

'I've got overalls in the van. We can make a start together, at least.'

Together? That word made Rory's stomach flip. 'Well, if you're sure you don't mind…'

He didn't need asking twice.

By the time Rory had made the tea and taken a cup to Belle, John had his overalls on and was scratching away at the orange paint with the wire wool he'd brought. 'Who lived in this house before you? Turquoise cornice, pink walls, orange fireplace – Dorothy from *The Wizard of Oz*?'

Rory kneeled beside him and started to scrape. 'I would say, you should see my bedroom, but you already have.' Instantly, she wanted to cram the words back into her mouth. It sounded like she was flirting with him. Was she flirting with him? Did she want to flirt with him? *Quick, say something else. Anything.* 'I'm not really in the mood to go out tonight, either. But I've got to: my friend is having some problems at work.'

John nodded. 'It's good to support your friends. You're a good person.'

He needed to stop complimenting her. Her insides couldn't stand it. 'I'm not sure about that. But it's nice to help people. Like you. You like helping people.' That wasn't flirtatious. Was it?

John looked up at her. 'I like helping some people.'

The alarm started to beep on Rory's phone. How was it seven o'clock? 'I need to go and get ready. Susie won't be happy if I'm late.' Rory hadn't been looking forward to going out tonight anyway, but now it was the last thing on Earth she wanted to do. She'd much rather stay here, drink tea and scrape away at pumpkin orange paint with John. *Together.*

John turned his eyes back to the wire wool. 'Of course. Of course. You go and get ready, I'll just finish this last corner bit.'

*

'You look great, Mum!' Belle was coming out of the bathroom when Rory emerged from her bedroom. 'You haven't worn that dress in ages. It looks good on you.' Her eyes carried on down to Rory's feet. 'Oh my G... What the heck are those shoes?'

Rory looked at the inoffensive black pumps she had chosen to wear. They might have to stand at the bar and she'd already been on her feet all day. 'What's wrong with them? They match the dress.'

'They might be the same colour, but they are *not* a match.' Belle looked disgusted. 'What about your black heels?'

'Too high.' Rory shook her head. 'They're only good for dinner parties, when you get to spend most of the evening sitting down.' Even then, they made her feet throb. Was she moving into the 'dressing for comfort' stage of her life? Did she even care?

'Hold on.' Belle disappeared back into her bedroom and returned with a pair of glittery black shoes with a small heel. 'You can wear these. They're really comfortable. Honestly.'

Rory was dubious, but she didn't like to turn her daughter down. 'That heel looks a little thin.'

Belle nudged Rory back into her bedroom and onto the bed. 'Just sit down and put them on.'

Once Rory had her shoes on, she did a twirl for her daughter's approval. This was the first time she had borrowed something of Belle's. It felt like an important moment. She wanted to pull her towards her and breathe her in.

But Belle was heading back to her own bedroom. Rory followed and watched her packing a rucksack. Where did she think she was going? 'What are you doing, Belle?'

'I'm going to Fiona's for a few hours.'

'But your gran's coming. I've asked her to keep you company.' Rory had learned the hard way to no longer use the word 'babysitting'.

Belle turned, her face thunderous. 'Mum! I'm sixteen! I've told you I don't need looking after.'

Rory didn't want to spoil the evening. 'I know that, but I'm going to be back late. You might get lonely.' If only Belle could understand how young sixteen really was.

'I've made plans now. Tell Gran she doesn't need to come.'

'But I won't be here when you get home.'

Belle shrugged. 'I'll be all right. Look, I'll call you when I get home just to confirm that I haven't been abducted or murdered.'

Rory turned to go. She would have been a lot happier knowing that Belle was home, with or without Sheila, rather than letting herself into an empty house later tonight. She could put her foot down. Demand that Belle stay at home. But what argument would she have? Belle was sixteen. Why should she stay home?

No one prepared you for this when you had children. The nappies and lack of sleep had been bad, but at least she'd known where Belle was at all times in those days. Not knowing was much worse. *The bigger the child, the bigger the problems.* Was it time to give her daughter a bit of freedom?

John had slipped off his overalls and was waiting for her with his van keys in his hand. 'I can drop you off in town if you like? I'm going that way anyway.'

*

John's van was surprisingly comfortable and warm. Rory's dad's old blue van had been a museum piece compared to this.

'Do you realise that this is the first time I have ever been in a white van?'

John pretended to doff his cap. 'I am very honoured to be your first. If we had the time, I could show you what she can do. Top speeds of 60mph are not unheard of.'

Rory rang Sheila on the way. Sheila was disappointed not to be needed, but she did have some news.

'I visited the new lady. I saw her husband go out with a shopping bag, so I went up to their flat. She was lovely, but very vague. She asked if I wanted a cup of tea and then brought me back a mug of juice. George, that's her husband, had gone somewhere but she wasn't sure where.'

Rory wanted to hear about this, but she also wanted to get off the phone, so she could talk to John. 'Did she say anything else?'

'We'd barely started talking when I heard his key in the lock. He was surprised to see me, I suppose, so I tried to explain that I was just visiting to welcome them to the building, but I'm pretty sure I looked as guilty as hell. He looked worried when he saw my mug and asked her if she'd made me a hot drink. Quite abrupt, he was. Then he thanked me for visiting and almost shuffled me out of the flat.'

Rory bit her lips together to stop herself from interrupting. Once her mum was mid-flow, there was no stopping her.

'I'll be honest with you; my mind was doing cartwheels. By the time I was talking to Barb over a game of whist in the lounge later – she'd just wound up Flo by telling her that we were practising our cards because we were going to invite Sid to play strip poker – I had practically decided that he was keeping the poor woman prisoner. I feel terrible now I know the truth.'

Rory couldn't bear it any longer. 'Which is?'

'Olive has Alzheimer's. George came and found me in the lounge to tell me. He wanted to apologise and explain. Apparently, she's had it for a few years, but it's got to a point where she can't be left alone for long. That's why they've moved to Seymour House. He couldn't look after their bungalow and her at the same time.'

Rory didn't want to rush Sheila, but it was rude to be talking on the phone like John was her taxi driver. 'That's really sad. The poor man. And Olive.'

Sheila nodded. 'I didn't tell him what I had been suspecting, but I felt terrible. He seems a very nice man and it must be difficult. I invited him to poker night but he said it's a bit tricky with Olive, although if she was having a good day, maybe they could come together. I offered to sit with Olive sometimes too, so that he could go out and do some shopping or even just go for a walk. But he thinks she wouldn't like to be left with someone she didn't know.'

'That's really nice of you, Mum. It'll be good to make more friends there, too.'

Sheila laughed. 'You sound like me when you started school! Is this the beginning of you treating me like a child?'

'Of course not.' But this was the exact same feeling that Rory had had when she'd put on Belle's shoes earlier. Roles changing. Time moving. Stages reaching. She wasn't ready for any of it. 'I've got to go now, Mum. I'll call you in the week.'

'Everything all right with your mum?' John glanced across at her.

'Yeah. All good.' But Rory couldn't say the same for herself. Time to shake herself out of this mood. Penny needed cheering up. Deep breath. Happy thoughts. It would be fine when she got there.

CHAPTER THIRTEEN

Rory and Susie were both teachers. They both enjoyed reading, a glass of wine, a good laugh. But there, the similarities ended. And taste in men? They were on different planets.

Susie most definitely went for brawn over brain. Or muscles over mind. Or packaging over contents. However you wanted to describe it, her predilections in the men department were based at a primeval level. Which is why, Rory believed, they never seemed to last.

When Rory arrived, it was obvious that Susie had had a few drinks before she came out. 'You're here!' She enveloped Rory in a hug. 'Just in time. We need a rational voice. So far we have considered, A: framing Nathan for stealing school funds, or B: killing him. What are your thoughts?'

Penny sighed. 'Lovely though it would be to staple him slowly to his own desk, I think we need to accept that he is going to be here for the duration, and think about how we can live through it.'

'Have you spoken to Derek?' Rory couldn't imagine their amiable headteacher letting anyone bully his staff.

Penny nodded. 'He was really nice to me, but says his hands are tied by the governors. They are the ones who employed Nathan and they love him, apparently. He's going to have a word with Nathan, but he didn't look too confident about it.'

Rory squeezed her hand. 'We'll fight this, don't you worry.'

'What's all this talk of fighting, ladies?' asked a man who had joined them at the bar. 'Who has upset you? Just tell me.'

Susie whipped around on her bar stool, crossed her short but shapely legs, and gave him her brightest smile. 'No one worth boring you with. You don't look like the fighting type to me.'

He held his hands up in surrender. 'You've got me. I'm a lover, not a fighter.' He dropped one of his hands, took Susie's and kissed it. 'Although for you, I would make an exception.' Susie looked ecstatic. Rory wanted to throw up. 'I'm sitting over there with my friend. Why don't you come over and join us?'

Before Rory could open her mouth to say that they were in the middle of something, Susie had pulled a reluctant Penny out of her seat and was dragging her over. 'Follow!' Susie hissed at Rory.

The rest of the evening was a predictable cocktail of flirting and innuendo. Rory only got through it by drinking. And drinking some more. Eventually, she realised that she wasn't even part of the conversation any more. Susie was talking to one of the Chuckle Brothers and Penny, albeit less enthusiastically, was talking to the other. Far from being disappointed by this, Rory welcomed it as a good time to leave.

She put her hand on Penny's arm and waited for her to stop laughing politely at whatever had just been said. 'I'm going to head off.'

Penny turned around in her stool and held Rory's arms. 'Oh no! Please don't go!' She lowered her voice. 'Don't leave me here on my own. We'll go back over to where we were if you're bored here.'

Rory waved her hand hazily. 'No, I'm not bored,' she lied. 'Just tired. All the work at the house – it's taking it out of me. You stay and enjoy yourselves. There's a taxi rank outside. I'll be fine.'

But Rory had timed her exit badly. The rank had a very long queue and there didn't seem to be any sign of a cab. The house was only about a forty-five-minute power walk away, though, and it would do her good to get some fresh air. There was DIY to be done in the morning, and she could do without a hangover for company.

For the first ten minutes, the walk was quite pleasant. There were plenty of people milling around on a Friday night. She felt completely safe. As she left the town centre, though, the streets emptied out, and walking didn't feel like such a good idea any more. Then it started to rain.

Rory was cross with herself. She'd have killed Belle for walking home alone at this time of night, and here she was doing exactly that. What a great role model. With any luck, Belle would be in bed and wouldn't see her mother falling in the (now fixed) front door, soaking wet and inebriated. Rory had done her very best to show her daughter what a single, independent woman should be like, and this wasn't the picture she wanted to paint.

When Rory had been Belle's age, her dad would always come and pick her up from any night out. He'd insisted upon it, often to her embarrassment. She would make him promise to wait around the corner, so that her friends didn't find out that she wasn't allowed to walk home on her own. She wished her dad was here to call now.

With the rain, the alcohol and the reminiscing, Rory's mind wasn't on her feet. When the road became darker, she picked up the pace and almost immediately lost her balance. As her foot slid sideways, it became a slapstick comedy routine as she tried to right herself, failed, tried again, and then hit the floor. Snapping the heel clean off her shoe in the process. Worse. Belle's shoe.

Uncharacteristically, tears pricked her eyes. The events of the last week had been mounting up on her: the house, Nathan Finch, Charlie's disappearance. And now she was sat in a puddle, with rainwater seeping into her knickers. Wrenching the stupid shoe from her foot, she threw it into the nearest bush, then dropped her face into her hands and indulged in what her mother would call a 'good cry'.

'Rory?'

Looking through running black mascara, Rory saw a large white van pulled over next to where she was sprawled. 'John?'

John Prince switched on his hazard lights and jumped out, holding out his hands to help her up. 'What happened? Are you all right?'

Taking a deep breath and wiping her face with the hem of her dress, Rory nodded. 'I'm fine. What are you doing here?'

'I got a call from a friend with a… er… a… stopcock emergency. I haven't had a drink because I'm driving, so I'm going to pop over and help her out.'

Did the man never do anything but work? 'Well, I am on my way home from my crappy night out, which was made worse by the appearance of men.' She accepted his hand as he pulled her up. 'Not you, obviously. You, I am very happy to see.'

'I'm glad to hear it.' He looked down at her feet. 'I'm not up on the latest fashion, but I'm pretty sure you didn't go out with only one shoe.'

The bloody shoe. 'No. I broke the heel of the other one.'

John nodded as if he understood. Though he obviously didn't. 'And where is it now?'

Rory's face grew hot. She felt stupid. 'In the bush.'

'I see.' He didn't pursue it any further, just opened the door to his van and waited for her to get in.

Rory closed her eyes and let her head rest on the back of the seat. 'Thank you so much for this.'

'No problem. So it didn't go well tonight?'

'Nope. We were supposed to be having a girls' night out but then Susie got chatting to some guys.'

'And you weren't interested?'

Rory shook her head. 'No. Not my type.' Which was why, even if she did want to date someone, it would be pointless looking for them with Susie. She opened her eyes and looked sideways at John. It was strange looking at him from this angle. And this close. 'Did you say *she*? A female friend?'

John rubbed his nose. 'She's a friend of a friend, really.'

Of course he had friends. And some of them were female. Nothing wrong with that. So why did Rory feel sick? Was she more drunk than she realised? Maybe she'd hit her head as well as her backside. *This is John Prince. Your builder. Don't make a fool of yourself. Stop staring at him.*

'Are you okay?' John glanced at her.

'Fine.' Her voice was almost a squeak. She coughed. *Pull yourself together.* 'Sorry. I'm fine. Just tired.'

'I'll bet you are. You've been working hard on that house. People don't realise what tough work all that prep is. Stripping wallpaper, soft soaping the walls, pulling up carpets. It's back-breaking.'

Rory let her head fall back again. 'Would you believe me if I told you that fixing the house was the least complicated part of my life right now?'

John smiled. 'Actually, I would. That's what I like about my job. You know where you are with a brick wall and pile of cement.'

Rory waited for him to ask her what was complicated with the rest of her life. But he didn't. Men were another species.

Within a few minutes, they were home. John jumped out from his side and came to open her door. Until she stepped out from the van, Rory had forgotten about the missing shoe. She put her bare foot straight into a puddle. This night got better and better. Tomorrow would be worse. Belle was going to kill her.

*

The next morning, Rory was awoken by her mobile pinging. Slowly, she peeled back her eyelids and raised her head from the pillow – but not slowly enough to prevent the banging headache that the daylight brought. Turning over in bed to reach her mobile, she yelped as she rolled onto her bruised bottom. With the pain came a visual memory which made her groan out loud. Had she really been sitting in a puddle with only one shoe when John had picked her up? How was she going to face him? Bugger.

The ping was a message from Susie. *Guess who gave out her number last night?* It was difficult to be pleased for her when all Rory wanted to do was crawl to the bathroom and lay her head against the cold tiles. It was obviously one of the men from the bar who'd been given the number, and Rory wasn't sure that was cause for celebration either. She'd reply later. Right now, she needed coffee. In a bucket.

Somehow, she managed to shuffle herself down to the kitchen – after checking Belle's room to see if she was still asleep. When she'd checked on her last night, Belle had been tucked up in bed as promised. Maybe Rory was worrying about nothing. Belle was a sensible girl. It would take more than a blonde-haired boy to turn her head.

Rory had filled the kettle, and pressed its surprisingly loud switch, before realising that they had no milk in the fridge. There was no way she could get through the next hour without caffeine. She had a very strange feeling in her stomach which needed set-tling. It seemed to get worse every time she remembered John driving her home last night. Maybe it was embarrassment rather than nausea? Either way, she needed to haul herself to the corner shop and get some milk.

Five minutes later, in a hoodie she had borrowed from Belle in case she saw anyone from school, Rory opened the front door and nearly tripped over something sitting on the step.

It was Belle's sparkly shoe. With the heel fixed.

The funny feeling was back. And this time, it wasn't the chemical paint stripper.

CHAPTER FOURTEEN

Despite a weekend spent hooked up to the coffee machine, Rory didn't feel normal again until she woke up on Monday morning. And then she was back in the classroom.

10-G had finished the first drafts of their letter-writing task. 'Is there anyone who is willing to read theirs aloud? I know some of them are quite personal, so you don't have to.'

'I will!' Harry's hand shot up.

'Okay…' Rory was tentative. Harry wasn't normally so keen to share his work. 'Everyone else, please be silent whilst Harry is reading aloud. As soon as you're ready, Harry.'

Harry's gave a large comedy cough, 'Ahem!' and then he began. 'Dear Kylie Jenner. I would really like to…'

'Hold on!' Rory interrupted. 'Harry, do I need to check this first?'

Harry frowned. 'I used full stops and capital letters like you told me to.'

Lacey rolled her eyes. 'She means, is it dirty?'

'Oh.' Harry grinned. 'It might be a little bit.'

'Then maybe I should take a look first and pick out the bits that are fit for classroom sharing.' Rory had dodged a bullet there. 'Well done for volunteering, though. Anyone else?'

Charlie's hand snaked into the air. 'I could read mine if you like?

'Is it rude?' Lacey had appointed herself the classroom censor.

'No,' Charlie looked disgusted. 'It's to my mum.'

Everyone was quiet. Rory's heart was beating hard in her chest. What was he going to say?

Charlie stood up and started speaking quietly, getting louder as his confidence built. 'Dear Mum. Firstly, I am sorry for being a lot of trouble sometimes. I know that you are not well and it makes you worry when I am messing about. I don't want to make you stressed but sometimes I don't think. When I'm older, I'm sure I will be better.

'It's just that it's not fair you are ill all the time. It makes me really angry. After all that stuff with Dad, you deserve to have an easy life and not be feeling ill and in pain. When I am older, I am going to get a really good job so that I can look after you. You really deserve it.

'I am going to make you proud of me, Mum. Really proud. I am going to work hard at school and not get into trouble so you don't need to worry about me at all. Mrs Wilson says I am a good writer, so hopefully that will help me to get a good job.

'The thing is, I am scared. I am scared that you are not going to get better. I am scared that one day you will go into the hospital and not come out. What will I do then, Mum? It's always been us – you and me. What do I do if I don't have you? You're the best mum I could ever have and I miss you when you're not here. That's all. And I'm sorry. Love, Charlie.'

He closed his exercise book and put his arms down on the desk, resting his head on them.

The whole time he had been speaking, no one had said a word. Rory wanted to say something to encourage him, but she didn't trust her voice. After a few moments had passed, Lacey got up, plucked a packet of biscuits out of Harry's hands as she passed and put them down on the desk in front of Charlie. Then she pulled a chair close to his, sat down and put a hand on his shoulder.

Rory opened her mouth to speak, but was interrupted by Nathan walking into the room. Apparently, he no longer felt the need to knock first. The pupils shuffled to sit up straight in their chairs. With obvious practise, Lacey's fingers crept around the biscuits and pulled them under the desk onto her lap.

Rory recovered herself quickly. 'Mr Finch. How can we help you?'

He gave his customary menacing glance around the room and then addressed her. 'Can I have a quick word outside?'

After following him into the corridor, Rory tried to keep a foot in the door, but Nathan motioned for her to close it. 'This is not a conversation for pupils' ears. I've been reviewing the data and we're going to need to move some pupils around from next week. Charlie, for example. His data shows that he is not making the expected progress, so I'm thinking of pulling him out of English for some small group work with a learning support assistant, and…'

'No.' Charlie would not react well to this at all. 'I think that would be a very bad idea. With respect, he's had a lot of change in his life lately. If he thinks he's being treated differently from everyone else, he'll be upset. Anyway, I can get his grades back up, he's just had a lot of absence.'

Nathan didn't look convinced. 'I'm sure you could give me a reason like that for every pupil in the class, but sometimes we have to make tough decisions in this job. Well, we'll leave that discussion for now, perhaps. More importantly, I wanted to tell you that your latest homework grades need inputting as soon as possible so that we can make an informed decision about set movements. Once the information is on the system, perhaps you and I can meet to discuss individual pupils.' He stopped and smiled at her. It wasn't the same politician-on-*Newsnight* smile he gave in staff meetings. It was more natural. More reasonable. Almost human.

Rory mumbled her agreement and backed into the classroom.

'He well fancies you, Miss.' Lacey was back at her desk, holding the biscuits just out of Harry's reach.

'That is not appropriate. And no, he doesn't.'

'Then why is he always hanging around here?'

Rory didn't have an answer for that, but Lacey had a point. Rory would have assumed his deputy head role would keep him much too busy to keep coming to her classroom just to ask her to enter her data. Why not just send her an email?

'What did he want, then?' Harry made a grab back for the biscuits, but Lacey was too fast.

Rory plucked the packet from Lacey's hands and put them on her own desk. That was break time sorted. 'Mr Finch had some important information to give me about our assessments for this half term.' Everyone groaned, even Charlie. He seemed to have regained his composure; either Lacey or the biscuits had worked their magic. *You don't need to worry*, Rory wanted to tell him. *I'll be here to help make sure you get exactly the grade you need to stay right where you are.*

*

After the pupils went home, Rory had a big pile of homework marking to wade through. Before she started, she went to make a drink to accompany Harry's confiscated biscuits. In the staffroom, she met Susie. A very bouncy Susie.

'Ask me what I'm doing tonight.'

'Marking?'

'Nope.'

'Planning lessons?'

Susie soon tired of waiting to make her announcement. 'No! I have a date!'

Rory was too fed up to conjure up enthusiasm, but if Susie had met someone, maybe that meant she might leave her alone and stop making her go out to noisy bars. 'That's great. Anyone I know?'

'That guy from the bar on Friday. I told you I gave him my number, and he called me this morning. We're going out for dinner tonight.'

This was all rather sudden. 'On a Monday? And why did he call you today? That's a bit short notice.' Rory was suspicious. Who had a first date on a Monday? And what made this man think that he could click his fingers and Susie would be available the same day? Although clearly, she was.

'Don't be so cynical. He said he'd been plucking up the courage to call me all weekend.' Susie was beaming and Rory didn't want to burst her bubble. He hadn't looked like the type of man who was lacking in confidence. Lacking the ability to complete a crossword, maybe. But confidence? No.

'Well, just be careful, Susie. You don't know what he's like other than what you saw in the pub.'

'And if I don't go on a date with him, I never will. Just think – he could be THE ONE!'

Rory smiled. Susie was almost as much of a romantic as Belle. An over-sexed romantic, admittedly. 'And I don't think you should go back to his place or invite him to yours until you know a bit more about him.'

Susie feigned shock. 'And break the third-date rule? Never!'

Penny joined them in the kitchen. 'Is there any milk anywhere? I need a cup of tea.'

'Bad day?' Rory opened the fridge and passed Penny someone's milk whilst Susie found her mug. 'Me too. I had a visit from Finch. He wants to move Charlie out of my class.'

'No way,' Susie shook her head. 'That boy needs stability, and he likes you.'

'Apparently, the data says otherwise.' Rory bent her arms and made a robotic movement.

'Doesn't surprise me at all,' Penny stuck out her bottom lip. 'You're lucky you only get brief visits. He pops in to my room unannounced about three times a week, and I can't get him to leave. He looks at the kids' books and then stands at the back of the classroom with folded arms like a bouncer at a nightclub.'

Susie put a tea bag in Penny's mug and filled it with hot water. 'That's just not right. Is he still using the C-word?'

Rory nearly gagged on her coffee before she realised that Susie meant Nathan's buzzword: *consistency*.

Penny nodded and took the mug of tea from Susie. 'Yep. "*You should have a ten-minute starter activity, Miss Phillips. They need to respond in green pen, Miss Phillips. You must rotate your seating plan every four weeks, Miss Phillips. Consistency. Consistency. Consistency.*"' She sighed. 'It just doesn't work like that for me.'

'We need to do something about this.' Rory wasn't about to let him treat Penny badly. 'Who does he think he is, coming in here and unsettling everyone? I'm going to see Derek.'

'I don't think he can do very much,' Penny shook her head, mournfully. 'I told you, the governors are in awe of the Fantastic Finch. They believe he's going to save us all from the Big Bad School Inspectors. I've chatted with Derek and he thinks we just need to go with it for now.'

'That's ridiculous. Nathan Finch has only been here five minutes. We can't sit back and let him get away with this.' Rory couldn't understand why he was singling Penny out in this way. He was nagging Rory about data too, but he wasn't taking up residence in her classroom. She pulled on her suit jacket. 'I'm going to see Derek right now.'

Penny fiddled with the locket around her neck. 'Be gentle with him. He's under a lot of pressure, too.' That woman was too nice for her own good.

However, when Rory arrived at Derek's office, his secretary told her apologetically that he was already in a meeting with Nathan. She offered to make Rory an appointment for later in the week, and Rory had no choice but to accept it.

What she wouldn't accept was Charlie moving out of her class. Time to get creative with that data.

CHAPTER FIFTEEN

Rory had been with kids in detention at lunchtime and was starving when she got in, so she made herself a quick bowl of porridge. Belle had gone straight to Sheila's after school and Rory would join her there when John left. She'd only mentioned the possibility of some shelves on the wall in the sitting room and here he was, with a couple of options. Apparently, he'd 'found' them in his workshop.

'How does this look?'

It took Rory a moment to pull her eyes away from his biceps and onto the shelf he was holding up. 'Uh, a bit too high.'

He brought it down. 'This?'

Rory swallowed a mouthful of porridge. 'Too low.'

He moved it slightly higher. 'Now?'

'Yes, just right.'

John made a small mark on the wall in pencil and Rory twitched. They were her beautiful new smooth walls he was writing on.

John stuck the pencil behind his ear. 'Of course, you're going to want to paint the walls first. Have you decided on a colour?'

She hadn't. She'd got as far as buying a range of tester pots but hadn't tried them on the perfect walls. 'Some possible ones are over there.' She nodded with her head.

John was a man of action. He opened the first pot and daubed it on the wall. Rory flinched. He turned to her. 'What about this beige one?'

'It's not beige.' Rory stood and put the porridge bowl onto the coffee table. 'It's mushroom.' She scrutinised it closely. 'And it's too dark.'

'Okay, then.' He popped the lid off another one. 'How about this?'

'Too light.'

John shook his head. 'I'm out of my territory on this one. Colour schemes are not my thing.' He sat down – Rory didn't like to tell him he was now sitting in *her* chair – and screwed up his eyes to look at the paint splashes. 'Nope. All look the same to me.'

'Well, they are not. I'll get my mum to help me. She's good at that sort of thing. Actually,' she looked at her watch, 'I need to get going.'

*

Between the two of them, Sheila and Belle had cooked up quite a feast. 'You two are amazing.' Rory sat at a table laden with dishes of steaming vegetables. 'I want to know why all these skills skipped a generation.'

'You were never interested in learning to cook.' Sheila passed her the mustard. 'You'd much rather be down the shed with your dad. He'd have been proud of you, you know. Doing that house up. I think you're bonkers, but your dad would have been right behind you all the way.'

Rory could feel her eyes sting. Fifteen years didn't diminish the loss.

'What would Grandad have made of me, Gran?' Belle had asked this question many times over the years. She just liked to hear Sheila's answer. And Sheila liked to tell it.

'Oh, he would have loved to see you grow up – Princess Belle, he'd have called you. After your mother, it would have been nice for him to have a little girl to play with.' The two of them laughed together.

'Do you two never get tired of this conversation?' Rory helped herself to gravy. She didn't mind. It was nice to imagine what her dad would have made of Belle. 'How are your friends downstairs?'

'They're fine. I've visited a couple of times and Olive is great company. We reminisce about the old days. Children's programmes, sweets we ate, songs we danced to. I've suggested we make it a regular thing on Tuesday afternoons. George can have some time to himself and Olive and I can watch a bit of daytime television together. He thinks we watch home makeover shows, but I've discovered that Olive likes a bit of Jeremy Kyle. She doesn't have a clue what a DNA test is, but she likes to giggle at the "funny people".'

'Her Alzheimer's isn't that bad, then?'

Sheila sat back in her chair. 'It's hard to explain. It sort of comes and goes. Today, she asked me who "that man" was, and it took me a while to work out that she meant George.'

'Ouch.'

Sheila nodded. 'I met their daughter today, too. She popped in while I was there. Olive was a bit confused about who she was but Karen, the daughter, gave her a big kiss and a hug and, I don't mind admitting, her tenderness with her mother brought a tear to my eye.'

'Oh, Gran.' Belle leaned over and gave Sheila a kiss.

'Thanks Belle, sweetheart. I hope you'll look after your old gran if my marbles start to go. I'm not sure what your mother would do with me.'

Rory winked. 'I'll find you an old people's place with a nice view and good-looking male carers.'

Sheila shook her head. 'Karen wants me to encourage George to go to some of our social events. She's offered to sit with her mum, but he feels guilty leaving her. I thought I'd get Sid to ask him.'

'That's a good idea, Gran.'

'Well, I thought so. But when George got back, she only went and told him that we'd talked about it! I don't know what it is with you all nowadays, thinking you have to be honest about everything. It's not healthy to know the inner workings of each other's minds. Much better to put it in such a way that they end up thinking it's their idea. When Karen went to the toilet, George asked me if my daughter tried to tell me what to do, too.'

'I hope you told him that your daughter is wonderful.' Rory helped herself to another potato.

'Of course, I did. But there's something to be said for spending time with your own generation. That's why I can't understand those silly men who want to date a girl half their age. What do you think they talk about?'

'I don't think they plan on doing much talking, Granny.' Belle raised an eyebrow at Rory.

Rory laughed. 'That's enough from you, young lady. Although, I think she's right, Mum.'

Sheila wrinkled her nose in disgust. 'I'm surprised they have the energy. How's your friend Susie getting on?'

'Actually, she has a date tonight. She says he seems to be normal which, according to Susie, is a small miracle in itself.' Susie's actual words had been: 'He's not a bloody freak for once!'

'And has he got a friend for you?' Sheila never missed an opportunity.

Rory sighed. *Remember that you love her.* 'It's not a "buy one, get one free" situation, Mother.'

'Well, it wouldn't hurt for you to get yourself out there,' Sheila pressed.

Rory put down her fork. 'Get myself out there? *Get myself out there?* When did you start talking like a character from an American sitcom?'

Belle did a rapper pose. 'Granny, you're so street.'

Sheila tucked her hair behind her ear. 'I got it from Barb. I can't help it if I'm more modern than my own daughter.'

'Well, Mum,' Rory raised her wine glass. 'When you get yourself "out there", I'll be right behind you.'

'Well, maybe you've just given me the incentive I need.'

*

Sadly, Susie's hopefulness about the man she'd met at the bar was short-lived. Rory had just got into bed and picked up a book when the phone rang.

The first thing Rory heard was a snuffling and a munching. 'He's married.'

'What? Oh no. What an arsehole. How did you find out?'

'One of his wife's friends came into the restaurant and he nearly gave himself a hernia trying to hide under the menu. After that, it didn't take much working out.'

That's why he'd called out of the blue on a weekday. It wouldn't be so easy to call women at the weekends when he was at home with his wife. Sleazebag. 'How awful for you.'

'I felt a complete idiot. There I was, prattling on about cities I'd like to visit, and he was trying to shush me and contorting his body like a cast member from Cirque de Soleil, trying to avoid being seen.' There was the crinkle of chocolate wrappers at the other end of the line.

'I hope you gave him what for. How dare he do that to you?'

The sound of a Pringles tube popping open. 'I ordered the most expensive dessert on the menu then left immediately after it was served so that he ended up with the bill. I hadn't even eaten much of the dinner because I was trying to be one of those delicate women who only manage a couple of forkfuls. Now I wish I'd eaten the lot. And his plate as well. He didn't eat anything after he'd spotted his wife's friend.'

'Well, it's his loss. I hope the wife's friend tells her and he gets found out.'

Susie gave a huge sigh. 'I knew he seemed too normal to still be single at his age. They've usually got some flaw that's left them on the shelf. Back to the bloody drawing board.'

'Maybe you should give yourself a bit of a break. Just let up on the husband-finding for a while. Don't they say, sometimes it's when you least expect it that you meet someone? If you just live your life and enjoy it, you never know what might happen.' Rory's heart thumped as she spoke. Was that what was happening to her, with John?

Susie coughed on either a Pringle or a lump of chocolate. 'I know *exactly* what will happen. I'll be found in forty years' time having been half-eaten by my large collection of cats. No, it's onwards and upwards for me. I've been on the Internet researching good locations for single men. I'm going to get scientific.'

There was no point in trying to persuade Susie otherwise. Rory also knew what was coming next.

'And you're coming with me. No arguments.'

CHAPTER SIXTEEN

'Hello, Rory. How nice to see you, come in.'

The headteacher's office was a museum piece, entitled *Teaching Circa 1950*. Dark varnished chairs sat around a large heavy desk with a green leather inlay. The walls were lined with hardback books and the carpet had a well-trodden shiny path towards the desk.

The 1950s theme continued as Derek's secretary appeared with two cups of tea on saucers. Derek leaned forward and took his cup. He was a kind and fair man, but Rory still felt a twinge of apprehension walking into the head's office. It must have been a deep-rooted sensory memory from her own teenage years, when she had spent a considerable amount of time standing *outside* the head's office.

'Thanks for seeing me.'

'Not at all. Not at all. I'm sorry that you had to make an appointment. It's not like the old days when you could just pop in, eh?' Rory didn't like to remind him that the 'old days' were only last term. 'Now, what can I do for you?'

Rory hesitated. It didn't sit naturally with her to make a complaint about a member of staff. There were enough people willing to attack teachers – pupils, parents, the national press – without them turning on each other. Then she pictured Penny's innocent face and ploughed straight in. 'I am unhappy with a member of staff. It's Nathan Finch.'

Derek's face clouded. 'I'm sorry to hear that. What is it you are unhappy with, exactly?'

Where should she start? 'It's the way he's treating people. Dropping into classrooms without even knocking. Harassing people if they haven't used the correct colour pens. Obsessing over data entry and deadlines. It's putting everyone on edge and it's unnecessary.'

Derek sat back in his chair and pressed the tips of his fingers together. 'I'm sure it all seems a bit awkward initially. But this is a transition period. I'm afraid we've been a bit stuck in the dark ages, it seems. Nathan's ideas are very modern and it will take us time to get used to them.'

'We don't want to get used to them.' Rory was warming up to her topic. 'And he doesn't even seem to care about the children. Their progress data is more important than whether they are actually happy and doing the best they can. They don't like him, either.'

Derek nodded slowly. 'Being liked isn't always possible in our profession, is it? The students here don't like change. They'll get used to him. You've been here so long, you've probably forgotten what it's like to be a new arrival.'

This was not going well. How could Rory make him understand? 'That's the point. We have all been here a long time. That's what is great about St Anthony's. We know what works with these kids. Take Penny, for example. She's a great teacher and she gets great results. But Nathan is making her life a misery. I know she's been to see you but she's too nice to tell you how bad it's been.' This was Rory's trump card. Everyone liked Penny. Even the cleaners bought her a Christmas card.

Derek looked sad, but he just continued to nod. 'We need to move with the times, Rory. All of us. I know it's difficult, but it's like this everywhere now.' He picked up his teacup again. 'I didn't realise it was that bad for Penny, though. I'll see what I can do. Ask Nathan to go gently.'

As she left his office, Rory bumped straight into Nathan. 'Hello, Ms Wilson. I see you've been in to see Mr Brown.'

Rory felt butterflies in the pit of her stomach. Guilt? Nerves? Panic? 'Yes. He's free now if you want him.'

'Actually, it's you I was looking for. Would you come into my office?'

*

The deputy's office had previously been on the floor above, but Nathan had taken over the finance office, next to the head, and moved its occupants upstairs. The three finance ladies were now crammed into a shoebox whilst Nathan was able to swan around his executive suite.

'Take a seat.' He indicated a pair of black leather armchairs beside a coffee table. There was a modern coffee machine next to them: no Royal Doulton for Nathan Finch. 'I'd offer you a drink, but I assume Derek already did that?'

'Yes, I'm fine thanks.' Rory perched on the edge of a chair. She didn't intend staying long.

Nathan sat down on the other chair and paused dramatically. He put his fingertips together in exactly the same way Derek Brown had. 'I'm afraid I have to speak to you about a delicate issue. It has come to our attention that there have been some rather negative conversations in the staffroom. Conversations which may be damaging to staff morale.'

Rory looked at him in amazement. Had she accidentally fallen into the plot of a George Orwell novel? Was he bugging the staffroom now?

He seemed to be waiting for her to respond. Proceed with caution. 'Okay?'

'I'm afraid you have been heard making critical remarks about the new processes in the school. You and a couple of your colleagues.'

Rory couldn't believe what she was hearing. She could feel the anger rising. 'Who has told you this?'

'That's not important. As deputy head, people tell me things.' He smiled smoothly. 'I can assure you that any new plans and procedures are fully backed by the headteacher and the school governors. Therefore, it is the duty of the staff, *all* staff, to follow them through.'

'Without expressing an opinion?'

'Of course, you are entitled to an opinion. However, you have been here a long time and you have quite a lot of influence amongst the staff.'

'So you would like me to keep my mouth shut and toe the party line?' Rory couldn't believe what she was hearing. This was Saint Anthony's – not MI6.

'I'm saying that we value your input, but it needs to be channelled appropriately, and the staffroom is not the appropriate channel.' He stood up. 'Anyway, I have taken enough of your time. I'm sure you have plenty to be doing. The data deadline is tomorrow, after all.'

*

At the end of the school day, Rory sent a text to Penny and Susie to come to her classroom; she didn't feel like finding them in the staffroom after her meeting with Nathan. Not without checking it for bugging devices first.

'Who the hell does he think he is?' Rory was pacing up and down between the desks, waving her coffee mug around dangerously. 'He's been at St Anthony's five minutes and he thinks he knows everything about everyone. Who's been talking about us?'

'I doubt it's anyone,' Susie was sat on one of the student desks, filing her nails. 'Who would talk to him? He's just suspicious and has taken a chance. He must know that everyone hates him.'

'Derek Brown certainly doesn't.' Rory sat down behind her desk, put her elbows on the table and rested her chin on her hands. 'He didn't bat an eyelid when I told him what people thought about Finch.'

Penny sat up sharply. Her face reddened. 'Oh. It might have been me.'

'What?' Rory looked up.

Penny fiddled with her ear lobe. 'I might have mentioned to Derek that I'd been talking to you and Susie about Nathan. I'm sure I didn't say anything bad, though. I'm so sorry.'

Rory sighed. 'It doesn't really matter. Although Derek is clearly going to be no help. We need to sort this out on our own.' Rory rested her chin back in her hands and stared down at the seating plans that needed changing again. *Rotate your seating plan every four weeks. Consistency. Consistency.*

'What can we do, though?' Susie started on the other set of fingernails, swinging her legs. 'We are only *The Staff.*' She made inverted commas signs with her fingers. 'He is in charge, and we have to follow what he says.'

'Well, I can't do that.' Rory got up and started pacing again. 'No man tells me what to do. We need to come up with a plan.'

'Well, we'll have to be quick.' Penny had gone back to her normal colour but was still fiddling with her earlobe. 'The inspectors are due very soon, and if they fail us on anything, people will be for the chop. Though I guess it would be worse if they give the school a better rating than last time – then he'll be untouchable.'

Rory frowned. 'Just give me some time. I'll think of something.'

Susie tapped the desk in front of Rory. 'Well, you can tell us all about it tomorrow night. Don't forget that you have promised me a proper night out. There's a nightclub I want to try.'

Rory groaned. 'A nightclub? Aren't we a bit old for that?'

'Not this one, wait and see.'

On the way to her car, Rory called Sheila to cancel the dinner she'd arranged to have with her on Friday. She really needed to get herself a diary.

'Never mind, dear. I think there's something on in the lounge on Friday, so I'll do that instead.' Rory's mother's social life was better than her own. 'I managed to persuade George to join us last night for a card game. He waited until Olive was asleep and then came down. His daughter has given him her old baby monitor so that he can listen in to check she's okay.'

'Good for you.' Rory was at her car and pushed her pile of books into her left hand so that she could rummage in her bag with her right to find her car key.

'He is a lot of fun when he isn't worrying about Olive. You'd like him. He used to be a headteacher.'

'Headteachers aren't my favourite people right now.' Rory managed to locate her key and clicked the lock. She threw the books onto the passenger seat. 'Okay, I'm in the car, Mum. I'd better go.' That usually worked. Sheila had a mortal fear of speaking to Rory on the mobile in case she was driving.

'Wait! I almost forgot to tell you – Barb has a gentleman friend! You're never going to believe this, but she met him online on one of those dating websites they advertise on the TV.'

'Oh God. She does know there are people on there who just want sex?'

'Really? I'm not sure. Maybe she does. Anyway, she's met someone and she's being surprisingly coy about him; won't even tell us his name.'

'Maybe you should give it a go, Mum?'

Rory could almost feel her mum shudder. 'Dating on the Internet? Not for me. I think you need to meet a man and get to know him. I mean, they would never have matched me and your dad, would they? He liked being outdoors and fixing stuff. I used to tell him he might as well move into his garage, the amount of time he spent out there. I prefer a nice book or visiting a friend for tea.'

Rory started the car. 'Mum, I really need to go.'

Before she went home that evening, Rory had another plan she wanted to investigate. She had a friend who worked as a social worker at the council, and she needed to talk to her about Charlie.

CHAPTER SEVENTEEN

If any profession had more paperwork than teaching did, it was social work. Siobhan's desk was awash with files and papers. It took Rory a few moments to realise that Siobhan was sitting behind it. 'Are you drowning under that lot?'

Siobhan pushed her chair back and rubbed her eyes before getting up to give Rory a hug. 'I am. Who knows what time I am going to get to leave tonight? Please tell me your questions are quick ones.'

They'd known each other long enough for Rory not to be offended by this. 'They are, they are.'

'Come out to the kitchen. I'll make a drink whilst you tell me.'

Rory declined the coffee, but whilst Siobhan made one for herself, she told her about Charlie and his mum. What a great kid he was. What a tough time he'd had. About him running away from the foster carers each time his mum went into hospital. 'So, I was wondering. If his mum had a friend he could stay with when she went into hospital, whether social services would accept that.'

Siobhan sipped her coffee and they walked back to her desk. 'If she wants to make an informal arrangement with a friend to look after him, social services wouldn't need to be involved.'

'And' – Rory paused – 'would it make a difference if that person was his teacher?'

'Oh.' Siobhan sat back in her chair and narrowed her eyes. 'Speaking as your friend, Rory, you need to think carefully about this. I know what it's like; I do. You see so many kids who need help in this job and you want to take them all home. But we can't. We have to do what we can to help them with the expertise we have. Your expertise is being a teacher.'

Rory had been expecting this. She'd given Siobhan a similar pep talk in the past. Some kids got under your skin and you took them home with you mentally each night. She'd never considered taking one home for real before now. 'I know what you're saying. But Charlie is a bit of a special case. He's a really good kid. I just want to know whether it's legal. Or ethical. Will I be allowed to do it if Charlie's mum says she is happy with it?'

Siobhan sighed and rubbed her eyes again. 'From a social services perspective, there's no issue. But you might want to check it out with your headteacher.'

That was another bridge that Rory would cross later. Last year, she would have been confident that she would get Derek Brown's blessing on this. In the current climate, she wasn't so sure. She stood up and gave her friend another hug.

'Of course, of course. Thanks Siobhan, you've been a great help. I'll leave you to your piles of paper and get home to mine.'

*

But she didn't get stuck into a pile of marking when she got home because John Prince's white van was outside waiting for her.

When he saw her, he climbed out of his van, holding a pile of brochures. 'What time do teachers finish work then?'

'Never.' Rory put her key in the lock of the door. She couldn't look directly at him and her heart had started thumping. 'Sorry. Was I supposed to meet you here?'

John shook his head. 'No, no. I just had a couple of bathroom catalogues for you to look at and thought I'd drop them in on my way home.'

Clearly, he could have put these through the letter box. How much should she read into the fact that he'd waited for her? 'Would you like to come in for a cup of tea? You can tell me which suites you think would fit in my bathroom.'

Over a cup of tea, Rory told him about her plan for Charlie. She had spent the last week thinking about this, but she hadn't spoken to anyone about it. She was aware how crazy it sounded. But the more she considered it, the more it seemed like the right thing to do. The thing she *wanted* to do. Now that she had spoken to Siobhan and knew that there was no legal reason why she couldn't do it, there would be nothing to stop her.

While she told John about it, he sat and listened intently. She wanted him to tell her it was a good idea. Would he think she was crazy? Would she be scaring him off?

'I think that's a wonderful idea.'

'Really?' She heard the eagerness in her own voice. 'You don't think it's madness?'

He shook his head slowly from side to side. 'Not at all. If he's a nice kid, he deserves a break. Especially if his mum is all he has. He must be pretty terrified every time she goes into hospital. Staying here with you and Belle could be just what he needs. He already knows you and knows that you're kind and caring.' He took a long drink from his tea. 'Good for you.'

Kind and caring? It was nice to think that that was how he saw her. 'Thanks. I'm going to visit his mum in hospital and see what she thinks. I'm not sure how Charlie will feel about it either. Living in his teacher's house will be a bit weird.'

John shrugged. 'Got to be better than staying with complete strangers. Especially strangers he doesn't sound that keen on.'

'You're right. Hopefully he'll see it the same way.' Rory sat back in her chair. She would also have to speak to Belle about it. This was her house, too. Not that she was spending much time in it lately. Rory had even threatened to start renting out her room for a bit of extra cash.

John leaned forward and put his cup onto the coffee table. He took a slow look around the room. 'This place is starting to feel really homely. You did a good job of painting that wall. Mushroom 04?'

Rory threw a cushion at him. She'd used about fifteen tester pots on the wall and had been in a world of pain trying to choose a colour, until John had pointed out that they were all essentially the same. 'Very funny. I surprised myself, actually. Doing the painting was okay – almost therapeutic.' She'd painted a picture of Nathan Finch's face on the wall last night and then spent a very enjoyable ten minutes splatting paint at it à la Jackson Pollock.

John threw the cushion back at her. 'And have you persuaded Belle to let you buy a new sofa?'

'Well, I was starting to agree with her about keeping it, but…' Rory shuffled around. There was something not quite right. Belle had been adamant that they should keep their original sofa because it was so soft – she had sighed dramatically that 'It almost hugs you' – but right now there was something sharp poking into Rory's bottom. 'For some reason I can't get comfortable tonight.'

John stood and leaned over. He smelled of aftershave and the outdoors. He got closer. And closer. Was he going to put his hand under her bum? 'Get up for a second, it might be a spring in the cushion. I'll have a look.'

Rory's legs felt strangely wobbly when she stood to the side so John could feel around the seat of the sofa. Maybe she needed to eat something.

John stuck his hands down the sides of the seat cushion and prodded about, getting caught up in the throw as he did so. Rory's mother had made her buy that. Frowning, he shook his arm to extricate it from the fringe. 'I've never understood why people put these things on sofas. What's the point in choosing an upholstery you like and then covering it over?'

Rory had said the exact same thing to her mother. 'Just chuck it on the floor. And the cushions.' Sheila had made her buy those too. Pointless things.

John passed her a couple of cushions as if they were exhibits from a museum and then peeled back the throw. Something small and hard fell to the floor and rolled under the table. John peered after it. 'What was *that*?'

Rory got down on her knees and reached under the coffee table. It was a small piece of pea-green Lego. 'How the hell did that get there? Belle hasn't played with Lego for years.'

John replaced the throw, trying to put it back in the same position he had found it. 'Did she like Lego, then? That's a bit unusual for a girl, isn't it?'

Rory crossed her arms. He'd pushed a button here. 'Not for a girl who has me for a mother. Why should Lego be for boys? Should she have played with washing machines and irons, then?'

John gave up trying to get the throw to stay in place and held up his hands. 'I'm not a sexist pig, honest. Just don't know much about kids and what they play with.'

'They play with whatever they want to play with. But I'll let you off, this time.' Rory pulled the edge of the throw back into place, chucked the cushions on top and sat down. That was better.

So John didn't have kids? He was definitely father material. Decent, kind, hardworking, fun. In a lot of ways, he reminded Rory of her own dad. He hadn't ever spoken about anyone special in his life, but that didn't mean there wasn't someone. Although if there was someone, she'd have to be pretty damn understanding about the amount of time he was spending at Rory's. Could Rory ask him?

Luckily, she didn't have to. 'It wasn't that I didn't want kids. It has never been an option really. Just never met the right person.'

That weird feeling started up again. A fizzing sensation in the pit of her stomach. *Push it down.* 'You've still got time, though. If you wanted them.' Bugger. Did that sound flirtatious? She was spending too much time with Susie; it was wearing off on her.

John rubbed his nose. Had she made him uncomfortable? 'Yeah. Maybe. Getting a bit stuck in my ways now, though.'

Rory could have kicked herself. Her mind raced for a witty comeback but it was empty. *Cheers, brain.*

After a brief awkward silence, John stood up. 'Anyway, I'm off. I'm going out for a curry with a mate of mine.'

Going out for dinner sounded great to Rory right now. 'I wish I was going to a restaurant rather than trying to cobble something together in that pathetic kitchen.'

John scratched the back of his head. 'Well, if you're not doing anything tomorrow night, we could go out together for something to eat?'

Rory's face burned. Now he really would think she was flirting. She'd practically forced him to invite her to dinner. Thank goodness she had an excuse. 'That's a kind offer. But I've promised to go out with Susie tomorrow night.'

CHAPTER EIGHTEEN

Music thumped through the double doors. There was no neon sign or name stencilled across the windows. The outside of the building looked more like a hotel entrance than a nightclub. Rory had never been here before, but it wasn't quite what she had expected. Where were the bouncers?

'What is this place?' As they entered the lobby area, there was a vibe in the room which instantly made Rory suspicious. She couldn't put her finger on it, but there was an air of… desperation?

'It's just a nightclub.' Susie's innocent expression did nothing to allay Rory's suspicions. 'It's just been so long that you've forgotten what one looks like.'

Although Susie was right about it having been a long while since Rory had been in a nightclub – she had quite possibly been wearing an acid rave T-shirt the last time she'd been to one – there was still something odd about this place. Most people seemed to be hanging round in ones or twos; there were no large drunken groups of people out for a night on the town. The room was strewn with banners and bunting decorated with hearts and small fat angels.

'Shall we put our coats in the cloakroom?' Penny looked even less keen on this than Rory.

'Cloakroom?' A young, attractive man appeared who seemed eager to help them. 'Right over there, ladies. But let me sign you in first and run you through the opportunities this evening!'

Rory's head snapped around in Susie's direction. 'Why do we need to be signed in at a nightclub?'

Penny was holding her duffel coat and looking confused. 'What does he mean by *opportunities*?'

Susie shrugged and smiled at them brightly. 'You know security these days. It's a good thing, isn't it, making sure we're all safe?' She lowered her voice, 'And I wouldn't mind getting a pat down from him if he's offering.'

Penny picked up a flyer from the desk and read aloud: '"Stupid Cupid. Where singles can mingle."'

Rory turned to Susie in horror. 'This is a bloody singles event!'

'Is it?' Susie feigned surprise. Badly. Good job she taught IT, not Drama. 'I didn't realise. Oh well, we're here now.' She turned to the man on the desk. 'Susie Clark. Without an E.'

'The Clark or the Susi?' He winked at her before locating her name badge, which had been clipped to two others. 'And you must be Aurora and Penny?'

Rory took the badges and gave Penny hers. 'I am going to kill you,' she hissed at Susie under her breath.

*

Two gin and tonics later, and Rory had forgiven her. Almost.

Rory fished the lemon from the bottom of her gin glass and sucked it. 'I still don't know what possessed you to book the three of us into a singles event.'

Susie pretended to knock on Rory's head. 'Hello? Because we're *single*.'

Rory rolled her eyes. 'But a whole event focused purely on matching people up? It's all a bit Last Chance Saloon.'

Susie put her left hand on her hip. Rory had seen that look directed at stroppy Year 11s. 'You can stop rolling your eyes, young lady. I'm not sure if you are aware, Aurora Wilson, but we have been in the Last Chance Saloon for so long that we each have a stool with our names on.' She dropped the hand and sighed. 'I'm bored of chatting to men in pubs who turn out to be married. At least this way, we know everyone here is a possible date. Please just give it a chance. Who knows, you might even find someone worth breaking your vow of chastity for.'

Rory scanned the room. In the near vicinity she counted three beer bellies, two shiny shirts and a toupee. 'I doubt it.' She took another gulp of gin. 'Anyway, you might have warned us, at least.'

'If I'd warned you, there was no way you would have come, and I didn't want to come on my own. Although, actually, you are more likely to be approached by a member of the opposite sex if you are alone. Men are intimidated by large groups of women.'

Rory rolled her eyes again.

'Well, the music's good.' Penny tapped her foot. 'It'll be nice to have a dance at least.'

'No.' Susie grabbed hold of their wrists. 'No dancing. Men don't approach women when they're on the dancefloor, and also we'll get hot and sweaty and that's not attractive in women of our age.'

'Bloody hell, I feel like I've just woken up in a Jane Austen novel.' Rory threw the rest of the gin and tonic down her throat. 'Sorry, Mrs Bennett, but I'm off to dance. Come on, Pen.'

Thankfully, the music wasn't too loud, so they could talk whilst they were dancing. 'I've hardly seen you this week, how's it been at school? Is Finch still breathing down your neck?'

Penny nodded gloomily. 'He appears all the time; it's so unsettling. Yesterday we were having a lovely lesson about Buddhism – your Harry was sitting in the middle of the room, dressed in my gold shawl with his legs crossed – and the others were writing Buddhist quotes out and sticking them to him.'

Rory smiled. Everyone referred to 10-G as her class. She only taught them for five hours a week, but it did feel like they were hers. 'I bet he loved that. Did he have a bar of fruit and nut hidden under the shawl?'

Penny laughed. 'Probably. Anyway, Mr Finch turned up and told the children to get up and get behind their desks. Apparently, the lesson would have been unsatisfactory because Harry wasn't getting the opportunity to write, and I was doing nothing to stretch the more able members of the group.'

'What more able members of the group?' Rory might love 10-G but she was under no illusions about their academic ability.

'I tried to explain that they *were* learning, and Lacey, bless her, started to tell him the main tenets of Buddhism, but he didn't want to hear it. I've got to have a meeting with him next week. I'm dreading it.'

Rory became aware of a short bald man dancing at her elbow. She moved herself around so that she had her back to him. 'I cannot bear Nathan Finch. He has no idea how hard it is to engage those kids. I wonder how many years it's been since he had a full teaching timetable? Do you know, he was only timetabled to teach three hours a week when he started with us, and he has given those lessons to a trainee teacher, so he just sits at the back of the room to supervise. He doesn't know what he's talking about. Just ignore him.'

Penny shuffled from side to side, not quite in time to the beat of the music. 'I wish I could. I've got a feeling he's not going to go away.'

The short man reappeared on the other side of Rory and smiled at her. 'He's not the only one,' she muttered. 'Come on, let's go and get another drink.'

When they got back to Susie, she was chatting to a real live man. She was also flicking her hair intermittently – her mating signal – so they sat on stools a few feet away. When she glanced over at them, Rory pulled a funny face at her. Susie turned back to the man with a smile and stuck two fingers up in Rory's direction.

'I don't know why she is so intent on meeting someone.' Rory had ordered two more drinks. They needed a lot of alcohol to get through tonight.

'I can't understand why she goes for men who are mean to her.' Penny looked over at Susie. 'Why doesn't she try and find someone nice?'

Rory completely agreed. The man Susie was speaking to was one of her classics. Huge biceps. Shirt too tight. A vacant expression.

'Can you keep a secret?'

Rory turned back to Penny, who was staring into her drink and chasing an ice cube around with her straw. 'Yes, of course.'

Penny took a deep breath and looked up. 'I might have met someone.'

She'd kept that quiet. And she wasn't even looking particularly happy about it. 'Really? Is it Colin the librarian?'

'No! How many times do I have to tell the two of you that we're just good friends!'

Rory held up her hands. 'Sorry! Sorry! Where did you meet him then? What's he like?'

Penny smiled, but she looked nervous. 'He's lovely. It's early days but he's really lovely. When I first met him, I was still engaged to that idiot. But now… well, things have changed.'

Rory hugged her friend. 'That's great, Pen. I'm really pleased for you and can't wait to meet him.' She kept her hands on Penny's arms and scrutinised her face. 'Why aren't you looking happier about it?'

Penny's bottom lip trembled. 'I'm so grateful to you both. After I threw that idiot out, the pair of you were so great. Taking me out with you, looking after me.' She stared into her drink, then looked up again. 'But it's not really me, all this.' She gestured at the dancefloor. 'I prefer a night at home. I don't want you to think I'm one of those women who drops her friends when she meets someone new. And I still want to see you both, but I'm worried that Susie won't want me to hang out if I'm not looking to meet someone. I'll just cramp her style.'

'Oh, Pen,' Rory took the drink out of her hand and put it on the bar. 'Stop drinking that gin, it's making you maudlin. Susie will be happy for you! She doesn't invite you only because you're single, you silly thing. We have fun together.'

Rory wasn't convinced that Susie wouldn't throw a hissy fit once she realised that Penny had picked up a man with seemingly little effort, but she wouldn't mention that right now. Penny's emotional response probably included a big dollop of worry about Nathan Finch too. That man had a lot to answer for.

'Thanks, Rory. I'm probably being silly.' Finally, Penny smiled. 'He *is* really nice. We have been out a few times and we have such a nice time. He's kind and thoughtful. Funnily enough, he does know Colin and they're about the same age.' She sat up in her seat. 'Too old for you, otherwise I'd ask if he had a friend.'

Rory nearly spat out her gin. 'Not you too, Penny? I've got enough to cope with dealing with stupid Cupid over there.' She turned to jerk a thumb in Susie's direction and, because Susie was now behind her, ended up sticking it in her boob, instead. 'Sorry! I didn't realise you'd come back.'

'Don't apologise. It's the nearest I've come to any action tonight.' Susie slumped down and picked up Penny's drink. 'Is this for me?'

'Yes.' Penny spoke before Rory could say it wasn't. 'That man no good?'

Susie took a large slug of Penny's drink. 'Nope. He told me it was great that a woman of my age still came out to events like this. That I hadn't given up hope.'

'Dick.' Rory shot him a death stare across the room.

'Idiot.' Penny patted Susie's hand.

Susie smiled weakly. 'Thanks, girls. Maybe I'm too late for even the Last Chance Saloon.' She took another large gulp. 'I'm going to the loo.'

As soon as she was out of earshot, Penny grabbed Rory's arm. 'Look, will you tell her for me? That I'm seeing someone?'

'Penny! You're being daft. Surely you're not scared of her?'

'Not scared, no. Just a bit worried about how she's going to react.'

'Well, I think you're worrying unnecessarily. Go to the toilet when she gets back and I'll tell her.'

Penny breathed out. 'Thanks.'

Susie came back from the toilet. 'Glad I went when I did; there's a massive queue now.'

'Oh, good!' Penny slipped off her stool and disappeared into the crowd.

Susie looked after her and then back at Rory. 'Did she not hear me properly?'

Rory patted the stool next to her and waited for Susie to sit down. 'I need to tell you something. Before I do, I want you to remember that we love Penny. She is our friend.'

'What's happened?'

'She has a boyfriend.'

'What? How? When? Who? Is it Colin the librarian?' Susie looked almost hopeful with her last question. Maybe it would be easier to bear if it had been nice, quiet Colin.

Rory shook her head. 'Apparently not.'

Susie crossed her arms. 'Fabulous. Whilst I'm running around like a walking, talking pheromone, she manages to attract a mate as if by magic. Don't worry,' she uncrossed her arms and held a hand up to Rory. 'I am pleased for her. I'm not completely bitter and twisted. I just want to know what I'm doing wrong.'

Rory rubbed her leg. 'You're not doing anything wrong. It's just down to luck.' It was also down to the fact that Susie was attracted to Neanderthals, but Rory kept that to herself. This wasn't the time for another lecture.

Susie slapped the bar in front of them and beckoned to the barman. 'Do you know what's not down to luck? Getting rat-arsed. My round; let's make them doubles this time.'

Great. There was no way out of this. Susie needed to get stinking drunk and she wouldn't want to do that alone. Which meant Rory would be nursing a massive hangover tomorrow and that would wipe out the whole day for any DIY or schoolwork. Sunday, she was planning on going to the hospital to speak to Charlie's mum. And hospitals made her feel queasy at the best of times.

CHAPTER NINETEEN

The antiseptic smell hit her as soon as she walked in; it made her stomach flip. Belle hadn't been an accident-prone child, so the last time Rory had been here had been the night with her dad. The night they'd come home without him. She hated hospitals. Particularly this one.

It took a while to locate the ward with Charlie's mum. Hospital signage was confusing and Rory was still feeling delicate after the session with Susie on Friday. If Susie had been trying to drown her sorrows, she'd succeeded in generating a tsunami. Eventually, Rory found the right ward and was directed to the right bed by a helpful young nurse, who asked her to use the hand sanitiser first. The alcohol in it made her want to heave.

Rory wasn't prepared for how Charlie's mum would look. Or for the sight of Charlie by his mum's bed. He jumped up. 'Hello, Miss! What are you doing here?'

She nodded in the direction of the bed. 'I've come to see your mum, Charlie.' She smiled at his mum. 'Hello, Mrs Lewis. Nice to see you again.'

Charlie's face darkened. 'Am I in trouble?'

'No, no. Not at all. I just wanted to come and give your mum an update, seeing as she can't make it to Parents' Evening this year. I want to let her know in person how well you're doing in English.'

Like the sun coming out, Charlie's face cleared. Then he looked a little bashful. 'Thanks.'

'Actually, Charlie, I'm dying for a coffee. Is there any chance you could run to the canteen and get me one if I give you some money?'

Charlie stood up and pulled himself as straight as he could. 'I've got money, I'll get you one.' He turned to his mum. 'Do you want anything, Mum?'

She shook her head weakly and then moved as if to pull herself up in the bed. Rory stepped forward. 'Please don't move on my account, Mrs Lewis. I'll sit closer, if that's OK?'

'Of course. And please call me Jane. Go on, Charlie. Go and get your teacher a drink.' As soon as he'd run off, she turned to talk to Rory. 'You haven't come in to give me his English report, have you?'

Rory shook her head. 'No. I've come with a bit of a proposition.' She paused, wondering how to start. 'I'm worried about Charlie. I'm worried about this running away business.'

Jane sighed a weary sigh. 'Me too. But what can I do? I'm in and out of here a lot at the moment. I keep getting dehydrated. It's the Crohn's. When I'm in here, I can barely move, much less go out and find him.'

'You've been in a lot of pain?'

Charlie's mum blushed and then nodded. 'I don't know how much you know about Crohn's, but it's not a pleasant condition.' She laid her head back into the pillows and stared up at the ceiling. 'I'm due for another operation at the beginning of November and I'll be in for a week. I don't know what I'm going to do. He hates being in foster care. Hates it. It doesn't matter if they put him with nice people. He just won't stay.'

'And there aren't any family members who can have him? Or friends?'

Charlie's mum's weary head sunk even lower into the pillow. 'No one. We moved down here to get away from his dad; I don't know if he told you that? I can't risk telling anyone where we are. I can't risk it.' She closed her eyes as if she was exhausted.

Rory didn't ask why. It didn't take a genius to work it out. She took a deep breath. 'What if he came to stay with me?'

Charlie's mum's eyes snapped open at the exact same moment as Charlie turned the corner back onto the ward. He proudly produced a paper cup of coffee.

'You're a superstar.' Rory smiled at him. 'Did you get sugar?'

Charlie hit the heel of his hand against his forehead. 'I knew I'd forget something! I'll be right back!' He scooted off again.

Rory turned back to Jane. 'You don't have to decide anything right now. It's a big thing, I know. But he could stay with me when you're in hospital or when things get difficult for you to manage at home. I can help him stay on top of his work too, and…'

'Yes.'

'Wait. I need to explain. My house is a bit of a mess because we are renovating it and…'

'Yes. Please, yes.'

Rory smiled. 'Are you sure?'

'I'm coming out of hospital tomorrow and have no idea how I am going to look after him and myself for the next few weeks until I'm back in for the op. I don't have any local friends.' Mrs Lewis looked down at the bedclothes, which she was twisting in her hands. 'I can't get out very much. I lost my job too, and I've been too ill to look for anything else.' She looked up at Rory. 'I know Charlie likes you. I know that you'll look after him. To be honest, it will be a huge weight off my shoulders to know that he is okay. He's been more of a parent to me than I have to him these last few months. And it'd only be until I've had the op and I'm back on my feet again.' Tears were brimming in her eyes.

'Hey, hey,' Rory leaned forwards and rubbed her hand. 'He's a great boy. You're doing a very good job with him. Look…' Rory hadn't planned for this, but in the circumstances, what else could she do? 'Why don't you both come?'

'No.' Charlie's mum shook her head. 'I need to be in my own place.' She blushed again. 'I'm back and forth to the loo all the…'

'You don't need to worry about that with us…' Rory stopped talking when Charlie's mum raised her hand.

'That's very kind, but I just wouldn't be comfortable. I'll be fine at home. Charlie can be in and out to see me whenever he wants, but he'll be at yours for meals and getting him to school and stuff.' She let out a long sigh. 'And when I go in for my operation, he won't have to go to foster carers.'

When Charlie reappeared with the sugar, they told him their plan. He was shocked by Rory's proposal but, after some coaxing from his mum, promised to think about it. Rory knew it would be weird for him to be living with his teacher, but she was determined to make it work. She hadn't liked the way Charlie's mum looked, lying in that bed. She didn't know much about Crohn's disease, but she hadn't expected her to look so poorly. They had obviously been through a lot more than Charlie had let on. Rory had an overwhelming urge to pick them both up and keep them safe. She also had an urge to visit her own mother and give her a hug.

*

'Well, this is a nice surprise.' Sheila was in her tiny kitchen, making them a drink while Rory leaned against the counter. 'I've just got back myself; I was at Barb's, catching up.'

Sheila had made the small kitchen in her retirement apartment look just like the one in Rory's childhood home, but in miniature. The old biscuit tin was there, the 1970s orange Tupperware salad spinner, the decorative plate from Sheila and Frank's Isle of Wight honeymoon. It was comforting.

'How's Barb's romance going?'

'From strength to strength as far as I know; I've hardly seen her these last few days. His name is Fred and he lives on his own about five miles from here. He's still driving, so they've been out to some nice places together. Sometimes I wish that I'd learned to drive.'

'Are you kidding me, Mother? You'd be a liability.' Rory could imagine Sheila, slowing down every time a sparrow wanted to cross the road.

Sheila carried two cups of tea through to her lounge. 'Don't be so cheeky. Anyway, my Belle says she'll take me wherever I want to go once she can drive.'

'You'll be lucky. She's hardly ever at home.' This was beginning to play on Rory's mind more and more. When the house had been a complete mess, she could understand it. But it was really taking shape now; the lounge was comfortable and Belle's bedroom was finished. Yet she still went out, rather than inviting her friends home.

Sheila sipped her tea. 'That's what happens.' She patted Rory's knee. 'They come back eventually.'

'Maybe you're right.'

'Speaking of daughters, I met George's daughter again. She got a bit teary, love her. Her mum had helped her out so much with her first boy. He's eleven now. Her youngest is five and Olive always thinks that he's his older brother – she only ever remembers one of them. Well, you know me, I ended up giving her a cuddle and she had a good old sob. Poor girl just misses her mum; even though her mum is right there, snoring in her chair.'

This story made Rory feel even sadder. Her mum drove her crazy sometimes but she couldn't imagine not… No, she wouldn't think about that. 'I'm sure that was really nice for her to be able to talk about it.'

'I hope so. I've given her my telephone number so that she can call me if she needs anything. She loves George and he adores her, but they aren't going to sit on the phone for twenty minutes, talking about what the boys have done at school that week. That's what mums are for.'

Rory reached over and gave her mum's hand a squeeze. That was exactly what mums were for. 'How are George and Olive?'

'Very well. I am going to cook dinner for them next Tuesday. I was thinking I'd get Auntie Jean's rosemary chicken recipe. Olive has been telling me that her mum cooks with rosemary. I know that her mum is long gone, but if I cook rosemary chicken it might bring back some nice memories.'

'That's thoughtful, Mum.'

Sheila nodded. 'It'll be nice for me too. You'll be able to cook properly once your new kitchen is installed. When is it coming?'

'During the half-term holiday.' That would give Rory a whole week to get it installed. Should be plenty of time.

'And are you going to give in and get this John Prince to do it for you?'

Rory sighed. 'He's a builder, mum. He has bigger jobs to focus on than my kitchen.'

'You say that, Aurora, but he's not doing building work for you, is he? He's doing all sorts of little jobs.'

He was. Shelves and fireplaces and unblocking drains. 'I am paying him to do them.'

Sheila raised both eyebrows. 'So, what is he charging?'

Rory couldn't answer this. She had paid for materials and she'd paid for the work the electrician had done, but everything else was a bit vague. Every time she'd asked John about paying for his time, he'd managed to fob her off somehow. There was the discount he'd offered if he could use the before and after photos – which she hadn't yet seen him take – but she was still expecting to pay him. 'I haven't seen the latest invoice yet.'

Sheila smirked. 'Just as I thought. I think he's interested in you. He's pretty much been at your beck and call these last few weeks.'

Rory and her mother's view of men was never going to coincide, but Sheila's words played on Rory's mind on the way home in the car. Could John be interested in her? And if he was, would he ever make a move? Or should she?

CHAPTER TWENTY

Firstly, Belle had tried the time-honoured trick of running past the sitting room door, calling out, 'Bye, Mum! See you later!'

'Hold on!' Rory called back. 'I haven't even seen you tonight.' Belle came slowly back down the hallway. Now Rory knew why. 'What the heck are you wearing? Or should I say, not wearing?'

Belle jutted out her hip and scowled. 'It's just a skirt, Mum.'

'That's not a skirt, that's a belt.' And that was Rory's own mother's voice coming out of her mouth. She didn't care right now. 'You are not wearing *that* Belle. What were you thinking?'

Belle rolled her eyes. 'This is *fashionable*, Mum. Everyone wears skirts like this. I've got thick tights on underneath it.'

Thick tights didn't help the fact that the skirt was so tight you didn't even need an imagination to see what was underneath. 'You cannot go out wearing that unless you have a pair of proper trousers on underneath. Or at least leggings. Where are you going, anyway? You told me you were going to Fiona's house.'

Belle's head flipped back and she groaned dramatically. 'I am. Bloody hell. What's with all the questions?'

Rory felt like she'd been slapped. When did she and Belle speak to each other like this? Clothing discussions had only ever arisen because Belle wanted to wear T-shirts with asinine pictures of Snow White and Minnie Mouse. Not because of outfits suitable for the red-light district. Surely she knew what she looked like? *Don't go crazy. Stay calm.* 'The questions are because you are supposedly going for a sleepover at a friend's house, and yet you are dressed for a nightclub. Perhaps you can see my confusion?'

'You pretend to be cool and modern, but you are just like every other mother. It's so unfair. Just because you don't believe in people fancying each other, you have to ruin it for me, too. If you're so bothered about it, I'll go and get changed into something that covers me from my neck to the floor. Maybe I can find a nice *hoodie and jeans*.' Belle flounced out of the room.

'That would be marvellous, thank you.' Rory looked down at her own red hoodie and jeans. It didn't look that bad, did it?

She hadn't even had a chance to sit back down before the doorbell rang. It was John. And Susie.

'Look who I found on the doorstep.' Susie winked. 'We've introduced ourselves properly. I was complimenting John on his long ladder.'

Rory shot Susie a warning look. She'd forgotten they were supposed to be moderating coursework essays tonight. She suddenly felt very tired. And what was John doing here?

'Sorry to just turn up without calling.' He scratched the back of his head. 'Those LED spotlights you wanted were on special offer at the hardware place, so I took a chance and got them for you. I can take them back tomorrow if they're not any good, so I thought I'd pop them round now and see if they're what you want?'

'Thank you. That's fantastic. Come in, both of you.' She pointed the way through to the lounge.

Just then, Belle came downstairs. She was dressed more appropriately, but she had a big overnight bag with her and Rory had a pretty good idea what one of the items of clothing inside was likely to be. She didn't have the energy to start the argument again. Fiona's mother was sensible: surely everything would be okay round there. Belle waved a hand at her as she walked past. 'See you tomorrow.'

'See you tomorrow.' Stay calm. This was typical behaviour for a teenage girl. Try not to take it personally. Even when it hurts.

'Everything okay?' Susie asked Rory when she walked into the lounge.

'Who knows? Where's John?'

'Gone to *screw* something, I think.' Susie raised an eyebrow suggestively. 'I think he's a little bit scared of me.'

'I'm not surprised.'

'He doesn't need to be; I'm taken.' She beamed.

'Really?'

'Yes. After Penny's announcement, I decided I should up my game. My local pub had a barbecue on yesterday. I went on my own.'

'That was brave.'

'Yes. And a little desperate, some may say. But that was the mood I was in.'

Rory smiled. 'And?'

'And… I got chatting to a very nice man called Jim. A *very* nice man.'

'And?'

'And I spent the rest of the day with him.' She paused and raised an eyebrow. 'And the rest of last night and this morning.'

'Susie!' Rory wasn't a prude. Well, not much of one. But going to a pub alone, picking up a man and taking him home with you was a risky game to play.

'Don't panic. He was the perfect gentleman. He walked me home, came in for coffee and we sat and talked all night. We fell asleep on the sofa. Nothing happened. Well, not much happened.'

Rory felt slightly better, but it was still risky. 'So, what did you talk about?'

'Quite a lot about me, actually. He was really interested in my job and the kids we teach. That's how we got talking originally. Someone at the bar asked me about St Anthony's and it went from there.' She sighed and put a hand to her throat. 'It was so nice to talk to someone who was interested in me rather than talking about their car or their gym routine.'

Rory didn't mention that this is what normal men were like – just not the ones that Susie usually went for. 'He sounds nice.'

Susie smiled. 'Thanks. So, as I say, your man John Prince in there doesn't need to be scared of me. You, however…'

Rory held up a hand. She didn't want Susie getting wind of any feelings she had for John. 'Don't even start on that. There is so much going on for me right now that I can't even contemplate throwing a man into the equation. That is the very last thing I need. Plus, as I think I have mentioned several times now, he is my *builder*. There is *nothing going on*.'

'That's what you think.' Susie sat back in her chair.

A finger of fear ran through Rory. 'What have you said to him?'

Now it was Susie's turn to hold her hands aloft. 'Nothing! Nothing! I just have a feeling that he might think of you differently.' She ran her eyes up and down Rory's torso. 'Although he may change his mind now he's seen you in that ghastly hoodie. Red? What were you thinking?'

Rory groaned. She loved Susie, but subtlety and tact were not her forte. The worst thing about people in the process of falling in love is that they wanted everyone to join them in their bubble of happiness. 'When are you going to understand? I am not interested in meeting a man.' The drilling stopped in the other room and she lowered her voice. 'You need to focus on your own love life. I mean it, Susie.'

'All right, I'll keep my nose out, I promise. But you need to start thinking about meeting someone. I don't know if you've noticed it, but that little girl of yours is growing up fast. You can't use her as an excuse any more.'

After the row Rory had had with Belle, that one hit hard. Susie cared; that's why she'd said it. And maybe she was right. But what could Rory do about it?

'Do you think we could leave the moderation tonight? I'm exhausted. You're welcome to stay and have a drink, but I'm just not up to reading the same essay forty times over.'

Susie picked up her bag. 'Okay, honey. I'll shoot off. I'm pretty exhausted myself, but for very different reasons.' She winked suggestively, then kissed Rory on the cheek. 'Promise me you'll think about what I said?'

'I promise. Right after I've been to bed and slept for three weeks.'

John appeared at the door, and Rory shot Susie a warning look. 'Sorry, is it my drilling scaring you away? I'm all finished now. Did you want to come and have a look at what I've done?'

Susie got up to go. 'Not me, I've got to be somewhere. You go and look at your super-duper spotlights, Rory. I'll see myself out.'

Rory followed John back out to the kitchen. He flicked the switch so that she could switch the lights back on again. He grinned. 'Now you can see me!'

'They're bigger than I remember – they look great. Thanks so much for picking them up for me. The kitchen cupboards are being delivered in a month so it'll be good to have everything else ready.'

'Have you got fitters booked?'

Rory remembered the incredulous look that Call Me Adrian had given her. She braced herself. 'No. I'm going to do it myself.'

John shrugged. 'Sounds like a plan. Have you done a kitchen before?'

Rory squirmed a little. 'Not exactly. I have put flat packs together plenty of times.'

John nodded. 'You should be fine knocking the cupboards together, then. Sometimes setting them out can be a bit tricky, especially if the walls aren't square. I'm pretty free next month; I can give you a hand if you like?'

Rory was tired, a little emotional and very weary. The idea of putting together the whole kitchen alone was not feeling like an attractive prospect. 'If you could just pop in and give me a bit of guidance, that would be great.'

'No problem at all.' John started to throw tools back into his toolbox.

Rory hovered. 'Look, I'm sorry about Susie. I know she can be a bit full on, but she's only playing around.'

'Don't apologise. She seems a lot of fun. Have you two been friends a long time?'

'Six years. Since she came to work at St Anthony's. I'm still not used to her, though.' It was true. Rory loved Susie but they were as different as chalk and whiteboard pen. 'Do you want a cup of tea?'

'No, I won't stay; I've got an early start in the morning. Actually, I wanted to ask you if you were free Friday evening.'

Rory's heart sank. Bloody Susie! She had put him up to this. What the hell had she said? Rory was completely out of practise with this kind of thing. Fifteen years out of practise. She panicked.

'Look, John. I know that Susie has probably been talking to you. And I'm sorry, but I'm not... Erm... I'm just not dating right now. It's nothing personal; I don't go out with anyone. It's just not something I do. I'm sorry.'

John nodded slowly. 'That's good to know. I'll bear it in mind. Thanks. However, I was just wondering if you would be in to take delivery of a few tons of gravel that is being delivered for your drive.'

CHAPTER TWENTY-ONE

It didn't take long for the word to go around at school. Ten a.m. on Saturday morning there was a knock on Rory's door and, when she realised who it was, she regretted going to the door in her pyjamas.

'Good morning, Miss!'

Rory quickly hid herself behind the door and peeped out. It had been strange enough letting Charlie see her in her nightclothes; she definitely wasn't about to parade her M&S dressing gown before the rest of the class. 'Good morning, Harry. And your five friends. Much as it's nice to see you at the weekend after seeing you every day at school this week, what is it that I can help you with?'

'We've come to see Charlie, Miss. Is he coming out?' Harry paused, and a crafty grin spread across his chubby face. 'Or shall we come in and visit?'

'Nice try. I'll get him for you, just a sec.' She closed the door behind her. She liked Harry, but she didn't trust him not to come trooping through the hallway after her. 'Charlie!' she called.

'I'm in the kitchen, Miss – I mean, Rory.' It was taking Charlie a while to get used to the change in their relationship too.

He was sitting up at the counter in the kitchen, eating the biggest bowl of crunchy nut cornflakes that Rory had ever seen. She'd heard that teenage boys ate a lot, but she'd had no idea that they replaced their own body weight every day the way Charlie did. 'Harry is here for you with the other five of your lot. Does your mum let you go out with them?'

Charlie nodded. 'Yes. As long as I tell her where I'm going and what time I'll be back. Is that okay?'

'I guess so. Where are you going?'

'Dunno. I'll ask Harry. Probably the rec.'

Rory followed him down the hallway, grabbing a coat for herself to put over the top of her dressing gown. Charlie opened the front door and joined his friends outside.

'All right.' Harry nodded.

'All right.' Charlie nodded back.

There was a pause. Were they going to move on anywhere? Rory waited for Charlie to ask, but he didn't seem about to. Over to her, then. 'Where are you planning to go?'

'Just over the rec.' Harry stuck a handful of crisps in his mouth, then nodded at Charlie again. 'Are you coming with?'

'Yeah, all right. For a bit.' Charlie turned to Rory. 'I'll be back by five, if that's okay.'

The other boys sniggered behind their hands. Rory ignored them. 'What about your lunch?'

For some reason, that question was hilarious.

Charlie looked embarrassed. Not for himself. For Rory. 'I'll be all right.'

'Just wait there.' Once she was inside the kitchen, she realised that she didn't have anything to give him. She grabbed a bag of apples and a couple of pounds from the key dish. Outside again, she thrust the bag of apples at him. 'Here, take these; you can share them with your friends.' She glanced at Harry, who had finished his crisps and was now halfway through savaging a Mars Bar. 'You would do better with a couple of these, Harry.' Then she gave Charlie the two pounds. 'You can get a drink or something at least.'

Charlie looked at the bag of apples as if she had given him a bag of crack cocaine.

Just then, a familiar white van pulled up at the end of the drive.

'JP Building Services,' Harry read aloud. If only he were so keen in class.

John did a double take at the sight of seven small males on Rory's driveway. 'Is it Bob a Job week?'

'Charlie's friends have come to see him.' Rory was regretting merely putting a coat over her PJs. She should have got dressed. Was John coming in?

John put his head on one side and looked at Charlie. 'And they've brought him a bag of apples?'

Rory let out an exasperated sigh. 'They're apples. I don't know what is so strange about giving you all a bag of apples. They are very nice – look!' She tore open the plastic bag and took an apple. On reflection, it probably wasn't necessary to take such a large bite to make her point about their tastiness. 'Mmmm, mmmm,' she exaggerated. And then a piece got stuck.

She coughed and wheezed. It wasn't coming back up.

'What's the matter?' John put down his toolbox and searched her face.

Her cheeks were getting hot. She couldn't breathe. Oh my god, she really couldn't breathe!

'She's choking to death! Do something!' Harry yelled.

John grabbed her from behind, just under her ribcage. He pulled her. Hard. And again. At last, a large piece of apple shot out of her mouth and narrowly missed one of the boys.

Rory leaned over with her hands on her thighs until she got her breath back. She'd had no idea the Heimlich manoeuvre was so rough. Or maybe John was punishing her for changing her mind about the kitchen tiles five times. When she stood up again, John was looking at her with concern, and all seven boys were looking at *him* with undisguised admiration.

'That was amazing.' Harry's eyes were wide.

'You saved her life,' breathed Charlie.

'All in a day's work, lads.' John winked and flexed his fingers before picking up his tool kit.

Harry leaned forward. 'Can you show us how to do that?'

Before John could answer, Rory stepped in. With her experience of teaching teenage boys, she had visions of them sticking chunks of apple down their throats and then projectile coughing them at each other all afternoon. 'Maybe we'll leave the first aid class till another day. Go to the park and run off some of those Mars Bars.'

*

'So, he's actually moved in?'

She'd left John sitting on the sofa whilst she hurriedly got dressed. Today was wash day so she'd had to pull on the sweatshirt and jeans still thrown on the chair in her bedroom. She'd picked up her make-up bag and then put it down again; make-up would look like she was making too much effort. She'd scowled at herself in the mirror. Why was she overthinking this?

Now she was trying to act normally. 'He brought his stuff over yesterday. Although there wasn't much. Thank you for getting his room ready so quickly. I would never have managed it on my own.' Despite Rory's protestations that she would paint Charlie's room herself, John had turned up on Wednesday and got on with it. He'd been 'in the area' and had found a 'random tin of blue paint' in his van. Everything seemed to happen so quickly with him around. 'I know he really likes it. It's funny for me, having a blue room. Everything with Belle was always pink. And covered in perfectly proportioned cartoon princesses.' Rory pretended to stick her fingers down her throat.

John laughed. 'You don't strike me as the princess-loving type. Surprising you called your daughter Belle.'

'I didn't! She's named Christabel, after Christabel Pankhurst, the suffragette. "Belle" was her own name for herself. Then she had my mother calling her it. Eventually, I had to give in to the inevitable. Do you want some tea?'

'Yeah, great, if it's not too much trouble. I'm only dropping off some more paint samples for you to look at for your bedroom. I know you're going to paint it yourself, but they've got an offer on at the Builders' Merchants so you might want to buy the paint soon.'

Rory was beginning to get a bit suspicious about the special offers John kept getting for her. She always paid him immediately for any materials, and he always told her that he'd got a discount or they were on special offer. He still hadn't invoiced her for any of his time. Which visits was he charging her for?

'Great. My mum is coming this morning, so she can help me to choose. She's good with colour.' Rory busied herself making the tea. She no longer needed to ask John how he took his tea: strong and sweet. 'Have you got any plans for the rest of the day?'

'A couple of small jobs that need the final touches before wrapping them up. Then I've got an appointment with a house around the corner to give them a quote for an extension.'

'That sounds like a big job.' Rory felt a flutter of nervousness. If he had a big project like that, he wouldn't have much time to come and see her. She was only concerned about getting the last of her work done, obviously.

'Yeah, it is. Should be a nice little earner. She seems like a nice lady, too. Knows what she wants.'

'Really?' Rory wondered what constituted a 'nice lady'. Hopefully she was ninety years old.

John wasn't to know that Rory was analysing every word out of his mouth. 'Yeah, the rest of her house is quite modern, so she wants something a bit different. Should be an interesting job.'

Modern? Maybe not ninety. Possibly happily married?

'What does her husband think of that?' Could she be more obvious? *Idiot.*

John took a large gulp of tea. 'She's on her own. Got a couple of kids. Well, I think they're almost teenagers; that's why she needs a bit more room.'

On her own? And it was likely to be a long job, he'd said. An *interesting* job. Rory's heart was doing something strange. Was it indigestion? Heartburn? Was she *jealous*?

'When do you think you'll be starting work?'

John shrugged. 'She needs to get her planning permission in place first. I don't even know if she wants me to do the work yet. People usually get a few quotes in for a job like that.'

Rory looked at him over the top of her mug. His hair stuck out at the side from having a pencil pushed through it so often, and he needed a shave. But even in his mastic-covered jeans and an old T-shirt, he looked good. She would stake a Costa Coffee giftcard that he would get this woman's business. And those feelings she was trying to push down so hard were definitely jealousy. It had been so long since she'd felt them that it had taken her a while to recognise. *Try not to show it.*

'You mean they don't just pick up random men in B&Q?'

John grinned. 'No, I think that's just you. Although I seem to remember I had to practically force myself on you.'

A blush started at the bottom of Rory's face. John was only joking. Not flirting. She needed to get a grip. Her red face was going to give her away. Dammit!

'Well, I mustn't keep you chatting like this. I have my mum coming over soon and I need to get some work done. I'm sure you're busy.' She jumped up and practically snatched John's mug from his hand.

He looked startled but took her lead. 'Oh. Okay. I'll be off then.'

'Yes. Yes. I'll see you... at some point. Can you see yourself out?' Rory practically ran to the kitchen to avoid him seeing her red cheeks.

'Yeah, I'll, er... be in touch.'

Once she heard the door bang closed, Rory leaned against the kitchen cupboards and hid her warm face in her hands. Irrational jealousy, embarrassment, butterflies. What the heck was happening to her?

CHAPTER TWENTY-TWO

Rory couldn't get the lady with the 'interesting' extension out of her mind. Sheila arrived mid-afternoon bearing homemade lasagne, and Rory didn't even attempt to stop her from rearranging the contents of her freezer to fit it in.

Sheila paused with a box of caramel Magnums in her hand. 'Is everything all right, dear?'

Rory needed to get a hold of herself. 'I'm fine – just thinking about the house, what still needs to be done.' There was no way she could talk to her mother about her feelings. Sheila would be putting out bunting and baking a cake if she got the merest whiff of a possible romance.

Sheila swapped the Magnums for a frozen curry, which clearly didn't meet with her approval. 'You've done wonders with the place. I take my hat off to you, I really do.'

'Well, I can't take the credit really. Belle helped out with the early stuff and John has done so much since.'

Sheila pushed the freezer drawer closed. 'Ah, yes. Mr Prince. I was hoping I might see him today. I wanted to ask if he could come and hang some pictures in my flat.'

Rory groaned. 'Mum! He's not at our beck and call, you know.'

Sheila reached behind her for the kettle and started to fill it. 'I would pay him, Rory. I don't expect him to do it for nothing. Anyway, how is Charlie settling in?'

'Really well; he's no trouble. I'm sure he and Belle will really hit it off. When she's here, that is.'

'Have you met her boyfriend yet?'

'No. And I know what I said, but even I am starting to find it a bit strange.' Belle still hadn't brought any of her friends from college home. Even Fiona hadn't been to the house, except for a quick look round when they'd first moved in, and she'd been like a second daughter to Rory when the two of them had been revising for GCSEs.

Sheila got two mugs out of the cupboard, peered into them and then took them to the sink to wash. 'Just talk to her, Rory.'

Rory wasn't keen on the idea of sitting Belle down for a talk. 'Anyway, how did your rosemary chicken go down?'

Sheila dried the mugs and set them down in front of the kettle. 'Okay.'

Rory had been expecting an enthusiastic recount of every ingredient. 'What do you mean, okay? Don't tell me they didn't love it.'

Sheila filled the mugs from the kettle. 'The dinner was fine. Olive asked if her mum had cooked it for us, so I pretended I'd used her recipe, which made her happy. It just got a bit weird afterwards.'

Rory could see that Sheila was upset. 'What do you mean?'

Sheila gave Rory her tea and leaned back against the cupboard. 'After the dinner, and the wine George bought, we were in a bit of a party mood. George put on a CD of old songs and we were up and dancing. Three old codgers jigging about the lounge. Then Olive got tired.'

Sheila stopped to sip her tea. Was her bottom lip trembling? 'And?'

'She wanted us to keep dancing. She wanted us to dance "properly". So, we did.'

Sheila started to fiddle with the cups on the draining board. She clearly needed prompting. 'And?'

Sheila sighed and leaned against the kitchen cupboards. 'He's a lovely dancer, Aurora. I haven't been guided around like that since your dad. There isn't much room in those flats, so we had to keep quite close together. We started out laughing, but then we quietened down. The track changed to something slower and so did we.'

Rory felt a prickle of concern. 'What happened, Mum?'

'Nothing. Nothing at all. It's just that, when the music stopped, we realised that Olive was sleeping in her chair and it felt… well… wrong… the two of us dancing like that. Luckily, Olive woke up and she asked for pudding, so I busied myself in the kitchen. By the time I came out, everything was normal again. But I feel awful. I love Olive.'

Bless her mum and her sense of propriety. 'I'm sure it will be fine, Mum. You haven't done anything wrong. She was right there with you.'

Sheila had found a cloth and was wiping the kitchen counter. 'I know. I'm probably being silly. It's bloomin' Barb and all her talk of men. Oh, we met the infamous Fred this week! Barb's fancy man. And you could have knocked me down with a feather!'

Rory was pleased to see her mum smiling; she hated it when she looked sad. 'Why? What was he like?'

'Chubby, bald and about ten years older than her – the complete opposite to the movie stars she always goes on about. No wonder she was reluctant to introduce him to us. He is a very nice man, though, and he clearly dotes on Barb. Treats her like a queen. She was like a young girl while he was here. I'll admit to feeling a little bit jealous.'

There was a lot of that going around. 'Really?'

Sheila shook her head and wrung out the dishcloth. 'Oh, just ignore me. It's been a really funny week. How are you? How's work?'

'Just as bad. The deputy head is observing my lesson on Tuesday for my performance management, joy of joys.'

'Performance what?'

'Management. They have to observe our teaching to make sure we're up to par.'

Sheila kissed her on the cheek. 'Well, you will be amazing as always, but good luck.'

'I don't need luck,' Rory smiled. '10-G have got my back.'

*

Tuesday rolled around quickly enough. At least she'd had Monday to warn the class that Mr Finch was going to be in their lesson. And maybe tell them a little bit about the lesson she would teach. And maybe practise some of it. Or all of it.

'I hope you don't mind that I've chosen such a low ability class to observe.' Nathan Finch almost slid into the room. 'But I'm very interested in seeing how you manage behaviour. You have quite a reputation with the tough classes.'

That was because no one else ever wanted them and Rory liked them. 'No problem at all.'

'And you don't mind that it's an afternoon lesson? Classes like this are always worse in the afternoon, aren't they?'

Of course, they were. The kids were knackered from four hours of teaching followed by a sugar-fuelled gallop around the playground. Afternoons could be hell. Rory wasn't going to give him the satisfaction of admitting this. 'I never mind being observed and, as a new member of the Senior Leadership Team, I was hoping you might have a fresh perspective. It's always important to keep focused on your professional development, isn't it?'

Nathan looked like the cat that got the cream. 'Quite so, quite so. If only all the staff here had a similar attitude. We would have our outstanding rating in the bag.' Rory almost laughed aloud at the prospect of everyone having her current attitude. He wouldn't be wishing for that if he knew what her current attitude was.

As the pupils started to arrive, she couldn't look them in the eye. Harry in particular gave her such a huge wink of solidarity it was like a *Carry On* film. The comedy didn't stop there. Perfect uniform, pencil cases full of equipment and silent, uplifted faces; they were like a class from a 'Become a Teacher' promotional video. Charlie had reminded them all that morning and he'd done well. When Lacey walked in calmly, greeted both teachers, 'Good morning, Miss; good morning, Sir', and then sat down – on her actual chair – Nathan Finch almost fell over in excitement.

The lesson went perfectly. Of course, it should have done, as Rory had taught them the exact same lesson the day before. They raised their hands to speak. Gave their prepared responses perfectly. They even wrote almost a full page each. She could have kissed them.

Nathan didn't stay until the end. Deputy heads were far too busily important to waste a whole hour in a classroom. As he left, Rory could tell from his expression that he was impressed. Very impressed.

As the door clicked shut, she quickly put a finger to her lips. 'Wait!' There was absolute silence as they listened to the snap of his footfall ebb away to the end of the corridor. Going, going, gone.

'That was bloody brilliant!' Harry pulled a Snickers from his pocket.

'When Charlie said that thing, what was it?' Lacey mimicked a posh accent. '"*That's a very good point Lacey; I hadn't considered that.*" I thought I was going to wet myself!'

Rory should stop them, but they were right – it had been an absolutely text book outstanding lesson. Nathan would really have to rack his brains to even think of a target for development. She was so proud of them. 'You were amazing, all of you. Although I hope you realise I am going to be expecting work like that every lesson from now on.'

*

She was still smiling about it at the end of the day when she was packing up their books to take home and mark. She did her usual check of Harry's book – to see if he had managed to introduce his pen to the paper – and she saw a little message: *Did we do good, Miss?* And a smiley face. She grinned back at it. She bloody loved that lot.

Charlie had gone home without her. There was 'no way' he was going to wait around until six p.m. for her to go home and it would be 'too embarrassing' to go home with her, anyway. Rory was just about to leave when Nathan appeared in her doorway. Did he never take a minute off?

He turned to make sure the door was closed behind him. 'I wasn't sure if you'd still be here.'

Rory held up her bag of exercise books. 'No rest for the wicked.'

'Ah. Indeed.' He looked a little nervous. That was strange. He was also slightly more dishevelled than earlier. His tie had been loosened.

'Did you enjoy the lesson?' Rory couldn't resist asking.

'Yes, yes, of course. That's what I'd come to talk to you about. Kind of. I haven't written up my notes, so I'll give you my formal feedback later in the week. But I was very pleased with what I saw.'

Pleased? Was that all? Bloody Socrates couldn't have done any better. 'Good.'

'Yes, well. I also wanted to ask you about something. I'm new to town and other than the staff here, I don't know anybody.'

Rory's last cup of coffee rose up in her throat. Surely he wasn't going to ask her out? 'Oh.' It was almost a squeak.

'Yes. And the thing is, I have this event which…'

Just then, the door smashed open. 'Let's get out of this hell-ho… Oh!' Susie screeched to a halt and the colour drained from her face.

Nathan stood up straight and nodded. 'Miss Clark.'

'Mr Finch,' Susie mumbled, then looked to Rory for help.

Before Rory could make up something about it being a comedy act that they were working on for the school talent show, Nathan made a move to go. 'I'll catch up with you later in the week.'

Susie breathed a sigh of relief as soon as he'd gone. 'Was that your feedback? How did it go?'

'It was pleasing, apparently.' Rory didn't tell Susie about the rest of their conversation. For a start, she would never hear the end of it. And secondly, she didn't want to say it out loud.

CHAPTER TWENTY-THREE

As soon as she tried the bedroom door, her heart sank.

It had seemed such a good idea, to put all the storage boxes into the loft. Tired of living in a mess, she'd thought it would help to get rid of anything that wasn't needed right away. Putting the Christmas tree, suitcases and empty plastic boxes out of sight would at least be a start in getting straight and organised. Then she had been distracted by the photograph box.

Almost an hour had passed as she'd sat in the small bedroom below the loft hatch and sorted through the photographs. Although she still hadn't managed to organise them into albums, she had at least stuck by her resolution to print photos of Belle every year. All together, they looked like one of those time lapse animations of a flower coming into bloom. Did everyone look at their child and think they were the most beautiful creature alive?

Then there were Rory's own baby photos, and pictures of her parents. Her dad had been very handsome as a young man. There he was, collecting his athletics trophies. He could only have been about sixteen. Not much older than Belle was now. The circle of life. Rory wiped her eyes.

Maybe it was the distraction that had gotten her into this mess. Although, how was she supposed to know that the stupid loft ladder would get stuck? And what a design fault, to have the loft ladder blocking the door which opened into the room. She couldn't get the door open with the ladder down, and she couldn't push the ladder back up. She was well and truly stuck.

It was 2.15 p.m. on a Saturday. Belle was at Fiona's house and wouldn't be back until dinnertime. Charlie was visiting his mum. Rory had already considered calling her own mother, but what exactly would Sheila be able to do? Susie and Penny would have come to her rescue but, after leaving them both a voicemail, she'd remembered that they were on a shopping trip. They were intending to find Susie some new underwear in case her new relationship got to the third date. For a moment, Rory considered calling Scott, but he was to a crisis what Kate Moss was to a chocolate fountain. There would be little point. She had no other choice. As she scrolled through to find his name, she realised that her phone had automatically made it one of her frequently contacted numbers.

Within fifteen minutes, John Prince was outside the window.

Rory leaned out. 'Thanks for coming. I'm sorry. I didn't know who to call.'

He pretended to salute. 'I'm the fourth emergency service, Ma'am.'

'Isn't that the coastguard?'

'Maybe. I'll be the fifth, then. What is that hanging out of the window?'

Rory looked sheepish. 'It's a couple of old blankets tied together. I found them in the loft. I was considering trying to climb down them, but I'm not sure they would have held my weight.' She pulled the makeshift rope back inside the window.

'Not a bad idea, actually. It might come in handy – I'm not sure that my ladder is long enough to reach to the second-floor window. I've got a longer ladder at home, but I was on another job when you called.'

'Oh! I'm sorry. I didn't know you were working today.' Rory's face grew warm. Was he working Saturdays on that job he told her about? The 'interesting' extension for the woman who Rory had imagined to be a lookalike for Megan Fox.

'No problem. It was just a favour for a friend. I'd pretty much finished but she was trying to press a third slice of cake onto me. You saved me from myself.' He patted his waistline.

She? He had *another* female friend he helped? Of course, John wasn't her friend: he was her handyman. Builder. Whatever. 'Well, thanks. You'll have to add the time to your bill.'

John pretended to write on his hand. 'Noted. You know it's double time on the weekends?' He looked at her in mock seriousness.

'Stop playing about and get me down from here.' Not only was she feeling ridiculous and like a weak and feeble woman, she didn't want to tell him that she'd started to need the toilet ten minutes ago.

John unbolted the ladder from his van and propped it up against the side of the building. He was right: the ladder was too short. 'I'm going to have to go home and get my bigger ladder.'

'No!' Rory was really regretting the huge glass of juice she'd drunk before going up into the loft. 'I need to get out *now*.' She racked her brains for an excuse that didn't involve her having to talk about her bladder. 'I'm feeling claustrophobic.'

John looked sceptical, but he didn't argue. 'Okay, I'll come up and try and force the loft ladder back up.'

Rory was surprised by how quickly he made it up the ladder. It was hard not to appreciate how fit and lithe he looked from this angle. When he got to the top rung, he attempted to grab the window sill, but it was just out of reach. 'Throw down your blankets.'

She anchored the knotted blankets to the bed frame and threw them out of the window. John used them to pull himself to waist height, before swinging his legs into the open window. Impressive. He did a mock bow and then made a start on fixing the ladder. By this time, Rory was crossing her legs. 'Can you fix it?'

John stood back and scratched his head. 'This thing is an antique. I'm going to need to get some tools out of the van.' He turned to go.

'No! I need to go.' Rory gave up the claustrophobia pretence. 'I need to *go*.'

A smile of realisation dawned. 'Oh, I see. Well, I have a bucket I can bring up from the van?' Rory looked at him with daggers in her eyes. 'No? Well, then I guess I have to take you back down with me.'

The ladder was steep and scary. But she was about to wet herself. Which was worse? Weeing. 'Will you go down first?'

'Of course. Come on.' Expertly, John swung himself out of the window and, holding onto the blanket ladder, lowered himself onto the top rung of the ladder.

Involuntarily, Rory called out. 'Be careful!'

John looked up and smiled. 'Luckily for you, my Health and Safety qualification is fully up to date. Although they might take it away from me if they saw what I'm about to do.' He tied the bottom of the blanket ladder to the top rung of the real one. 'Out you come.' Clumsily, Rory stuck one leg out of the window and then tried to bring the other out to meet it without falling forwards. 'It's easier if you back out.'

That was worse. Imagining the sight of her backside lowering downwards towards John's outstretched arms. But his hands felt strong and capable. He guided her feet, legs and hips down towards the proper ladder. Why was she thinking about his arms? *Concentrate.* 'This is scarier than I imagined.'

'It's okay, I've got you.' As they inched their way down the ladder, he stayed just behind her, his hand on the small of her back. There was a warm feeling in her stomach, and it wasn't just her need to use the bathroom.

Finally, they were on solid ground. Rory breathed for what seemed like the first time in the last ten minutes. 'Thank you.'

'My goodness! How exciting, what happened?'

Oh no. Susie. She was going to make a meal out of this. Rory turned to see her excited face. 'What are you doing here?'

'We got your voicemails.' Penny fiddled with the button at the top of her blouse. 'We came flying round here to save you.'

'But it looks like someone else got here first.' Susie tucked a stray curl behind her ear and looked John up and down admiringly.

John backed up towards his ladder. 'Well, if you're fine. I'll get back to the other job. I'll see you in the week.'

Rory felt that damn blush again. 'Yes. Thank you. Thank you so much. I owe you, I really do.' She turned and hissed to Susie and Penny. 'Get inside! I am about to wet my pants!'

*

When she came out of the toilet, Penny had already put the kettle on.

Susie didn't waste any time. 'What were you doing in the bedroom with your builder?'

Now her bladder had been emptied, Rory had regained composure. 'You know why. I was trapped up there. He came to…'

'Rescue you?' Penny had her head on one side and there were practically hearts coming from her eyes. She was as bad as Belle for a romantic story.

'*Help* me.' Rory took the cup of tea that Penny had made. 'I got stuck in the loft and he came to help me out. No newsflash. No story. How was the shopping trip?'

Penny sighed, but Susie soon rallied when she showed Rory the contents of her shopping bag.

Rory whistled. 'Wow! There's nothing ambiguous about those pants.'

Susie poked out her tongue. 'Do you think they're too much?'

'On the contrary, I don't think they could be any less.' Rory had seen G-strings before, but these were much further up the alphabet.

'I'm really nervous.' Susie rewrapped the pants in their tissue paper and tucked them back into her bag. 'It's the first time I've been in this position for a long time.'

'Are you thinking about positions already?' Rory raised an eyebrow and smiled.

'No, seriously.' Susie did look serious for once. 'It's been a while since I made it to a third date.' Rory and Penny nodded together. They knew all about Susie's 'no sex until the third date' rule. Although they weren't convinced that she always kept to it. 'I really like him. What if the sex isn't good?'

'Sex isn't the be all and end all, is it?' Penny tucked her skirt over her knees. 'If someone is good company and makes you feel good about yourself, surely that's more important?'

Susie looked at her in amazement. 'What do you mean? Of course it is! I'm not looking for a human equivalent of the *TV Times*. And you can stop rolling your eyes,' she pointed at Rory. 'Just because you're a born-again virgin doesn't mean the rest of us are.'

'Hey, don't start picking on me just because you're feeling nervous. I never said I didn't like sex.' It was true. With the few men Rory had met in the last fifteen years, it had never been the sex part that she had a problem with. It was the rest of it.

Susie blew her a kiss. 'I'm sorry. I just really like him and I don't want to mess it up.'

Rory couldn't help thinking that she could have used those very words herself.

CHAPTER TWENTY-FOUR

Possibly the reason she had been so haphazard with the chisel was because she had come home from work in such a foul mood.

She'd guessed that Nathan had been impressed with her lesson because he had taken so long to give her his feedback; it would take him a while to be able to think of a target for improvement. He would never admit he couldn't think of one.

Eventually, he'd invited her into his centre of operations and proffered a chair. 'Sorry it has taken me so long to feed back to you. I'm sure you can appreciate how busy I am. There's a lot for me to do around here. You know what a mammoth task we have on our hands.'

Not too busy to pop into my classroom every other day, Rory wanted to say. 'That's fine.'

Nathan consulted the paperwork in front of him. 'Well, I was very impressed with your lesson, as you can imagine. Obviously, there is always room for improvement, but I will commend you on your ability as a teacher. I am aware that the group you have are not the most able pupils in the school, and you have engaged them well.'

Of course she'd shown him an outstanding lesson; she had staged it, for goodness sake. There was no way he could have done any better. 'Thank you. What suggestions did you have in mind for improving it?'

Nathan sat back in his leather executive chair and pressed his fingertips together. Clearly, he'd been looking forward to this.

'Firstly, I think the task you chose lends itself to group work. Which made me realise that, whenever I happen to be passing your room, I have not seen you undertaking group work with that class.' He pushed a sheet towards her. 'You could use my sheet which gives each pupil in the group a different role. It's very effective.'

Rory laughed. Then stopped. He wasn't joking. And the sheet he was showing her had come straight from a teaching resources website: she'd seen it on there a few weeks ago. 'You can't be serious. You've met them. How on earth would they manage a group work task without getting side-tracked by last night's *EastEnders* or who is fighting whom after school that day?' She had only recently learned when it was appropriate to use 'whom', and she could bet a week's wages that Nathan wouldn't know. Small victories. 'The only way to ensure that they are engaged in their learning is to let them have a desk to themselves, which is why we always work that way. They prefer it; I've asked them.' Aha! He couldn't argue with the power of pupil voice.

Nathan sidestepped and continued. 'I also noticed that you didn't seem to have a system for your questioning. I wondered whether pupils might benefit from a more strategic style. For example…' He opened a drawer and brought out a neatly bound set of lolly sticks. 'I have used this method very effectively myself in the past. You can write each pupil's name on a stick and then pull it out at random. That way they don't know who will be asked, and they all have to listen attentively in case it's them.'

Lolly sticks? This wasn't his idea either – it was from a TV programme about 'super teachers' that had been on last summer. Did he have *any* original strategies? 'But if I use this random method, how will I ensure that the questions are tailored to the pupils?

Nathan wasn't conceding defeat. 'Just some ideas for you to consider. I am happy to grade the lesson as outstanding nonetheless, and I think that we should find a way for you to share your expertise with others in your department and, indeed, the whole school.'

The whole school? Was he suggesting promotion? 'Thanks.'

'As one of our most highly rated teachers, I was hoping that you would be happy to represent the school for us at an evening event which is coming up shortly.' He picked up an invitation from his desk. 'I believe it's an event honouring local community leaders.'

Rory's heart sank. She hated events like that, but what could she say? At least it would be a free night out with wine. Maybe she could persuade Susie to come with her; the school was usually given two tickets to things like this. 'Of course. Can I invite another member of staff to accompany me?'

Nathan frowned. 'I think you misunderstood, Rory. You will be coming as my guest.'

*

When she got home, Rory threw her bags into the hallway and didn't even bother to go in and speak to Belle and her mum. She was looking for a fight and, in the circumstances, those stubborn bathroom tiles would have to be her chosen opponent.

Which was how she had ended up flat on her back with them standing over her.

'You're going to have to give her the kiss of life, John.' Was that her mother's voice?

'With all due respect, Mrs Anderson, I don't think that's necessary.' John?

'She's waking up. Mum? Mum? Are you okay?' That was Belle.

Rory opened her eyes. Their three faces were directly above hers. What had happened? How had she got here? She tried to push herself up from the floor, although it was a little difficult with them all bending over her. Ouch!

John put a hand on her shoulder. 'Slowly, slowly.'

'Do you think she'll need to go to hospital?' Belle was wringing her hands. 'She's not keen on hospitals.'

'I am here, you know.' Rory put her hands on the floor to push herself up. 'Ouch!' It was her finger. There was a nasty gash running the length of it. Her head swam.

'Put her head between her legs.' Sheila was in mother hen mode. 'She's always been like this with blood. When she was about twelve she came with me when I donated blood at the church hall and she passed out from just being in the next room. I was halfway through giving my pint when a nurse came in waving Aurora's scarf and asking if anyone knew the girl it belonged to.'

For god's sake, Rory had heard this story a thousand times. No way was John taking her to the hospital. It was mortifying. She could look after herself. She just needed the facts. Could they hear her with her face between her knees? 'What did I do?'

'We believe you were trying to take the tiles off the bathroom wall with a chisel.' John bent down beside her again. He reapplied the cloth that Sheila had been holding onto her finger. 'I think you might need a couple of stitches in that.'

Sheila seemed overjoyed at this information. 'I think you should take her straight there, John. Otherwise she might lose too much blood. She's always been prone to anaemia.' Rory didn't want to call her mother a liar in front of a relative stranger, but she knew for a fact that she was not prone to anything of the sort. 'The women in our family are very delicate.' Was Sheila flirting with him?

Rory raised her head. 'No, John doesn't need to take me. I can get a taxi. Belle can come with me.'

Belle glanced at her grandmother and backed away. 'Sorry, Mum, I can't. I've promised to help Fiona with her maths homework. It's due tomorrow.' Traitor.

'Then you can come with me, Mum.'

'You know, I've come over a bit strange myself at the sight of all that blood.' Sheila held a theatrical hand to her temple. 'I think I'm going to need to sit here quietly for a while.' In case she hadn't made herself completely and utterly obvious, she added, 'And you can't possibly go on your own; it'd be dangerous.'

Rory's would not be the only blood spilt that evening. 'I'll be fine. I'll call Susie or Penny. One of them will meet me at the hospital.'

'Stop being ridiculous.' John sounded impatient. 'Belle, can you get your mum a coat?'

Rory gritted her teeth and avoided looking at the huge smirk that she knew would be on her mother's face.

*

This was only the third time Rory had been in John's van and last time she was a little worse for wear. 'I'm so sorry about all that. My mum thinks she's being subtle.'

John smiled. 'Don't worry, I'm used to it.' What did that mean? Had her mum said something before or did he mean that old ladies were always trying to fix him up with their daughters?

'Really?'

John nodded. 'There's something about being a single man of a certain age that everyone wants to fix you up with their friend or daughter or mother.'

'That sounds like a twist on a Jane Austen novel.'

'It's true. Even more so when they realise that you've never been married and don't have any children. Plus, I've got all my own teeth.' Without taking his eyes from the road, he turned the bottom half of his face towards Rory and grinned widely to prove his point.

She laughed and relaxed. 'It's not just men of certain age, you know. My mum has been trying to fix me up since I split with Belle's dad. Apparently, you must be part of a couple to be happy.

My friends are no better. Susie is insufferable on the subject. I hoped that she'd quieten down once she met someone but she's been worse.' Susie couldn't believe that Rory wasn't upset that both she and Penny had met someone. At least she wasn't dragging her to any more awful singles' nights. But her latest endeavour was trying to persuade Rory to come on a double date with her man and his friend. Rory could just imagine what he would be like.

'For some reason, they don't want to accept that you're more than happy being on your own.' John tapped the steering wheel as he spoke.

Rory nodded. 'Exactly.'

'That you do not want to meet someone and settle down.'

'Absolutely.' At least that's how she *had* felt.

'That you are completely content with being single and have no plans to let someone into your life. Ever.'

'Hear, hear.' Did she sound convincing? Because she didn't feel it. *Never* seemed a very definite decision.

But John sounded sure. Very sure.

CHAPTER TWENTY-FIVE

Parents' evening at Belle's college. It was always strange being on the other side of the desk. Fortunately, Belle had always been a good kid and a good student, so Rory usually just sat and glowed whilst the teachers told her lovely things.

However, tonight was different.

Firstly, they ran into Fiona and her mum. Belle tried to steer her away from them, which alerted Rory's suspicions: Fiona was Belle's best friend and they had been inseparable for three years. Rory shrugged Belle from her elbow and walked over to say hello.

Fiona's mum turned and smiled. 'Hello, I haven't seen much of you lately. How are you doing?' Rory opened her mouth to say she'd been busy, but... Fiona's mum was talking to Belle?

Belle mumbled something about having lots of schoolwork and exchanged worried glances with Fiona. What was going on?

'Really? Hasn't Belle been over at yours all the time lately?' Rory asked. She should have checked up. But this was Belle. Honest, trustworthy Belle. Hadn't she just wanted to get away from the dust and the DIY noise at home? Where the hell had she been going, then?

Fiona's mum shook her head. 'She's stayed over a couple of times but arrived really late and they disappear upstairs. It's a shame she doesn't come and hang out during the day like they used to.'

Rory recognised the 'I'm so sorry' eyes that Fiona was directing at Belle. Rory would get to the bottom of this later. Not here, not in front of an audience. She put a hand on Belle's shoulder. 'Go and check out the queue in the Maths department and see if it's worth me making my way up there yet.'

When the girls had left, Rory turned to Fiona's mum. 'I obviously need to keep a tighter check on my daughter. I don't suppose Fiona has mentioned anything about her to you?'

'Only that Belle has a boyfriend now and she spends all her time with him. I'm sorry; I assumed you knew.'

Rory wasn't about to admit to Fiona's mum that she hadn't met him. This woman would judge the parenting skills of Saint Mary. 'I know about her boyfriend. I hadn't realised they were spending so much time together. Belle is such a dreamer; I don't think I considered it to be serious.'

'I know what you mean. I suppose we need to accept that our girls are growing up. How's the house renovation going? I've seen John Prince's van outside your house quite often; is he doing the work?'

Why would she assume that Rory wasn't doing most of it? 'He's just doing the bits I can't do. Do you know him?'

'A little. He's lovely, isn't he? When I split from Fiona's dad, he came and did lots of small jobs for me. You know, the kind of thing you get used to having a man to do?' Rory didn't know, but she nodded anyway for ease of conversation. 'A friend recommended him as being very good for women *on their own*.' She looked knowingly at Rory, who was at a loss for the second time in the last ten minutes.

'What do you mean?'

'You know. Trustworthy. Reliable.' She paused and lowered her voice. 'Easy on the eye.'

This was uncomfortable. Fiona's mum obviously believed she was speaking to a like-minded woman. 'Apparently, he was brought up by only his mother. His dad left when he was young. He seems to have a compulsive need to help out single mothers.'

Rory felt a little sick. And stupid. 'Really?'

'Of course,' Fiona's mum continued conspiratorially. 'I threw myself at him a little. Fiona's dad had only been gone a couple of months and I was feeling very lonely.' She seemed to go into a short daydream. She sighed. 'Nothing happened, though. He was the perfect gentleman. Makes him seem all the more attractive, doesn't it? I'm sure his bill was about half the price it should have been. It was the same for my friend.'

Was anything in Rory's current life as she had assumed it was? Belle and Fiona returned to say that the queues in the Maths department were terrible, but Rory couldn't stand there any longer. 'We may as well just join a queue. See you soon.'

In actual fact, there was hardly anyone queueing. Rory frowned at Belle. 'You said it was busy?'

Belle scrutinised her fingernails. 'It was. You were talking for ages to Fiona's mum.'

Belle's Maths teacher seemed very pleased to see Rory. He stood up to shake her hand. 'I'm so glad you could make it. Belle wasn't sure you were coming.' Rory looked at Belle. Why would she tell him that? But Belle just stared ahead, avoiding her eye. Then her teacher sighed and leaned forwards. Rory had enough experience of parents' evenings to know that leaning forwards was not a good sign. 'I'm a bit concerned about Belle. She's a bright girl, but I feel like her motivation and concentration are slipping.'

'Really? I have to say I'm a little shocked.' Rory turned to her daughter. 'Belle, what is this about?'

Belle shrugged. 'I'm not really interested in Maths any more.'

Not interested? Since when was Belle not interested in anything at school? Rory turned back to the Maths teacher. 'Thank you; I think Belle and I need to have a conversation at home. Is there anything specific she needs to work on?'

It was the same story in Chemistry: 'Bright girl, slipping in concentration.' And in English: 'There's not a big problem, or we would have called you.' With each successive meeting, Rory progressed into a strange land she'd never been in before. One in which she didn't know her own daughter.

On the drive home, Rory tried not to attack Belle straight away. 'Look, I know A levels are a big jump up from GCSEs. But what's going on, Belle? The student they described didn't even sound like you.'

Belle was slumped into her seat with her arms crossed. She stared out the car window. 'Nothing is going on. I'm getting enough done. The teachers want blood this year. Whatever you do, they just want more.'

Deep breath. Stay calm. 'And where have you been going when you told me you were at Fiona's? Why have you been lying to me, Belle?'

Belle's head snapped round. 'I haven't been lying! I do go to Fiona's. Her mum doesn't know what she's talking about. Sometimes me and the other girls just knock for her and we go somewhere else. Her mum probably doesn't notice me in the group. You can ask Fiona if you don't believe me.'

Fiona was unlikely to be a reliable source. But Rory left the conversation alone for now. She needed to work out how to handle this.

When she got home, Belle went straight to her room. Rory joined Sheila and Charlie in the living room.

'How was the glowing report? Are they sending her to Oxford yet?' Sheila looked up from the jigsaw they were doing together.

'Not so glowing.' Rory sat down heavily.

Sheila paused with a jigsaw piece in her hand. 'Shall I make you a cup of tea and we can talk about it?'

Rory shrugged. 'I'll have the tea.'

Sheila looked at Rory as if she was the stroppy teenager, but she spoke to Charlie. 'I'll be back in a minute, Charlie love. You carry on with the jigsaw.'

She nodded in the direction of the kitchen. Rory sighed and followed her out.

In the kitchen, Rory held up her hands. 'Really, Mum. I don't want to talk about it.'

Sheila filled the kettle. 'I was just going to tell you that Olive's been poorly. George is worried that it's a lack of exercise. We tried to take her out for a walk together, but she gets out of puff very quickly and wants to go home. It's a bit like taking a small child out. I suggested a wheelchair, but that defeats the object of her getting some exercise and, as she does get fresh air in the garden, it seems a pointlessly difficult endeavour.'

Rory wasn't listening. She knew what her mum was doing. This had been her tactic when Rory was young. Keep prattling on until it was a mercy to shut her up by telling her what was on your mind. But Rory wasn't ready to talk about tonight yet. 'Uh-huh.'

Sheila wasn't put off. She started to talk about George and how the strain of looking after Olive was beginning to take its toll on him. 'She is very demanding. She calls for him to come and then doesn't know what she wanted him for. Karen is really worried about him and he does look rather grey. I've started popping in more often. I take little treats for Olive and I've made lunch for the three of us a few times.'

'People are going to start to talk, Mum.'

Sheila crossed her arms. 'Let them. I don't care. His daughter doesn't seem to mind, so they can just keep their noses out.' They stood in silence for a few moments. Then the kettle clicked and Sheila opened the cupboards to find the cups. 'Speaking of daughters. What happened tonight?'

Rory sighed. 'It was awful. She's not focused in class. Home-work is poor. I don't get it, Mum. She has always been the perfect student. And now they are telling me that she's disinterested. Lacking in motivation. She'd rather have a chat than complete her work. I don't know what to do.' She looked up sharply. 'Oh my god! Do you think she's taking drugs?'

'Don't be ridiculous! Of course she isn't. She is just being a teenager. She has this boyfriend now and her head is full of other things. It's a perfectly normal stage.'

Rory slumped against the washing machine. 'I still feel like I don't know anything about him.'

Sheila continued with making the tea. 'His name is Alfie. He has blonde hair. Not too long; not too short. He is really good looking and he's had lots of girlfriends but he's never liked anyone as much as he likes Belle. Oh, and he supports Arsenal.'

Rory had a vague recollection that Belle had started to show an interest in the football scores. 'Why hasn't she told me all this?'

'Because you're her mum. That's how it works. Anyway, she thinks you are anti-romance.'

Rory practically growled. 'I am *not* anti-romance. I'm just pro-realism. How many girlfriends has this Alfie had, anyway?'

'Oh, I don't know. They are only sixteen. I'm sure none of them were very serious.'

That's where Rory did have more information than her mother. She hadn't been teaching for the last fifteen years without knowing how early kids got serious these days. But Belle?

'It gets worse, Mum. She's been telling me she's going to Fiona's house, but I saw Fiona's mum this evening and she told me that she hasn't seen Belle properly in weeks. Belle's never lied to me before.'

Sheila put a cup of hot tea in front of Rory and then put her hands around her own. 'Aurora. I know you're worried. And you are right to be upset that she has lied. But you need to keep this in perspective. Belle is a sixteen-year-old girl. You must remember what that felt like? She's a good girl. You've brought her up well. Leave it tonight and talk to her about this tomorrow, when you've both had time to sleep on it.'

Rory sipped her tea. Her mum was right. But Belle's deceit wasn't the only surprising information she'd received this evening, and she couldn't talk to her mum about the other thing without revealing how it had made her feel.

CHAPTER TWENTY-SIX

Rory had been flicking through Year 9 assessments and wallpaper samples for the hall when she got the call from Barb: Sheila was in hospital. Barb took an interminably long time to explain what was going on, but Rory just wanted to get off the phone, find her keys and get to Sheila as soon as she could.

Roadworks en route to the hospital did nothing to calm Rory's nerves. As the traffic snaked slowly past the orange cones, she tapped the steering wheel and worked her way through the pre-set radio stations, which seemed to have been hijacked by loud, thumping dance music. Who would have predicted Rory would be nostalgic for the soundtrack to *Beauty and the Beast*?

Parents' evening had been two days ago. Belle had stayed home for the last two nights. Rory hadn't used the word 'grounded' but had told her she needed to focus on the targets her teachers had set, and Belle hadn't argued. She knew that she was on thin ice. Rory had planned to talk to her on Friday evening, but Belle had come home from school saying she had a headache and spent the night in her bedroom. So it was Saturday morning by the time they had a conversation. This was probably a good thing. Rory had had longer to cool down and attempt a calmer approach. To start with a positive.

'Can we sit down and have a chat?' When Belle had emerged from her bedroom to get herself some cereal, Rory had patted the sofa next to her. They had spent many evenings on this sofa together, cuddled under a blanket. Belle would fall asleep watching a Disney DVD with her thumb in her mouth, whilst Rory tried to read a book without her noticing. That seemed an eternity ago.

Belle rubbed her eyes with the back of her wrist and yawned. Her mobile was in her hand; it was a permanent fixture these days. 'Yeah, if you like. What do you want to talk about?'

She leaned against the arm of a chair, her legs stretching out forever, and brushed her hair away from her eyes. Against Rory's advice, she'd decided she wanted to 'grow out her fringe' when she was six. There had been many months of trying to keep her hair out of her eyes with a variety of different clips. But her hair had always done what it wanted. Seems like the rest of her was now following suit.

'We need to catch up. Can you put the mobile away for a bit?' Rory was fighting hard to keep her tone as neutral as possible. What the hell did Belle *think* she wanted to talk about? World peace?

'Sorry, I'm just waiting for a...' Belle scanned the screen and smiled. She started to tap out a response.

For a girl who should have been waiting for the fallout from parents' evening, Belle was remarkably laid back. Rory's voice got a little firmer. 'Belle, I want to talk to you. Now.'

Belle dragged her eyes in Rory's direction. 'I'm here, Mum; talk away. I just...' The mobile pinged and her eyes were sucked back to the screen.

'Belle!' Rory snatched the phone from her daughter's hands. She didn't look at the message, but the fear that flashed across Belle's face made her wonder if she should. What was on that screen? Did she need to worry about more than the lack of school work?

When Rory placed the mobile face down on the table, Belle's fear turned to relief and then to anger. 'I am not one of your kids from school, you know! You can't just confiscate my stuff for no reason!' She made a grab for the mobile, but Rory's hand was on top of hers before she could lift it from the table. Rory might not have had to deal with this behaviour from her daughter before, but she dealt with stroppy teenagers on a daily basis. Belle would need to get up pretty early in the morning to beat her.

Rory looked into her daughter's flashing eyes. 'Just leave it there for five minutes.'

Belle pushed herself further back onto the armchair and crossed her arms. She stared at the mobile as if she could move it telekinetically in her direction.

Where to begin? It had never been difficult for Rory to talk to her daughter before. In fact, it had been quite difficult to stop Belle from chattering endlessly about anything that came into her head. Sheila had joked that there must be a hole in the back of Belle's head and, when the wind blew, it make her tongue waggle. But that was Belle the little girl. The tall, beautiful creature in front of Rory now was almost a woman. It wasn't a case of banning Coco Pops for a week if she didn't do what Rory wanted.

Rory took her hand from the mobile and laid it on Belle's arm. 'I love you, you know.'

Belle looked up with surprise. Then suspicion. 'I love you too, Mum. Of course, I do.'

Rory took a deep breath. 'You are the most precious thing I have, Belle. I want you to know that.'

'I do know that.' Belle shuffled in her seat. 'Is there something bad you're going to tell me? You haven't got a disease, have you?'

Rory shook her head. 'Thankfully not. This is about you. About your boyfriend.'

Belle stopped shuffling and flushed. 'I don't need to talk about that, Mum. You already did the birds and the bees thing.'

Rory had told Belle the facts of life early on. Sheila had tutted that it was too early. But Belle had asked, and Rory hadn't been about to make up some story involving storks and cherubs. She'd explained about mummy eggs and daddy seeds and Belle had accepted the whole thing without any trauma.

But there was a vast difference between a scientific explanation of procreation and the idea of her own daughter having sex with a real-life boy. A boy Rory hadn't even met. Maybe she should start with that.

'I was wondering when I might get a chance to meet this young man of yours.' Young man? Why the hell had she said that? She really was turning into her mother. 'I mean, meet Alfie.'

Belle actually groaned. 'What is this, Mum? The eighteen hundreds? We're not getting married or anything. It's not serious. I'm just… seeing him. If I ask him to come and meet my mum, he'll think I'm a complete weirdo.'

Rory was quite relieved to hear it wasn't serious, but they still needed to talk. 'Okay, well maybe it's too soon to bring him home, but I wanted to talk to you *before* it gets serious.'

Belle rolled her eyes and slumped back even further into the sofa. 'I'm not *stupid*. I'm *sixteen*, not *six*!'

Rory knew that. She really knew it. And to think she had complained that six was a difficult age. She wished she hadn't started this. But she had, and now she needed to keep going. 'At some point you might want to… to take things to the next… I mean, not necessarily with him, but at some point you might…' For the love of God. She'd taught Sex Education before. Why was it so difficult to say the damn word?

'Sex.' Belle practically pouted. 'You want to talk to me about sex.'

Now it was Rory's turn to squirm. It was so different talking to Belle than it would be talking to a whole class.

'Yes. I want to talk to you about sex. But not about doing it, exactly.' She took a deep breath and tried again. 'Belle, you are so precious to me.'

The mobile pinged. Twice in quick succession. The boy was keen, you had to give him that. Belle glanced at it longingly. Rory needed to hurry before she lost her attention.

'The thing is. Having... sex... it changes things. There is nothing wrong with a healthy sexual relationship' – she was beginning to sound like the school nurse on sex-ed day – 'but there is an emotional side that you might not be ready for. I just want you to know that you can talk to me, Belle. Any time. About anything.'

Belle raised an eyebrow. 'Did you talk to your mum about having sex?'

Dammit. This girl was clever. 'Well, no, but, you know, times were different then. You and I are closer than that. We've always talked about important stuff in the past.'

Belle stood up, leaned over and hugged Rory. It was a nice gesture, but it made Rory feel about a hundred and five. 'Oh, Mum, we are close. I will talk to you, if... if I'm planning anything. I'm not at that stage yet, honestly. Can I please have my mobile back?'

Maybe Rory didn't need to push the point. This was Belle. Her sensible daughter. Rory shouldn't have paid any attention to her mother. If Belle wanted to talk to her, she would. And anyway, it wasn't a serious relationship, so she could just relax. *What a relief.*

That was, until she picked up the mobile to give it back to Belle and saw the picture Alfie had sent her. He had taken a full-length photograph of himself in the mirror wearing a large smile. And nothing else.

*

And now she had to worry about her mother too. It took Rory about ten minutes to find a parking space at the hospital. Ambulances were coming and going and people in various states of distress were walking into A&E. That smell of bleach and antiseptic. She hated this place. Too much sadness. Now, where was her mum?

Sheila was sitting in the waiting room with her ankle bandaged. Something about the way she sat, with both hands on her handbag, made her look vulnerable. 'I told Barb not to bother you. I could have got a taxi home. Olive is still poorly and I was going to take the Reader's Digest in there tonight and read her the funny letters.'

Rory was so relieved to see that she was okay. Tears pricked the back of her eyes, but she didn't know if they were for Sheila or herself. 'Don't be ridiculous, Mum. Of course I would want to be here to take you home. Come on. Let's get out of this place and you can tell me what you've been doing to yourself.'

She also had a few things she wanted to get off her own chest. But Rory would need to make sure Sheila was sitting down again when she told her what was going on with Belle. Otherwise she might end up spraining her other ankle.

CHAPTER TWENTY-SEVEN

Rory wanted to take her mum back home with her, but Sheila had insisted on going back to her own flat. Rory made her a cup of tea. Water, with a hint of tea bag and the merest suggestion of milk. Just the way Sheila liked it.

'Lovely. Thank you. They made me a cup of tea at the hospital but it was like sludge. Couldn't drink it.' She took a sip. 'It's good to be home and out of that place. The nurses were all lovely but I couldn't bear it.' She squeezed Rory's hand. 'Thanks for coming, love. I know you hate it, too.'

Rory's throat constricted. 'My heart stopped when Barb called to tell me you were at the hospital.'

'I knew it would. That's why I told her not to call you.' Sheila patted the hand she was still holding. 'It's just your silly old mother having an old lady fall. Turns out Flo was right about people dropping their wet smalls in the laundry room. Can you imagine how embarrassing it was telling that young male nurse that I'd slipped over a pair of wet Y-fronts?' She smiled, but her bottom lip trembled a little.

It was that vulnerability which made Rory's eyes fill.

Sheila held out her arms. 'Oh, come here, you silly thing.'

Rory lay her head on her mum's chest and let her hold her close. Imperial Leather and humbugs. That was a far more comforting smell than the disinfectant in the hospital. It was a while since they'd done this. A long while.

'I thought…' Rory's voice cracked. She didn't trust herself to continue.

'I can imagine what you thought. You're not getting rid of me for a long while, my girl. So you can put that right out of your head.' Sheila stroked Rory's hair. Then kissed the top of her head and pushed her back into a sitting position. 'This isn't like you. The tears. What's going on?'

Rory wiped her face with the back of her hand. 'I took your advice and spoke to Belle.' She shot a look at her mother which warned her against being smug. 'It didn't go so well.'

Rory gave a short summary of their conversation and then explained about the photograph. Sheila's eyes nearly bulged out of her head.

'Well.' She took a deep breath and let it out slowly. 'Well.'

'I know.' Rory nodded. 'I made her show me their whole conversation. She is absolutely livid with me.' Livid didn't come close. Belle had threatened to call Childline. 'Most of their conversation was pretty standard teenage rubbish but the last couple of texts were pretty flirty and suggestive.' Rory's heart had sunk lower and lower as she'd read them. How dare some boy talk to her beautiful, perfect daughter like that?

'So, what are you going to do now?'

Rory shrugged. 'I have absolutely no idea. I've confiscated her mobile, which apparently puts me on a par with Adolf Hitler, but she will still see him at college so that's not going to make a huge amount of difference. I tried to talk to her about respecting yourself and knowing your own worth.' She put her hands on her face. 'Although, as half of that was done at the top of my voice, I'm not sure it had the effect I was hoping for.'

She had really lost her mind after the photograph. It was weird how she could be so calm at school with the shenanigans she had to deal with there, but it had been impossible to keep her cool with Belle. She was almost as angry with herself as she was with her daughter. Almost.

Sheila sipped at her tea. 'It's difficult being a mum sometimes, isn't it?'

Rory sighed. 'I used to think the tough bit was the night feeds and the nappy changing. Turns out I was wrong.'

Sheila looked at her. 'The bigger the child, the bigger the problems.'

Rory started to nod in agreement and then noticed the pointed expression on her mother's face. 'I'm not a problem! It's not me sitting here with a bandaged foot.'

Sheila ignored her. 'I think you did the right thing telling Belle how precious she is. Hopefully that'll be enough to ensure she's not pressured into doing anything she's not ready for.' She paused and took Rory's hand again. 'You are precious too, you know.'

Rory squirmed. 'Mum. This is not about me.'

'No. But if you're allowed to worry about Belle, then I'm allowed to worry about you. It's time you started to have a life of your own. Between that school and Belle and now this house of yours, I'm not sure what life you are allowing yourself to have.'

Rory pulled her hand away and sat back on the sofa with folded arms. 'I go out with my friends.'

'I know. And I also know that you often go home early and refuse to even enter into conversation with anyone of the opposite sex.'

Damn Susie. She should never have let her swap email addresses with her mother. It had only been so Sheila could practise before emailing her friend Jean in Australia. Now they were ganging up on her.

Sheila had obviously been preparing this speech. 'You don't seem to realise that you are running out of time to meet someone. You need to hook them whilst you've still got your looks. What man is going to be attracted when your boobs are round your waist and you could get a week's shopping in the bags under your eyes?'

Her mum was joking, trying to lighten the mood. But right now, Rory wasn't in the mood for jokes. 'I keep telling you, Mother. I don't need a man.'

'None of us have ever *needed* a man, Aurora. It's just nice to have one around sometimes. Even if it's only to open jars and catch spiders.'

'You bought me that jar opening contraption from the Kleeneze catalogue last Christmas. Job done.'

'I knew I shouldn't have done that!' Sheila softened her voice. 'Have you dated *anyone* since Scott? Maybe you just haven't wanted to tell me?'

She sounded so hopeful that Rory didn't want to disappoint her. But there had been no one of any consequence. 'I just haven't been interested. I mean it when I say I don't need someone.'

Sheila leaned over and put her hand on Rory's cheek. 'I know that. I know that you can do everything on your own. I'm proud of that. I'm proud of you, my clever, brave, beautiful daughter. The way you've brought up Belle, your career, even that damn house of yours. I know that you don't need anybody else to do anything you set your mind to.'

Rory was amazed to hear these words. 'So why do you go on about it all the time?'

Sheila sat back in chair, but she didn't take her eyes from Rory's. 'Because need is different to want, Aurora. Don't you want to have someone at home to carry the load? To be there when you can't? To talk things through with when you have a big decision?'

This was too much. 'I've got you, Mum.'

Sheila paused before she spoke. 'But I won't always be here, Rory.'

Rory's chin trembled. She fought to get it under control. 'Don't say that, Mum.'

Sheila shrugged. 'You asked me why I go on about you meeting someone. That's why.'

The two of them sat in silence for the next few moments. Rory wasn't able to speak. Too much had happened today. There was too much to think about. And all of it hurt.

Eventually, Sheila took a deep breath. 'On the subject of saggy boobs and wrinkles though, I think Flo and Sid might be getting it on!'

Rory took her lead. They needed to balance these feelings with some humour. 'Really?'

'I've seen him come out of her flat a couple of times. When he saw me, he mumbled something about helping her put up a shelf, but I know that can't be true. That man is to DIY what Arnold Schwarzenegger is to needlework. Plus,' Sheila held up a finger like Hercule Poirot, 'there was no sign of a toolbox. I told Barb and she's having a field day. Every time she sees Flo she winks at her and asks her how she's been sleeping. Flo asked me yesterday if Barb has an eye infection.'

Rory laughed. It felt good. She reached over and kissed her mum on the cheek. 'Well, if even Flo is starting to date, maybe you're right and I should get a wriggle on.' She put her palms under her boobs as if to weigh them. 'How long do you think these babies have got left?'

Sheila pulled her arms back down again. 'That's not what I meant. I'm just saying, be open to meeting someone.'

'Yes, Mum.'

'There might even be someone under your nose.'

Rory knew where this was going. 'Mum…'

'Like, what about John?' The expression on her mother's face as she tried to pretend that this idea had come to her out of nowhere was almost endearing.

There it was again. That odd fluttery feeling. Maybe she needed to get her blood pressure checked. 'He's my…' She was going to tell her mother for the hundredth time that John was only her builder, but she didn't have the strength. 'He's not interested in women, Mum. He told me himself.'

Sheila looked very disappointed. 'Really? He doesn't look…'

'Gay? Number one, there's not a "look", and number two, I don't think he's gay. He's just happy on his own.'

Sheila huffed. 'Well, they're *all* happy on their own, it's our job to…' She stopped when she saw Rory's face. 'All right; I won't say another word. It's just a shame. I like him. He reminds me of your dad.'

He reminded Rory of her dad too. That was probably why it was so easy to talk to him. Maybe that's all it was.

'Obviously he's a builder like your dad, but I mean he has a similar personality, the way he teases you a bit. Your dad was always pulling my leg. When we were camping once, he told me that spiders don't like torchlight. He had me walking around for about thirty minutes with a torch tied to each ankle before he and Jean's Roy fell about laughing. Buggers, they were.'

Rory smiled. 'We've got a lot of good memories, Mum.'

'That we have.' Sheila patted Rory's hand. 'And it's time for you to make some new ones. What about this fella of Susie's? In her last email, she told me he might have a friend for you.'

This was like being fifteen again. Rory had some understanding why Belle had been so defensive. 'Maybe, Mum. Maybe.'

Sheila sat back as if her job was done. 'Good. Call her tonight and tell her. Her boyfriend sounds very exciting. Apparently, he has a huge tattoo on his back of a medieval dragon.'

CHAPTER TWENTY-EIGHT

Rory had just got home with the flat-packed IKEA shoe cabinets she'd had delivered to work – one for her, one for Belle – and was about get them out of their boxes and put them together, when an attractive young woman knocked on the front door. An attractive young woman in overalls.

'Hi. I'm Chris.'

'Chris?'

The attractive young woman held up a wrench. Her ponytail waved behind her. 'Your plumber. For your bathroom? You are Rory?'

Of course! John had offered a couple of weeks ago to contact a plumber friend of his to plumb in Rory's new bathroom suite, but Rory clearly hadn't written the date down in her diary. Also, she'd assumed that Chris would be a man. How embarrassing. She should have known better with a name like her own. Sexist.

'Of course, come in.'

Chris picked up a heavy-looking toolbox and followed her inside. 'I don't normally work evenings, but I can never say no to John. He's a special case.'

Rory was beginning to realise that. She paused at the bottom of the staircase. 'Have you known John long?' Chris looked to be about three years older than Belle. Practically a child.

'A couple of years. I met him on a job shortly after I qualified. He puts a lot of work my way. Shall I go straight up?' She pointed upwards with the wrench.

'Yes, of course. The bathroom is at the top of the stairs. The basin and bath are already in there. The toilet is in the hall. I'll make you a drink. Tea?'

Chris grinned. 'I'd love a black coffee, thanks.' Of course she took it black. You wouldn't stay that slim and attractive drinking builders' tea with two sugars.

*

Chris had already started hefting things into place when Rory took her coffee to her. Standing in the doorway with the mug, Rory watched her getting everything into position. Attractive and capable; no wonder John 'put a lot of work' her way. 'So, John keeps you busy?'

Chris grunted as she gave the bath a shove, then stood to take the coffee from Rory. 'Thanks. I haven't stopped today. Yeah, John usually recommends me to his female customers. They feel more comfortable having a woman round.' This made perfect sense. Some women on their own might feel vulnerable with a strange man in the house. *Don't read anything into this.*

'He has a lot of female customers, does he?' Was it possible to say that without sounding like she was fishing for information? Or desperate?

Chris took a gulp of her coffee, put it on the window sill and nodded. 'Yeah, quite a few. Which is great for me.' She dropped down onto her haunches and started to lay out pieces of plastic tubing. 'This bathroom suite is nice. Must have cost a bit?'

It was the kind of bathroom Rory had assumed would be out of her price range. Stand-alone bath, shower with six body jets, taps that looked like a modern water feature. Fabulous. 'Actually, John managed to get it for a really good price. Some of it was ex-display, I think. I really love it.'

Chris looked up sideways, lips pressed together and a twinkle in her eye. 'He's good like that, our John.' She winked at Rory, then went back to her plastic pipes and elbow joints.

Rory felt a warmth rising in her cheeks. 'I'll be downstairs if you need anything.'

Chris nodded and started to whistle softly to herself.

Back in the sitting room, Rory opened the cardboard boxes and pulled out the components of the shoe cabinets, laying them across the floor in a production line. Beneath her, the floorboards looked great now they'd been sanded down. By John. The walls and cornice were smooth and crisp now they'd been properly plastered and painted in the same neutral shade. Which John had helped her choose. And the fireplace? Well, that had been a joint effort. Would she have managed all this without him?

She hadn't appreciated the twinkle in Chris's eye: it was time to reassert herself. She had her hammer and screwdriver set and was ready to go at the shoe cabinets when the doorbell rang again. When she saw who it was, her stomach flip-flopped.

'Hi, Rory. Just checking Chris found you okay?'

Rory held the door open. 'Come in and see for yourself.'

John walked through the hall, pointed up the stairs and, when Rory nodded approval, took them two at a time up to the bathroom. There was a little mumbled conversation, a few laughs. What could be so funny about plumbing? When she heard him coming down the stairs, Rory dashed back into the sitting room.

John knocked on the frame of the door and came in. 'Look, I was thinking. I don't have anything on tonight, so I'll hang round and help Chris. The sooner we get this finished, the sooner I can get the tiles up. You could have a fully functioning bathroom in the next week.'

Tempting though his offer was, Rory had to stick to her principles. 'You've done enough and I know you have other work on. I can get someone in to do the tiling later.'

John frowned. 'But the tiles are here and I've got time this week. Plus, I won't charge as much as it would cost you to get a tiler in because it's part of the whole job. It makes sense, doesn't it?'

How could she tell him no without sounding rude? 'Actually, I'm going out shortly. I wouldn't feel right, leaving you here slaving away whilst I'm drinking wine at Penny's.'

John shrugged. 'I don't mind. I've been here on my own several times and anyway, it'll give me a chance to catch up with Chris. Haven't worked with her in a while.'

He was making it impossible for her to refuse his help without making a big deal out of it. And the promise of a beautiful bathroom by the end of the week was appealing. She couldn't stay here while he worked, though. Her stomach was already doing somersaults. It hadn't got the memo from her brain. *He is not interested in you. He just helps people. Needy women. You are* not *needy.*

'Okay. If you're sure. But I am going to have to shoot off.' She prayed that Penny was home and in the mood for alcohol. 'You've got a key, haven't you?'

John fiddled around in his pocket, brought out her spare key and held it up. 'Certainly have. You go and enjoy your night with Penny.'

But when Rory called Penny from her car, she was out to dinner with the new boyfriend. 'I'm so sorry. Shall I come home and meet you there?'

'Don't be silly, it was just a last-minute thought. You enjoy yourself and we'll catch up another time.'

Sheila didn't answer her home phone, Susie was already out, Charlie was with his mum, and Belle was with Fiona. Allegedly.

There was no way Rory was going back in. She headed to a service station ten minutes' drive away. At least there would be coffee.

Fifteen minutes later, she was sitting at a plastic table drinking Costa Express and thumbing through her phone. She'd tried to read a book on the Kindle app but couldn't focus without her mind wandering back to her bathroom and whether John and Chris were enjoying their 'catch up'.

This was ridiculous. Hiding here, when she should just go home and get on with her shoe cabinets. So what if John had a lot of female clients? What business was that of hers? And to feel jealous about him and Chris – because that's surely what was causing this burning feeling in her chest – was absurd. Chris was young enough to be his daughter. And who was Rory to have an opinion on that, anyway? Especially as she had a date lined up with Susie's boyfriend's friend at the end of the week. Rory shuddered. She still wasn't convinced the date was a good idea.

Susie had been very excited at the prospect of setting her up. There is no one as infuriatingly in love with love as someone in the early stages of a relationship. 'This will be so much fun! The two of us out with two friends! I'll come over to yours beforehand and we can get ready together. I can't wait!'

Why had Rory agreed?

But, if she didn't make an effort to meet someone, was tonight going to be the shape of her evenings to come? Rory enjoyed her own company, but you could have too much of a good thing. The blind date was already arranged, so she just needed to put on her big girl's pants and turn up. What's the worst that could happen?

Belle sent her a text at 9.30 p.m. to say that she was home with Charlie and they were keeping John and Chris in black coffee and sugary tea. Belle seemed quite enamoured with Chris, who was, apparently, 'a right laugh.'

Even though it was childish, Rory left it until 11.00 p.m. to return home, wired on caffeine and lemon drizzle muffins. There were no vans outside and the house was quiet. She was safe.

Belle and Charlie were both in their rooms, so Rory completed her usual tour of the downstairs, checking locks and switching off lights. In the sitting room, where she'd left the components of the shoe cabinets laid out, were two completed cabinets and a note from John: *Sorry. Couldn't resist.*

Caffeine and muffins could really make your stomach feel weird.

CHAPTER TWENTY-NINE

'I don't want to do this.'

Susie wasn't listening.

'I've changed my mind.' What had Rory been thinking, agreeing to this date? It was her mother's fault. Looking all vulnerable and making her cry. If Sheila hadn't been so adamant, Rory would never have gone along with it.

'You don't get to change your mind at the last minute. Jim has told his friend all about you. This is going to be fun.' Susie, looking stunning in a fitted red dress which matched her lipstick, continued to flick through Rory's wardrobe with a face of increasing incredulity. She pulled out something dark green and voluminous. 'Culottes? What were you thinking?'

Rory snatched them from her and stuffed them back into the wardrobe. 'I bought them after I'd had Belle. They were forgiving.'

Susie sighed and sat down on the bed. 'Haven't you got anything a bit more… sexy?'

Sexy? It had been a while since Rory had worried about that. Functional and smart were more her requirements when she shopped for clothes. And that was rare. She'd spent more time in Topshop with Belle in the last six years than she ever spent in clothes shops for grown-ups.

Susie leaned back onto the bed and propped up her head with her hand. 'I have to say, I really like this room. Your man John, he's done a great job.'

There it was again: that fluttery feeling whenever anyone mentioned John's name. *He is* not *looking for someone. He is your* handyman. Rory pushed the feeling down. But she turned back to the wardrobe so that Susie couldn't see her face.

'Yes. He has. I'm really pleased with it. And he's not "my man".'

Susie sighed. 'More's the pity. You shouldn't have let that one get away. Great arms.'

Time to change the subject. 'What do you know about this man I'm meeting tonight?'

Susie sat up again. 'Not much. But I can confirm that he is breathing, solvent and has not got a wife.' She smiled proudly. 'I checked.'

*

In all her thirty-eight years, Rory had never been on a blind date. Walking into the restaurant, she kept up a running commentary in her head. *You are a grown up. You are just meeting someone new. There is nothing to be worried about.*

Except she was worried.

Susie had never had the best taste in men. In fact, the main reason Susie was still single was because she was only ever attracted to the type of man who would make normal women run a mile. Overly familiar? Rough around the edges? Brains of a Brussels sprout? That was Susie catnip.

Therefore, Rory wasn't surprised when Jim looked like he might have just got back from holding up a post office.

Maybe she was being unfair. He was dressed well. A crisp white shirt and smart trousers. The long sleeves hid the tattoos which Susie found so attractive, but when he turned to speak to the waiter, Rory could see the pointed tail of a dragon peeking out from the collar of his shirt. According to Susie, it covered the whole of his back. She'd gushed how his tattoos made him look like Tom Hardy. Maybe if Tom had just recovered from glandular fever. Although to be fair to Susie, there was something strangely familiar about him.

But Rory wasn't here to pass judgement on Jim. Susie was a big girl and could take care of herself. Rory really should pay attention to the man who had been brought here for her. She'd promised her mother that she wouldn't judge him in the first five minutes. Just think about the jars he could open and the spiders he could catch. Look for the positives.

'So, what do you do, Andy?'

He leaned back in his chair. 'I'm in business.' He winked at her. 'Bit of this, bit of that.'

Rory's heart sank. But Susie's eyes told her she had to continue. *Jars and spiders.*

'How do you know Jim?'

'He started drinking at The Crown a few weeks ago. That's my local. We've had a few bevvies together the last few Fridays.' The wink again. Then he went silent.

Marvellous. A wheeler dealer *and* a drinker. Her cup runneth over. Plus, Jim had only known him for a few weeks; so much for the glowing recommendation. How long before she could get out of here?

'You're a teacher like Susie, aren't you?' Susie's boyfriend, Jim, was at least trying to engage her in conversation.

'Yes, we've worked together for about six years. At St Anthony's.' And this is how Susie repaid her.

'Yeah. St Anthony's,' he nodded his head, 'I've heard of it.'

'Oh, did you go to school round here, then?' This had to be the dullest conversation she'd had in a while.

'No. Only moved here recently. And then I met this one.' He took hold of Susie's hand and squeezed it.

Susie's face was sickening.

Jim turned back to Rory. 'Do you like it? Teaching?'

'Yes. I love it. The kids at St Anthony's are great.' Whenever Rory talked about her students, it made her smile. Teaching was a tough job – and Nathan Finch was making it tougher – but she wouldn't change her students for the world.

'I hated school, me. I hated teachers too.' For a moment there was a glint in Jim's eye that wasn't particularly attractive, then he tried to smooth it over with a smile. Rory definitely had the feeling that she'd met him before. It was odd.

'There're probably a few of our pupils who might say the same.' Susie tried to lighten the mood.

Jim didn't take his eyes from Rory. 'Rough, are they? The kids at your school?'

Rory bristled; those were *her* kids he was referring to. 'I wouldn't say that.'

'That's not what I've heard,' chipped in Andy. 'Some of the kids on my estate go to St Anthony's. I reckon you've got some right toe rags.'

'We've got some difficult kids. But they have difficult lives. It's understandable.' Why wasn't Susie joining in with her? She loved the kids at St Anthony's as much as Rory did. And why was Jim the Dragon Tattoo Man still staring at her so intently?

Jim laughed harshly. 'Oh, the broken home story? Don't wash with me, I'm afraid.'

Great. He was going to be one of those. *I was given a clip round the ear and it never did me any harm.* Rory wasn't in the mood. 'I just need to go to the bathroom, excuse me.'

'I'll come with you.' Susie pushed out her chair and got up to follow her. So she hadn't lost her voice after all.

*

As soon as they were inside the Ladies, Rory turned to speak but Susie held up her hands and spoke first.

'Okay, before you say it, I know that Andy is all wrong for you. I'm sorry. It was worth a go. Just stick it out until the end of the meal and I promise you never have to see him again.'

Rory couldn't last that long. 'The end of the meal? How about I get an emergency call from home and have to leave in ten minutes?'

'No! It will look too obvious. Just wait until after dessert and then say you're tired or have got an early start or something. You know, the lines I've had men use on me. Please?'

Rory groaned. When Susie put it like that, what could she do but agree? Susie grinned and turned to reapply her lipstick in the mirror. She was so lovely. If only she could see that her bad luck with men had less to do with her attractiveness and more to do with her poor judgement.

'What do you think of Jim, then?'

Rory had dreaded this question. Jim was awful. Unattractiveness aside, he seemed intense, aggressive and opinionated. And they hadn't even had their main meal yet. There was no point saying any of this to Susie, though. Every man she met was a potential life partner until they did something awful and her rose-coloured spectacles fell off. Rory hoped he wouldn't hurt her too badly.

But Rory was saved by the bell. Or her ringing mobile. It was Sheila. 'I need to take this; it's my mum.'

'Hello Rory? It's Mum.' The waver in Sheila's voice stopped Rory from telling her that caller display had told her that already. 'Can you talk? You're not driving, are you?'

Sheila started every phone call like this. Whatever was bothering her was obviously not serious enough to prevent her Health and Safety checks. 'No, Mum, I'm fine to talk.' Rory made a gesture to Susie to go back on in without her. That would save her from having to give her opinion on Dragon Man. Hopefully, by the time she got back out there, the meal would have arrived and she could eat and go.

Sheila sounded wobbly. 'Something awful has happened.'

'What? Are you okay? Is it your foot?'

'No, nothing like that. It's George, I've upset him.'

Rory breathed out. No need to panic. She leaned back against a hand basin. This might take a while. For once, she didn't mind. 'I can't believe that, Mum. What happened?'

'Olive was in bed, so George moved two dining chairs into their bedroom so all three of us could listen to some old music and have a sing song; we've done it a few times. Sometimes Olive joins in and sometimes she just sits and taps the rhythm on my hand.'

'Sounds nice.' Sheila was obviously upset, so Rory didn't want to rush her. Also, it would buy her more time away from Dragon Man and his boring sidekick.

'It's really nice. Olive often falls asleep and then George and I talk about years ago. Things we got up to as kids, movies we loved, music we used to listen to. Do you know he likes The Beatles too? I can't believe we have known each other for almost two months and not found that out.'

Listening to The Beatles always reminded Rory of her dad. She couldn't listen to 'Yesterday' or 'Hey Jude' without thinking of him, singing along in his van. Happy memories.

'George went to make tea. While he was gone, Olive woke up. She was a bit confused, so I held her hand. Then she asked where my husband was. I reminded her I'd lost my husband. She got agitated then, cross with me even. "No, your husband," she kept saying, "your husband. The one you were singing with. That tall man with the grey hair." She meant George! I said, "He's your husband, silly." And then she laughed at me. "No, he's your husband. You can tell by the way he looks at you."'

Rory could see how this might be awkward. But Olive had Alzheimer's. It was to be expected. 'If she'd just woken up, Mum, she was probably just a bit disoriented. It's nothing to get upset about.'

Sheila sniffed. 'I know that; I didn't think anything of it. She's been really unwell and there are more and more days she doesn't know who people are. The problem was that George appeared with the tea at that exact moment and he heard every word.'

'What did he say?'

'We didn't talk about it, but he drank his scalding hot tea in record time and then made up some jobs that he had to get done before bedtime. It didn't take a genius to work out that he wanted me to go. Olive had already dozed back off, so I gave her a peck on the cheek and left.'

'He was probably just embarrassed. It'll be okay next time you see him.' Rory really needed to get back to the table. She was cross with Susie, but not cross enough to be rude.

'That's just it. I asked him if he wanted me to pop in again tomorrow but he said we should leave it because Olive could do with some uninterrupted sleep. He made a feeble joke about staying in his pyjamas all day, but I knew what he was telling me. Don't come.'

'Give it a couple of days, Mum. I'm sure it will be fine.'

Sheila sniffed again. 'I hope you're right. I can't stop feeling guilty, but it's not as if we've been doing anything wrong. I just visit Olive, giving George a break when he needs it. I've enjoyed his company, but there's nothing wrong with that, is there?'

'Nothing wrong with that at all. I'm sure it will all sort itself out, Mum. Look, why don't you come over a bit earlier tomorrow night, we can have a chat before I go out.'

'Oh yes, I'd forgotten you've got your date.'

'No, that's tonight. Right now, in fact.'

'You should have said! How is it?'

'Terrible. I'll tell you when I see you tomorrow night.'

Tomorrow night. When she had to go out to the Community Awards with Nathan Finch. Her weekend just got better and better.

CHAPTER THIRTY

'Are you sure you don't mind doing this, Mum? I don't have to go, you know; it's only a work thing.' Rory had been fussing about like this since Sheila had arrived. She would rather be going to the dentist than an awards dinner with Nathan Finch. Susie and Penny had been teasing her about it all week. What the heck were they going to talk about? Seating plans?

Sheila, on the other hand, was quite excited. 'I don't mind a bit. I'd only be sitting at home, fretting about George and Olive. Plus, it'll be nice to spend some time with Charlie. Now go and get dressed. Your date will be here in a minute.'

Rory threw her hands up in the air. 'For the last time, Mum, he is *not* my date! This is a dinner for the Community Awards. I am merely accompanying the deputy head.'

Sheila nudged Rory in the direction of the door. 'Yes, yes. I know. Just go and get dressed or you'll be keeping *the deputy head* waiting.'

Charlie walked in, dragging his feet. 'I don't want to see Finchy. Does he have to come in?'

At the same time, Sheila said 'Yes,' and Rory said 'No.'

Sheila gave Rory another little push. 'If you're still sitting here in your jeans when he arrives, I'll have no option but to let him in. Go and get dressed!'

Rory's new dress was hanging on the outside of the wardrobe. She'd needed something more formal than her usual black dress and had made the mistake of allowing Susie to come shopping with her. Somehow, Susie had persuaded her that the dark green brought out her eyes. Rory didn't want to dwell on what that neckline was going to bring out. There was no point worrying about it now. Susie had even kidnapped the black dress so that Rory couldn't change her mind at the last minute.

The doorbell rang. Damn. Nathan was early. That meant that poor Charlie might have to see the dreaded deputy out of school hours and, worse, her mother would get the chance to talk to him. As quickly as she could, Rory wriggled into the dress and hobbled across the landing to Belle's room. 'Quick! Zip me up!'

Since the naked selfie incident, Belle had been subdued. Rory had made her come straight home from college for the first few days afterwards, but had relented and let her study at Fiona's last night whilst Rory was on the awful double date with Susie. When Rory appeared at Belle's door, dressed to go out, Belle did a mock double take. 'You look really good, Mum. You should dress like this more often.'

'Thanks. Maybe I'll get one to wear to Sainsbury's?' Thank God they were friends again. Despite Rory's evil parenting. Rory watched Belle's reflection in the dressing table mirror as she zipped her dress. Her look of concentration was so endearing that Rory couldn't resist kissing her.

But, as she walked downstairs, Rory realised that the voices she could hear didn't include that of Nathan Finch. That was John's voice.

Rory's stomach still did its familiar flip when she saw him. She was a fool. He didn't fancy her; he just felt sorry for her. John and Sheila turned to look in her direction. Charlie had his head in a box, from which he was extricating a variety of implements.

'Wow.' John almost dislocated his jaw, his mouth fell open so fast.

'Darling. You look beautiful!' Sheila clapped her hands together and kept them there, as if in prayer.

Rory fiddled with the neckline of the dress. John couldn't take his eyes off her. Sheila looked happily from one to the other of them, and Rory wanted to strangle her.

Charlie came to the rescue.

'Rory. Look at this lot. John has bought me my own set of tools.'

'Wow, lucky you.' She smiled at John. 'That's very generous of you.'

John shrugged. 'A mate of mine got them cheap. He was getting some for his own boy and I thought Charlie might like some. He can earn his keep that way.' He winked at Charlie, before turning to check with Rory, 'It's okay isn't it?'

'I would think so. As long as I don't have to return him to his mother missing a finger.' She felt a pang. She'd got used to having Charlie around. He didn't belong to her, but it was going to be difficult to say goodbye. With Belle spending less time at home, Rory had enjoyed having someone to look after.

John rubbed his palms together. 'How's your bathroom working out?'

It was fabulous. 'Great. How's Chris?' Another pang. A different kind.

John frowned. 'Er, fine. As far as I know. Your mum reminded me that your kitchen is being delivered next week. What day do you want me?'

Damn her mother. After the parents' evening revelations, Rory didn't want John to help at all. How could she put him off? *Think.* 'Actually, it's been delayed. Not sure when it's coming now.'

Sheila looked confused. 'But that's not what...'

'Yes. Yes. You know how these things are. Never go to plan.' Rory's nose started to itch and she rubbed it with the back of her hand. An itchy nose meant a cold was on its way, just in time for the half-term break. Great.

John shrugged. 'Okay. Well just let me know when you want me.' He narrowed his eyes. 'Is your nose all right?'

'Just a cold. I'll be right back.' Rory dashed to the downstairs loo to blow her nose. She needed to be quick before her mum said anything to make John suspicious about the kitchen delivery.

This time, when the bell rang, she grabbed her coat. It had to be Nathan. 'Don't worry, Charlie. I'll go straight out.'

'Hold up,' John jumped up. 'I'll come out with you.'

He followed her out to the hallway. 'Sorry, I should have checked with you before giving him the tools. I know it's not my place. I just feel sorry for the kid, you know. My mum was on her own. I know what it's like.'

So, it was true. The doorbell rang again, insistently. Rory tried to ignore it. 'It's fine. Honestly. It was a kind thing to do. It's good that you like to... help people.'

'It's a great thing you're doing for him. And for his mum. It must make it easier for her knowing that he's in such a nice place with... such nice people.'

Rory's heart thumped. 'Thanks. Really. Was that all you wanted to talk to me about?'

The doorbell rang again. Followed by a loud knock on the door. John hesitated, 'Those girls are desperate to get going, aren't they?'

'Oh, it's not the girls. It's...'

Just then, the door opened. When Sheila had let John in, she clearly hadn't closed it properly. A sharp rap from Nathan Finch and it had opened, revealing a surprised Nathan in an expensive tuxedo, knuckles still in mid-knock. 'Sorry, I'm not sure how that happened.'

Rory couldn't even look at John. 'John this is Nathan. He's the deputy head at my school. We have an event to attend. A community awards evening. Nathan, this is...' Her mind went blank. How did she introduce John Prince? Her builder? Her friend? 'This is John.'

Nathan nodded curtly. 'We need to get going, really. I hate to be late.'

Rory's red face was probably providing a lovely contrast to her green dress. 'Of course. Sorry, John. I have to go.'

'No problem.' John wasn't meeting her eye either. 'I completely understand.'

*

The Civic Hall had been decked out with tablecloths and flowers in an attempt to make it seem classy. The seating plan – seems they couldn't escape the damn things – placed Rory and Nathan quite close to the front of the stage.

Rory was tearing a piece of bread into small pieces. 'Do you often have to come to these events?'

'From time to time.' Nathan looked amused by her bread dissection. 'Are you going to eat that?'

Rory put the bread on her plate and looked around. 'Actually, I'd like some wine. Where is the waiter?'

On reflection, she probably shouldn't have started drinking so early. Red wine on an empty stomach was all very well for a night out with the girls, but not so much for an evening engagement with a deputy head she trusted less than the education minister.

The other people on their table were all from one primary school so, after a brief period of polite conversation, they left Rory and Nathan to entertain themselves. Nathan's previous employment experience was something of a mystery which, after a fourth glass of wine, Rory decided to investigate. 'So, what made you leave your last job?'

Nathan shrugged. 'I had gone as far as I could there. The new head wasn't looking to replace his current deputy and I didn't want to hang around and wait for someone to die.' Rory hoped he was talking metaphorically. 'How long have you been at St Anthony's?'

'Gosh.' Rory counted on her fingers. She had been there since Belle was one. Was it really that long? 'Fifteen years this coming September. Although it seems to have gone very quickly.'

Nathan nodded slowly and sipped his wine – still his first glass. 'Why are you still just a teacher?'

Here it was. Rory's pet career hate. 'Because being *just* a teacher is what I want to be. I want to teach kids, not manage other people to teach kids.' She could never understand why some people seemed desperate to climb the career ladder when it meant leaving the classroom.

Nathan shook his head. 'That's very admirable, I'm sure. But aren't you bored of that by now?'

Rory took a gulp of her wine. 'How can I be bored when people like you keep changing things every year?'

Nathan raised his glass in recognition of her quick response. 'All I'm trying to do is ensure we have consistency across the school.'

That bloody word again. 'But kids aren't consistent, are they? They are all different, so the way we teach them must be different. The teaching has to fit the pupils.'

Nathan wasn't persuaded. 'Consistency is the most important thing. At my old school, everyone taught the same lessons and marked in exactly the same way.'

'Isn't that a bit dull and repetitive? Look at Penny, her RE lessons are creative and interesting: pupils love them.'

'Enjoyment is not a priority. Even though it's only RE, all lessons need to follow the same form as everyone else's. Students learn better when they know what to expect. When they have routines.'

'That's rubbish. And RE is important. Penny tackles lots of…'

Nathan coughed, then put his glass down. 'It's inappropriate for us to discuss another member of staff. Anyway, I was hoping to speak to you tonight about a new position we are creating. It's something I'm… *we're* hoping you might be interested in. We need a lead teacher to coach the members of staff who are… How can I put it…?'

'In danger of being fired?' Four glasses of wine made Rory blunt.

'You could put it that way. You'll note that I didn't.' Nathan paused and took a sip of water. 'I was thinking that you might be just the person. The staff like you. You're an excellent teacher.'

He was praising her again. It was uncomfortable. 'What are you asking me to do?'

Nathan pressed the tips of his fingers together. 'If we have concerns about a teacher's effectiveness, we have to *show* that we are helping them to improve. It's not like the real world; we can't just sack them.' He looked as if this was a great sadness to him. 'We need to show that we've provided coaching.'

What did he mean? Was this a genuine job offer to coach other members of staff, so that Rory would have a chance to help her colleagues? Or was it a poisoned chalice? Was she the priest being sent in to read an innocent man his last rites? 'Are you offering me the job?'

Nathan tapped his fingertips together and shook his head. 'There is no job as yet. It's just something we're thinking about. Obviously, we would have to make sure we found the right candidate. Would you apply?'

'It would depend on what the job entailed.' Honestly, it might also depend on how much money he was offering. Finances were a little tight right now and some extra income would be most welcome.

'Well, it would mean that we gave you one or two teachers to work with each term. You would observe their lessons, give them some targets and then check that they were meeting them. Obviously, we would need to reduce your teaching timetable to enable you to do that. We could take your 10-G class from you pretty much straight away.'

Rory sat up. That was Charlie's class. 'I couldn't give up that class.'

'Of course you could. We'd probably give them to a trainee teacher. It's only babysitting really, isn't it? There's not a hope for a decent grade in that room.'

Now he was really pushing his luck. 'I disagree. There's a couple of kids in there who are doing really well. And anyway, that's not the point. I like teaching them and they deserve to get good lessons.'

Nathan leaned back in his seat. 'But that is you thinking as a classroom teacher. Think how much of a wider impact you could have as a lead teacher. You would be improving lessons for hundreds of pupils; not just those twenty. If I had stayed a classroom teacher, I would not have had one tenth of the impact I am having now.' If Rory imagined his 'impact' as being similar to that of a nuclear bomb, she'd be forced to agree. 'Just think about it over the half term holiday.'

Rory drained the last of her glass. She didn't really need anything else to think about over the holiday. Particularly as she was supposed to be fitting a complete kitchen, and she didn't want to ask John Prince to help.

CHAPTER THIRTY-ONE

The entire sitting room was taken up with cardboard boxes. What was the collective noun for boxes? A pack of boxes? An Amazon? A bloody mess?

Call Me Adrian's delivery friends had made several trips back and forth to their large van to bring in the flat-packed kitchen units. The man who seemed to be in charge had given Rory a large delivery note and she had attempted to cross off each item as they brought it in. Very quickly, the combination of serial numbers and box sizes had confused her completely and she had resorted to pretending to tick things rather than admit she was lost.

The whole process was made even more difficult because she had no voice. It was typical to get ill at the end of term, and what had started as a sore throat had now left her barely audible. So, when the man in charge asked her – for the third time – if she was really intending to put this kitchen together on her own, she was only able to nod rather than quote chapters from Caitlin Moran. Probably a good thing.

Now she was sitting on the front step with a cup of tea, psyching herself up to go in and get started. Belle was out for the day and Charlie was with his mum. John had offered to come and help her but, after the parents' evening epiphany, Rory did not want to be another single mum in a list of his charity cases. Just thinking about it made her blush. How had she misread the signs so badly? Idiot.

It was cold outside, but Rory's face was burning. Was her sore throat the beginning of flu or was she still hot from pulling the boxes around to check that she hadn't missed anything on the list? It was more likely to be flu because her face was hot, but her body was cold. She had the throw from the couch on her lap and had wrapped it around her legs like an old woman. Or a geriatric mermaid. She nodded 'hello' at one of her neighbours – motioning to her mouth and shaking her head to explain why she didn't speak.

Then a familiar white van pulled up outside the house.

'Morning. Did I get here in time?'

Rory's lack of voice reduced her to holding out her hands and doing her best 'quizzical' face – *a la* Marcel Marceau. She'd had plenty of practise over the years with 10-G.

John scratched his nose. 'The kitchen? It's being delivered today? Your mum called me and said that they'd made a mistake and it was coming today after all.'

If Rory had had a working larynx, she would have growled. She should never have given Sheila his number. Putting up some picture frames, indeed. How had she not seen that Sheila had an ulterior motive?

Rory nodded in the direction of the house, pointing to her throat and shaking her head.

'Oh! You've lost your voice?' He grinned. 'That explains why you didn't call me yourself.'

Rory shook her head as she walked through to the sitting room. Where could she find a notepad and pen under these damn boxes?

John whistled. 'That's a lot of cabinets. They don't seem to be in any order. Did they not put them in groups of the same? Where's your delivery note?'

The delivery note! Rory could write on the back of that. Finding it, she scribbled: *It's okay. You don't need to help.*

John leaned forwards to read it and laughed. Then he saw the look on her face and coughed to hide it. 'Just let me stay and get you started. It's no trouble, honestly.'

Rory started to write again and then stopped. Who was she kidding? She had no idea where to start with this lot. And now her head was beginning to throb. She scribbled again. *Thanks. I appreciate it. But I WILL pay you.*

John shrugged. 'Yeah, whatever you want. Now give me that delivery note.'

*

John was so fast at putting cupboards together. Rory had just about finished one in the time it had taken him to do three. He tried to take hers when she was struggling to push a dowel in, but she pulled it away from him with a scowl of disapproval. She might not be as capable as Chris, the perfect plumber, but she could shove a damn dowel into a damn hole. Eventually.

John just laughed. 'Don't take this the wrong way, but you remind me a lot of my mum.'

Great. Just what every woman wants, to be compared to someone's mother.

'She was a strong woman, too. Really determined.'

Maybe that wasn't so bad.

'Had to be, really. My dad left when she found out she was pregnant, and her parents didn't help much.'

John pulled over another box and tore it open. Rory leaned over and wrote on it: *You must have helped?*

John pulled the box away from its contents in one swift movement. 'Yeah, when I grew up. I was a bit of a bugger when I was younger.'

He started to arrange the pieces of cupboard in front of him. He had a definite process with each one. He laid everything out in the order he would need it, including the screws and dowels. Then he became a mini production line. It was soothing to watch.

'Wish I'd been able to help her more, really. Although she did get to see me start the business before she passed away. She was dead proud. You know what mothers are like.' He smiled up at Rory, then went back to his work.

Rory knew exactly. She had albums full of Belle's childhood creations to prove it. She picked up her pen again. *You like helping people?*

'I s'pose I do.'

They continued to work in silence. John wasn't a talker and Rory couldn't. Usually that wouldn't have been a problem. But today, there was something nagging at her.

You've helped a lot of single mothers? She tapped at the cardboard to get his attention.

John shrugged. 'I guess so. I see them on their own with their kids and I remember what it was like. If I can help them out by charging what they can afford, I do.'

This was very admirable. But memories of Fiona's mother's face made Rory uncharitable. She felt hot again. There was a burning in her chest.

What about the single dads? She wrote.

John laughed. 'I'd help the single dads too, but there seem to be less of them who have the kids living with them. And they're usually too proud to ask another man for help.'

Too proud? Were women not proud, then? Did he think she had no pride? Rory felt hotter and hotter. And it wasn't just because she was unwell.

John paused and frowned. 'Are you okay? You've gone very red.'

Rory nodded. She didn't have enough room on the cardboard to tell him how she felt right now. Did he think he was some kind of saviour to these women? As if they weren't completely capable of doing these things themselves. Like this kitchen. She hadn't asked for his help. Well, her mum had, but that was not Rory's fault. Rory's head swam. She stopped hammering and took a deep breath.

John tapped the small corner cupboard he had just put together. 'Shall we put this one up? See what it looks like?'

He was up and holding the cupboard against the wall before Rory could get to her feet. There was no way she was going to admit she wasn't up to this. But she wasn't. Her legs felt so heavy. Within seconds of standing, her vision blurred and her legs went out from under her.

'Rory!' John let the cupboard slip to the floor and crouched down beside her. 'Are you okay? What happened? Are you hurt?'

John held onto Rory's arms and looked into her eyes. He had very deep blue eyes. Beautiful blue eyes. *Must not look at them.*

Rory closed her eyes and opened her mouth. 'Fine. Flu.' She managed to squeak.

John slipped an arm around her back. 'I'll carry you to the sofa.'

Rory jerked in alarm. She would have to be dying before she'd let him pick her up. She managed to scrabble herself into standing. The ground swayed beneath her feet.

John helped her into the sitting room and pulled the last few boxes from the sofa before helping her to lie down. He brought her some water and then hovered over her. Rory closed her eyes.

'I'll go back to the kitchen and carry on; I'll come back and check on you.'

Rory kept her eyes closed but shook her head. Even that small movement was painful. She managed to squeeze out a couple of sounds. 'No. Go.'

'It's fine. I really don't…'

Rory opened her eyes. 'Please. Go.'

'But, Rory…'

Rory propped herself up on her elbows and croaked, 'I am perfectly capable of doing this on my own.' She took a deep breath and tried again. 'I didn't even ask you to come here today. And now you won't leave. How many times do I have to say that I don't need your help? Just go.'

She closed her eyes again and listened as John walked back to the kitchen and packed away his tools. Her throat tightened even further. She was being unreasonable. Acting like a child, even. But she couldn't let him see her like this. She wasn't a charity case who needed helping. She shouldn't have let him do so much. That had never been her plan. And if she had fooled herself into thinking that there might be something more… Well, that was her own stupid fault and she needed to get back to the way things were. Standing on her own two feet.

John crept back into the sitting room. 'I'll be off, then. Are you sure you'll be okay?'

Rory held up an arm and waved. She couldn't speak. She couldn't write. All she wanted was to curl up in a ball and feel better.

The front door slammed shut.

*

Rory was in bed for the whole of the next day. Susie brought over some whisky to make a hot toddy and, when Rory woke up, Susie was sitting on the end of her bed, sipping at it.

'So, you *are* alive. How are you feeling?'

Rory tried to push herself up into sitting but the effort was too much. 'A bit better. The paracetamol seems to be working and my voice is much better. Where are Belle and Charlie?'

Susie took another sip of the whisky. 'Charlie went out with Harry. Belle is in her room doing her half-term homework.'

Rory's eyes widened. 'Really?'

Susie put the whisky tumbler on the side table. 'Of course not! How drugged up are you? She's gone out.'

When Belle was sick, Rory would cook all her favourite foods and make her a bed on the couch so she could sit and watch her favourite programmes. What did Rory get in return? Nothing.

'No one wants to look after me, then?'

'I'm here, you ungrateful moo.' Susie prodded her through the quilt with a shiny red fingernail. Her face was made up, too. Was she on her way somewhere?

'You look nice.'

Susie arched an eyebrow. 'Compared to you right now, anyone would look good. Tell me you didn't let the dashing John Prince see you like this?'

Oh, no. The way she'd treated John yesterday! Where had that come from? There was only so much she could blame on the flu. Rory pulled the duvet up over her reddening face.

Thankfully, Susie didn't notice. 'I'm meeting Jim after I've checked on you. I'm hoping we might actually go out somewhere if I'm dolled up.'

Rory pulled the duvet away from her face. 'What do you mean?'

Susie picked up a cushion from the bottom of the bed and held it on her lap, smoothing it over. 'We don't seem to *do* anything. All he wants to do is hang around my place; says he prefers it to the place he's staying in. Not that I've ever seen it.'

Rory managed to wriggle upwards a little. 'Forgive me for being forward, but I thought you enjoyed *hanging out* at your place.'

Susie threw the cushion at her. 'We don't even do that. He says he's tired all the time. Just wants to lie on my sofa and drink beer.'

Even through her paracetamol daze, Rory was annoyed by this. She knew that Dragon Man had been a bad choice the first time she'd met him. How dare he treat her lovely friend like this? 'You can't put up with that. Does he not even talk to you?'

Susie retrieved the cushion and recommenced stroking it. 'That's the weird thing. When we do talk, he just wants to ask about my job, the school and…'

'And?'

Susie looked up. 'And you.'

Rory hadn't been expecting that. She may have got her voice back but she didn't have a response to this. 'Me? Are you sure?'

Susie nodded. 'Yes. At first, I thought he fancied you but I'm not sure that's it. He just uses you as a reference point when he's on a rant about schools. "Teachers like your mate," he says, "teachers like your mate who think they know best."'

This was sounding weirder and weirder. Rory would end up being interviewed for one of those Channel 5 serial killer programmes and people would be shouting at their TVs, asking why she hadn't got her friend the hell out of that relationship.

'Susie. Are you sure he's…'

Susie put up a hand. 'Don't say anything. He's had some problems finding work. He's a bit low at the moment. I need to give it some time.' She sat up straighter and prodded Rory again. 'And as for you, you'd better get yourself better before the end of half-term. Haven't you got your high-powered meeting with The Great One on the first day back?'

CHAPTER THIRTY-TWO

Since he'd started in September, Nathan Finch had been stalking Penny, criticising her teaching and her marking. But Rory hadn't expected to be the one he asked to coach her. He knew they were friends. It was unprofessional.

Nathan had called her into his office, where he was now leaning back in his black leather chair, fingertips pressed together, swivelling from side to side. All he needed was a white cat to stroke.

Rory had recovered from the flu but had spent the rest of the week off trying to put the damn kitchen together on her own, before giving in and contacting Call Me Adrian. She'd been far too embarrassed to call John after the way she'd spoken to him. Call Me Adrian had been unnecessarily smug before sending out the kitchen fitters. Her kitchen was finished, but so was her self-esteem. She was not in the mood for Nathan's games.

'You do know that she is one of my closest friends?'

'Oh, is she?' He was clearly faking. 'Well, if that's the case, I'm assuming you will jump at the chance of helping her.'

Rory would do anything she could to help Penny, and not just because she was her friend. 'Like I keep saying, Penny is a great teacher and her results are good. Plus, the kids like her.'

Nathan started to sort through some papers on his desk. 'Apparently, the head thinks very highly of her, too. He wants me to ensure that she feels supported, rather than… What was the word he used… Attacked?'

'So why do you still think she needs coaching?'

He looked up. Raised an eyebrow. 'She doesn't do things the way I want them done.'

Arrogant pig.

But Rory had begun to have a suspicion that there was more to Nathan's behaviour than pure arrogance. 'Maybe *you* could teach a model lesson for her?'

'What?' Nathan looked as if she'd just suggested that he teach Buddhism through interpretive dance.

'Teach a lesson to her class whilst she observes. Show her how you want her to structure it.' It had probably been a while since Nathan had been at the front of the classroom; it would do him good to remember what it was like.

Nathan coughed and flexed his shoulders. 'I don't think so.'

Rory wasn't going to let it go. 'Why not? You said yourself, it's *only* RE.'

He returned to shuffling papers. 'Penny is not a trainee teacher. She should know what a good lesson looks like. Anyway, I have a meeting with the finance office in—' he flicked a wrist to expose his expensive watch '—ten minutes. So I will catch up with you later.'

Interesting. Obviously no one wanted to teach an extra hour that they didn't have to. But Nathan Finch hadn't looked annoyed. He'd looked scared.

*

Rory went to find Penny immediately to tell her what Nathan had asked. 'But I will refuse if you think this is too weird. You've been teaching longer than I have and I know what a great teacher you are. There is going to be nothing I can teach you that you don't already know. I don't want this to cause problems between us.'

Putting a gentle hand on Rory's arm, Penny smiled. 'Stop worrying. I'd much rather have you in my classroom than Nathan Finch.'

It was Rory's turn to smile. But not for the same reason. 'Don't speak so soon. I have a little plan up my sleeve for Mr Finch to feature in your classroom in the very near future.'

Penny gulped. 'What do you mean?'

'Wait and see.'

*

Belle was staying at her dad's that night and Charlie was going straight to Harry's after school, so Rory was planning on a night in front of the TV after finishing her marking. She didn't want to even look at the kitchen. The perfectly placed cabinets were mocking her. Just as she got to the last book, the doorbell rang.

Sheila was on the doorstep with a cake that she had made for Rory and Belle. 'Don't worry, I'm not stopping. I was making a cake for Olive and George and it was just as easy to make two.'

Rory watched her mum bustle past in the direction of the kitchen. 'Thanks, Mum. Does that mean everything is back to normal between you now?'

Sheila was already looking in the cupboard for some cake plates. Clearly the 'not stopping' had been merely a pleasantry. 'No. That's why I've made the cake for them, as an excuse to pop in. But I haven't got the courage up to do it yet.'

'You still haven't spoken to George?'

Sheila shook her head. 'Karen came to see me yesterday. She could tell that something wasn't right. I couldn't lie to her. I told her what happened. She looked a little shocked, but she didn't blame me at all. She suggested I just give him a few days because he can be stubborn. But it's been a while since I've seen them and I'm missing them terribly.'

'Why don't you stay for a cup of tea and we can have a slice of cake now?' That was clearly her mother's intention anyway.

'What? Oh, yes. I will. I don't really know what to do with myself. I've got used to spending time there. It's like going out without going out, just popping downstairs. It's been a long time since I've had someone nearby like that to chat to. Since your father went, I've got used to being on my own. But it's surprising how much you can miss having someone to just watch TV with or make a cup of tea for. It's nice to be needed.'

Rory put an arm around her mum's shoulders. 'We need you.'

'Oh, no you don't. Not really. In fact, I don't know that you've ever needed me. You've always been Miss Independent. I mean, look at this kitchen. It's marvellous.'

Rory bit her lip. She hadn't admitted to her mum that she and Call Me Adrian had been right about needing kitchen fitters. This wasn't the time to do it. Rory bent down to hide her face in the fridge in the pretence of getting milk.

'Do you miss him, Mum? Do you still miss Dad?'

Sheila sighed, leaning back against the cupboards. 'Every day, love. Sometimes I still get two cups out in the morning and then have to put one back. He was a good man, your dad.'

Rory's eyes prickled. She slid the milk onto the counter and Sheila put her hand over Rory's. They stood in silence for a few moments until Rory could trust her voice. 'Do you think we'll ever get used to not having him around?'

'Probably not,' Sheila smiled at her daughter. 'But that's all right. We were lucky to have him while we did.'

Rory nodded and blinked her eyes. 'They don't make them like that any more.'

'Rubbish.' Sheila patted Rory's hand firmly and then went back to her tea making. 'There are plenty of nice young men out there. And your dad wasn't perfect, you know. You don't need someone perfect.'

'I don't need someone anything right now.'

Sheila sighed. 'I don't want you to be on your own forever. One day, I won't be here and I'd like to think…'

Rory held up her hand. 'Mum, please. Don't do this again. Let's change the subject. Did Karen say anything about Olive's health?'

Sheila picked up her cup. 'Yes. Olive is a little better but George is still worried. He is so good with her, Aurora. I have never known a man so caring and patient. I know you are used to all this equality business but it's unusual for a man of my generation to look after someone like that. I can't imagine what would have happened if your father had had to look after me.'

Rory laughed. 'You'd have been living on bacon sarnies and breakfast cereal.'

'I would! And I dread to think what he would have dressed me in. Do you know, when I had you, he had to bring clothes into the hospital for me on the day we took you home. He brought in a mini-skirt and a pair of knee-length boots.'

Rory could just imagine her father standing in front of her mother's wardrobe with a confused expression on his face. 'I doubt much housework would have got done either.'

'Exactly. I always said the pair of you would let the place go to rack and ruin if anything happened to me. No, it's a good job I've got all my faculties.'

There was that damn lump in Rory's throat again. Why was she feeling so emotional lately? Just the thought of her mum not being there…

'I would look after you, Mum.'

'I know you would, love. But let's hope it doesn't come to that. Anyway, my point was that George is a very good husband.'

Sheila was always singing George's praises. He was a good husband. A good man. Rory was pretty sure she had also described him as good-looking the first time she'd seen him. 'Mum? Do you like George?'

'Of course I do. I just told you that.'

Rory sipped her tea and raised an eyebrow. 'No, I mean, do you *like* him?'

Sheila stood up straight. 'Aurora. He is a married man.'

'I know that, but it must be like being alone sometimes, with Olive the way she is.'

Sheila readjusted her cardigan. Then patted the back of her hair. 'I suppose it is, but we aren't alone. We never leave Olive out of the conversation. I would never do that. George would never do that.'

Now it was Rory's turn to take her mum's hand. 'Mum, I wasn't accusing you of anything. George is a nice man. If you feel attracted to him, that's not a crime.'

Sheila pulled her hand away. 'We are just friends, Aurora.'

Rory chose her next words carefully. 'But what if Olive wasn't there? What would happen then? Would you and George still spend time together?'

Sheila blushed. 'I have no idea. I suppose that would change things. I don't want to think about it, Rory.'

After Rory's dad died, Sheila hadn't even moved the newspaper from the arm of his chair for the first three weeks. Rory had hated going home; every time she walked into the lounge and saw that chair, it had been like losing him all over again.

Rory heard the front door open and close. Charlie would appear in the kitchen any minute, probably wanting more food. She needed to cut to the chase. 'She is going to die from this, isn't she?'

Sheila deflated a little. 'Not from her main problem, but... she does seem very frail... I'm not sure...'

'And what will happen to him then?'

Sheila busied herself putting away the tea bags and milk. 'That's not for us to say, is it?'

Rory wasn't suggesting that Sheila steal George from under his poor wife's nose, but they could be friends. 'When she dies, he's going to need someone. Someone who understands. Why not the friend he already has?'

Sheila put her hands to her face and rubbed her eyes. 'Oh, Aurora. I've done all that. I don't want to start caring for someone new. At a certain point you realise you're too old to go down that road again.'

'You're no different from me, Mum. You keep telling me to be open to letting new people into my life, but you're not prepared to even think of it for yourself.'

Rory left her mum wiping the kitchen worktop and went to check on Charlie. It was strange that he hadn't appeared. Had he gone straight upstairs?

CHAPTER THIRTY-THREE

'Where have you looked?'

Rory hadn't wanted to call John for help, but Charlie was more important than her pride. Belle was with her dad tonight and Rory couldn't get hold of her. Sheila wasn't answering her phone either. Who else was there?

'Everywhere I can think of. I've walked the school route, been to the park, called the hospital. No one knows where he is.' She was trying to stay calm, but her heart was beating right out of her chest. When she'd got home from school she had popped up to Charlie's bedroom to ask how his day had gone. That's when she'd seen that all his clothes were missing from his room. What had happened to make him leave?

John was calm and practical as always. 'Have you spoken to his mum? She might know where he is likely to have gone.'

Rory shook her head; her face was pale. 'I don't want to worry her until I have to. That poor woman is in constant pain and extra stress just makes it worse.' She put her hands to her forehead and pulled them down her face. 'She trusted me to look after him, John.'

John put an arm around her shoulder. 'I can understand how you feel, but she would want to know. I think we have to speak to her.'

*

It had already been a tense day. Rory and Penny had agreed a plan to discover whether Rory's suspicions about Nathan were correct, and he'd been surprisingly easy to flatter into action. Mind you, Rory had laid it on pretty thick.

'If I'm going to take on this new role, I'd really appreciate your experience in lesson observation. If we can observe Penny together, it would give me a clear baseline from which to begin.' She'd been particularly proud of her use of the word 'baseline'. Nathan loved a bit of data terminology.

They were sitting in the back of Penny's classroom watching her deliver the beginning of her lesson – a PowerPoint presentation no less – when Penny was struck down with a mysterious stomach pain and had to leave the room immediately.

Rory stood and turned to Nathan. 'You'll have to take over. I'll go and check she's okay.'

He jumped to his feet. 'No! You take over. You're the one coaching her.'

Rory frowned. 'And you're going to follow her into the Ladies' toilet?'

A film of sweat appeared on Nathan's top lip. 'Be quick. Very quick.'

Of course, she wasn't quick. She met Penny in the staff toilet. Stood and chatted with her for about fifteen minutes – allaying her fears that they were both about to get fired – and then took the long route, via the football pitch, back to Penny's classroom.

When she got back, the entire class were in silence, copying from a set of old text books which Nathan must have found at the back of the classroom. Nathan nodded at her curtly as he stalked out of the room and left her to finish up.

Rory followed him into the corridor, keeping an eye on the class through the window in the door. 'Why didn't you carry on with Penny's PowerPoint?'

Nathan turned and looked at her. He was barely keeping his anger under control. 'It's not my subject. I wasn't prepared.'

Rory feigned surprise. 'But it's *only* RE. Surely you could have just…' She trailed off at the look on Nathan's face.

'We will speak about this at a later date. In private.'

She was right. He couldn't teach. Now she just needed to work out how they could use this information to their advantage.

*

When Rory went to see her, Charlie's mum drew a blank about where her son could be. She wanted to check herself out of the hospital straight away and come and look for him, but Rory promised her that they would find him soon and that she would call her every fifteen minutes with an update. She managed to persuade her she needed to stay there in case he turned up at the hospital. Rory prayed that he would.

Rory called Belle for the third time that evening. Why wasn't she picking up her phone? She had tried Scott's house phone and mobile several times, and he wasn't answering either. What were they doing over there? She sent Belle a text with a brief explanation of what had happened and then returned to John outside the hospital, where he was waiting for her in the van.

'Still no luck?' he asked.

She shook her head. 'His mum doesn't know where he might be. Let's go to Harry's house. I'll be able to tell if he's telling me the truth if I see him face to face.'

*

On the way to Harry's house, Rory tried calling her mum again. It was a very long shot that Charlie would have gone there – and Sheila would surely have called her if he had – but at least her mum could go to the house in case he came home.

Sheila also sounded desperate. 'Aurora! Thank goodness. I'm so pleased you've called me back so quickly. I'm just so upset. Sorry for the long message I left on your machine. It probably didn't make any sense.'

It was this conversation that wasn't making any sense. 'Mum, what are you talking about?'

'Olive. She died, Aurora. She's gone.'

Rory's heart, already in her stomach, plummeted further. This was awful, but she really didn't have time to talk about it now. They would be at Harry's house in about three minutes.

'Oh Mum, I'm so sorry. What happened?'

Sheila was crying, so it was quite difficult to make out what she was saying. There was no way Rory could tell her that Charlie was missing too.

It seemed that Olive had died a couple of days before and Sheila had only found out because Barb had told her. Sheila had then called Olive's daughter, Karen, to say how sorry she was. 'She was in their flat so she came up to see me. Olive seemed to be getting better but then she started to get very vague. She didn't even know who they were. It's so terribly sad. It was a stroke in the end. To think you and I were having a conversation about her dying and she was already…'

Two minutes away. 'Mum. You couldn't have known that. Don't feel bad. How is George?'

'I don't know. I haven't seen him. Flo offered to take some meals into him but he's been staying with Karen. What should I do, Rory? He made it quite clear that it wasn't a good idea for me to visit any more. I really want to see him because he must be so upset. But maybe he won't want to see me? I couldn't ask Karen because the poor dear has enough to think about. She promised to let me know about the funeral.' She started to cry again.

Rory wanted nothing more than to go straight to her mum and have a good cry with her. Every bereavement brings back old feelings of the people you've lost before. Sheila wasn't just crying for George and Olive. She was crying for Frank, too.

But right now, Rory needed to find Charlie. 'Mum, just hold on for a bit. I'm in the car. I'll call you back really soon, I promise.'

*

Harry's house was on one of the rougher estates in town. Rory had only been around here a couple of times and seeing it served as a reminder that some kids had it pretty tough. Harry's mum was a nice woman, but there didn't seem to be a whole lot of time in her life for Harry. When they got to the house and knocked, Rory was ready with an apology for turning up unannounced. But it was Harry who opened the door and let them in.

Once Harry had gotten over the shock of opening the door to his English teacher at 8 p.m., he was quite open. 'I haven't seen him since school. He said that you wanted him at home. I was taking the mick about him being a good little boy and going home to do his homework and he stuck two fingers up at me as he went in.'

'You saw him go in the front door? So he went home? To my house?'

'Yeah. He went in and I rode off home. You can ask my mum, I got in at ten past four.'

They hadn't seen any sign of Harry's mum since they arrived, so they couldn't ask her to corroborate his evidence, but he did look like he was telling the truth.

'So where could he have gone after that?' Rory was trying to piece everything together in her head. She hadn't really spoken to Charlie last night because, when she'd gone upstairs to check on him, he'd told her he was tired and was just going to 'crash'. He'd only come back downstairs to grab some food out of the fridge. Mornings were always manic, so she hadn't spoken to him properly this morning either. She could have kicked herself. Offering to go to bed early was clearly a sign of something being up. Idiot.

Harry shrugged. 'I'm really sorry, Miss, but I haven't got a clue.'

When they were back in the van, John and Rory tried to work out where to go next. John tapped the steering wheel. 'Did something happen last night? Did you have an argument about anything?'

'No. I barely saw him. To be honest, I was preoccupied with Mum. We were having a heart to heart. I was asking her what she thinks will happen when Olive dies, and she said…' Rory trailed off and an expression of horror came over her face. 'Oh John, he can't have overheard and thought I was talking about his mum?'

CHAPTER THIRTY-FOUR

The ward was quiet, the lights down low. The only noise was the beep from the monitors and the occasional shuffle or groan from a patient. Rory had got special permission from the ward sister to sit with Charlie's mum long after visiting hours had finished. They had notified the police about Charlie's disappearance, but Rory was clinging to the idea that he would turn up at the hospital eventually. She'd left at note at home to ask him to call her if he went back there, but she knew he was more likely to come here.

She and Charlie's mum had gone through a list of all the places Charlie might be. The park. Harry's house. The flat he shared with his mum. All the places that Rory had already checked. Rory *and John* had already checked.

After her performance over the kitchen, Rory was surprised that John had been so quick to help her. Mind you, that could just be because he liked Charlie so much. It had nothing to do with Rory, really. But he hadn't even been narky with her – he'd been in the same level mood as always. It was possible that he hadn't even noticed how awkward and annoyed she'd been when she'd asked him to leave the other week. Or was it that he hadn't really cared?

Now wasn't the time to think about John Prince, though. Charlie's mum was motionless on her pillow, but her eyes darted around. They settled on Rory. 'I feel so helpless.'

Rory took her hand. 'Me too. I'll go back home and get my car, start driving the local streets. Maybe he's just walking around.'

Charlie's mum shuddered. 'I can't bear the thought of him out this late. I told him that the last time.'

Rory couldn't bear it either. In the past, Charlie had run from foster carers to be with his mum. This time he was running from Rory. What had she done?

She stood and took her coat from the back of her chair. Then Charlie turned the corner into the ward.

When he saw Rory, he stopped short and scowled. 'What are *you* doing here?'

Rory almost cried with relief, but she didn't want to scare him off. 'I've been searching for you. We were worried sick.'

Charlie leaned over the side of his mum's bed to kiss her and she put her arms around him and held him close. 'We were really worried about you this time, love.'

'I've told you that you don't need to worry about me. I can take care of myself. I always have.' Charlie extricated himself from his mum's arms and stood stiffly beside the bed with his back to Rory.

Rory wanted to explain before he took off again. 'Charlie. I think I know why you left, but you got the wrong end of the stick.'

Charlie glanced at her and then turned his eyes towards the floor. 'Nice try, Miss. But I'm not as stupid as you think. I heard what you said about…' He trailed off. Not able to bring himself to say the words in front of his mum.

'Charlie, listen to me.' His mum took his arm and pulled him towards her, then placed a hand on either side of his face, making him face her. 'Rory wasn't talking about me last night. I am not going to die. This bloody disease might render me incapable of always being the mum I want to be, but it is bloody well not going to take me away from you. I promised you. Didn't I? When we left. It was you and me, together. That hasn't changed.'

'I was talking about my mum's friend, Charlie.' Rory's throat was tight but she managed to speak. 'An old lady with Alzheimer's disease, not your mum. Why did you run off like that without saying anything?'

Charlie looked unsure whether to believe them or not. His lip quivered but he stuck his chin out to calm it. 'I heard you talking and your mum saying she wouldn't want to look after someone new.'

'We weren't talking about you,' Rory sighed, exhausted with relief and emotion. 'And we would never say we can't look after you; you have a room at our house whenever you need it.' She looked at Charlie's mum. 'You are both welcome there.'

Charlie's mum smiled at her weakly. 'Thank you. But I'm coming home soon.' She looked at Charlie. 'No more running, eh Charlie? We've done our running for one lifetime. Time to start trusting people again.'

After making him promise that he would come home with her, Rory made herself scarce so that Charlie could have a private chat with his mum. Still not sure she had his trust, she waited outside the ward doors; unless he climbed out of the window, he would have to go past her to leave. While she waited, she tried again to call Belle but couldn't get reception on her mobile on the ward. She smacked the screen and shook it hard. As if that was going to make a difference. Stupid bloody phone.

Ten minutes later, Charlie came out and they headed to the hospital exit to call a cab. As they got nearer to the front door, Rory could hear the ambulance sirens; their wail still cut through her like a rusty knife.

Charlie coughed. 'Look, Miss, I mean, Rory: I'm sorry and everything. About tonight.'

Rory took heart from the fact he was using her name again. She put a hand on his shoulder. 'I'm sorry that our conversation made you feel like that. It was just bad luck. But your mum is right, you have to trust me, Charlie. You have to be able to tell me things. I'm on your side.'

They had reached the reception area and the outside door, but Charlie slowed to a standstill and began to scuff his foot back and forth across the doormat, staring at the ground. When he spoke, his voice was full. 'I know that you are. I am grateful. Honest.'

Rory's eyes filled. It was this place. It always made her emotionally unstable. She didn't trust her voice, so she nodded. What she wanted to do was take Charlie in her arms and squeeze him tightly.

It was a while after visiting time now, so the reception area was empty. The shutters were down on the hospital shop and the chairs stood to attention, awaiting their next round of human misery and hope in the morning. Rory's teacher sense made her realise that Charlie had more to say. He was still staring at his feet as he dragged the toe of his shoe backwards and forwards. He'd need new ones soon. This was new to her, the way boys went through clothes. Belle had been such an easy child to care for. Although she was certainly making up for lost time now.

All Rory wanted to do was get home, speak to Belle on the phone and collapse into bed. But she couldn't pass up this opportunity to listen. 'Do you want to sit down for a minute, Charlie?'

He nodded. They sat in the nearest chairs, those square, wooden, PVC-covered chairs only ever found in hospital waiting rooms. Was it some kind of sensory memory that made Rory's stomach lurch? Surely they didn't still have the same chairs here that they'd had fifteen years ago?

As soon as Charlie's bottom hit the chair, his mouth opened. 'It's just been me and Mum these last two years. Since we… moved here. It's just us, no nan or grandad or aunts or anything.'

Rory needed to tread carefully. 'It's quite a long way for them to come, I suppose. It's Yorkshire you're from, isn't it?'

Charlie shook his head. He still hadn't looked at her. 'No. I mean, yes, we're from Yorkshire but that's not why we haven't seen them. We… couldn't risk it.'

He kept his head down but moved his face sideways so that he was looking at her. His eyes were red, and his face was pale.

'My dad. He wasn't a good man. He wasn't a good man at all. He hurt her. My mum. He hurt her for a long time. And then when I got a bit bigger, he started to threaten to hurt me. That's when we left. When he was at work one day we just packed up and came here.' He gave her a watery smile. 'When we got to the station, mum gave me a map and told me to close my eyes and stick my finger down. She said if it was completely random, he'd have less chance of finding us.'

Rory put her arm across Charlie's shoulders. 'You've both been so brave.'

Charlie swallowed. Then swallowed again. 'But no one knows. No one knows about him. Mum never reported it. I told her to, but she was too scared. So, what happens…' He turned his face back to stare at his shoes. 'What happens if something happens to Mum? Will they call him to come and get me?'

Rory squeezed him tightly. 'Your mum isn't going anywhere Charlie, you heard her in there. But if your mum can't look after you, we'll fight to make sure that you can live with me instead.'

He turned himself into her as she enveloped him tightly and held him as he sobbed, her own tears dripping into his hair.

After Charlie had rubbed his face with the back of his arm – 'I don't look like I've been crying do I?' – they ventured out to find the taxi rank. The outside of the hospital was quiet. Charlie pointed across the road and Rory followed his finger to see John Prince, dozing in the cab of his van. They crossed the empty road and she knocked on his window. 'What are you still doing here?'

John yawned and stretched. 'Couldn't just leave you here, could I?' He winked at Charlie. 'You materialised eventually then, son?'

Charlie blushed and nodded.

Rory put an arm around his shoulders and then smiled at John. 'I think we've got it all ironed out. Now I just need to go home and have a hot bath. I'm annoyed that Scott and Belle haven't called me back, though. They must have got my messages by now.'

As she spoke, her phone finally managed to find a signal and it pinged. A voicemail from her ex-husband, Scott. Finally.

Rory had to press the phone closely to her ear because there was some kind of hippy music playing in the background. 'Sorry, just got your seven messages. We've been practising our hypnobirthing exercises so I had the ringer switched off. Did you get confused? Because you said that you were looking for Belle, but she's not due to stay at ours until the weekend? Call me back and let me know everything is fine.'

Rory looked at the message log. Scott had left that message four hours ago. An icy shiver crept down her spine for the second time that evening. Where the hell was Belle?

CHAPTER THIRTY-FIVE

When you bring your baby home from the hospital, you drive home as if you have eggshells on the roof. As they grow, you stand beneath the climbing frame ready to catch them, hold their hand tightly when you cross a busy road. Before you know it, they get bigger and more independent and you have to trust that you have done your job well.

Rory had been proud of the job she'd done on Belle. She was a sensible girl. Caring, bright and *sensible*. She'd never given Rory cause to worry like this in the past. What had happened to her? That boy.

John wouldn't hear of it when Rory had asked him to drop her back to her car. 'No way. You're in no fit state to drive and I want to see she's all right too.'

They dropped Charlie home with strict instructions to call them if Belle appeared. Then Rory called Fiona's house and got an answer machine. Then she tried Fiona's mobile number which – thank God – she'd saved onto her own mobile when the girls had gone on a school trip last year. Belle had always been forgetting to charge her phone in those days. Not any more. The damn thing was welded to her hand.

Fiona didn't answer. So Rory sent her a text: *Are you with Belle?*

What an idiot. Why hadn't she questioned it when Belle had told her she was staying at Scott's? She never stayed over at her dad's mid-week. It was easy enough for her to get to college from there, but she preferred to go from home where all her stuff was. Idiot. Idiot. Idiot.

John glanced at her. 'Why are you slapping your own head?'

Rory hadn't realised that she was. 'Partly to punish myself. Partly to try and get my brain to work.'

John's strategy was more logical. And slightly less physical. 'What other friends does she have? Who else might know where she is?'

Of course Belle had other friends than Fiona, but right now Rory couldn't think who they were. She hadn't really been speaking about anyone else other than Alfie lately. She'd made some offhand references to 'new friends' that Rory 'wouldn't know' but life had been so busy – the house, school, Charlie – Rory hadn't had a chance to really find out who they were. She thought back to Harry's invisible mother. Maybe Rory was just as bad?

They'd used to talk all the time. Long afternoons shopping or evenings drinking hot chocolate – always with a tiny marshmallow for each year of Belle's life. When had that changed?

Rory was a terrible mother. She was a neglectful mother. This was all her fault.

The phone was ringing. It was Fiona. A very tearful Fiona.

'My mum says I have to call you.'

Thank God. Rory vowed silently never to resent Fiona's smug, irritating, know-it-all mother ever again. 'Is Belle with you? Do you know where she is? What's going on? Is she with that boy?'

John put a hand on her knee. 'Let her speak.'

Fiona was sniffling down the phone. 'I told her not to go. I told her you'd find out. I told her…' She started to cry again.

Another icy chill crept down Rory's spine. What the hell was going on?

There was a muffled noise and some muttering at the other end of the line.

'Hello? Rory? This is Michelle. I understand you're looking for Belle?'

'Yes. Do you know where she is?'

More muffled conversation. 'According to Fiona, she's at Alfie's house. Apparently, his parents are away for the night.' Michelle paused. '*Some* parents don't seem to keep their children on a very tight rein.'

The judgement poured into Rory's ear. Ordinarily, she would have had a sarcastic reply, but this woman was her saviour right now. 'Do you know where he lives?' She would have got down on her knees and begged if she had to.

'Fiona does. I'll put her back on.'

*

The address wasn't far and they were there in a matter of minutes. John's van could move faster than Rory had expected. Maybe she was giving it extra power from the steam coming out of her ears.

'If he has so much as touched her...!'

John continued to be the voice of reason. 'You need to calm down. Wait and see what Belle says. Whatever is going on, you need to play it cool in front of him.'

Rory nearly snapped her neck, her head spun so fast in John's direction. 'Cool? Are you serious?'

John remained calm. 'She's sixteen, Rory. You can't humiliate her in front of her boyfriend.'

Rory liked John. And he was doing her a big favour by driving her around at – she peered at the dashboard – almost midnight. But parenting advice? Really?

'You don't have a clue what it's like to be a parent.'

'No. I don't.' He sounded sad. But she had no time to worry about him.

*

Alfie's house was large and grand. There were even sweeping steps up to the front door. Of course his house was like this. He'd be some arrogant little prince, used to getting his own way. Rory knew the type and she hated them. She hated him.

John had barely parked when Rory threw open the van door and jumped out. Just in time to see the front door to the house open, and a dishevelled-looking Belle come running out. She had her coat and bag clutched in her hand and her clothes looked wrong somehow. Make-up streamed down her face. She almost ran straight into Rory.

'Mum! What are you…' Her face crumpled into tears. 'I'm so sorry, Mum. Everything is awful. I'm so sorry.'

Rory wrapped her arms around Belle tightly. Relief nearly made her legs crumple beneath her. Her baby was safe.

Gently, she held Belle away from her and looked into her face. 'Are you okay? Are you hurt? What were you doing here?'

Belle hung her head. 'Mum, please can you just take me home?'

Rory was torn between comforting her daughter and storming into the house to kill the boy inside. Belle was shivering in the cold evening. John got out and ushered them towards the van. Alfie would have to keep. Belle needed to get home.

John took off his jacket and put it around Belle's shoulders. 'Come on, love. I've got the heater up nice and warm.'

*

However hard Rory tried, Belle didn't want to talk about what had happened. At least, she didn't want to talk about it right now. All she wanted was to have a shower and go to bed.

John had tried to shoot off after taking them home, but Belle had asked him, practically begged him, to come in for a drink first. She was a clever girl. Rory couldn't interrogate Belle whilst John was there. As soon as they'd got in, Belle disappeared upstairs to the shower.

John followed Rory out to the kitchen. She took four mugs and the hot chocolate powder out of the cupboard. John ran his hand along the counter. 'You did a good job on this. Didn't need me after all.'

Rory put a jug of milk into the microwave. She should confess to having recruited Call Me Adrian's kitchen fitters. In her defence, she *had* put most of the remaining units together; it was just the levelling up she hadn't managed. The walls in the kitchen were about as straight as Julian Clary. But she didn't tell John that she had needed help. Just like tonight.

'Only because I had a very good instructor. Shame I can't get someone to show me how to manage a teenage daughter.'

Rory spooned hot chocolate powder into the mugs and filled them up with the hot milk. She counted sixteen marshmallows into Belle's mug. Where had those years gone?

Being a teacher meant that she'd been around teenagers for half her life. The mood swings, the drama, the erratic behaviour. She had fooled herself into believing that she was doing a great job with Belle, but she had just been lucky up until now. Parenting a teenager was very different to teaching one. How had she got it so wrong?

John sipped the hot chocolate she gave him, grimaced at the sweetness, and put it down. 'Don't be so hard on yourself. I don't think anyone finds it easy.'

Rory shrugged. 'Fiona's mother seems to manage it.' She was not looking forward to the condescending looks she'd be getting from that direction in future. Maybe she deserved it.

'Yeah, well. Appearances can be deceptive. I can remember the merry dance I led my own poor mother.'

John had mentioned this on the kitchen day, and Rory was eager for more details. Right now, she wanted to hear about anyone else who wasn't perfect. 'Really?'

John scratched the side of his head. For a moment, he looked like a young boy. 'Yeah. Staying out late, not telling her where I was. The usual stuff. She was soft, my mum. I used to give her a hug and a kiss and she'd forgive me anything.'

Their relationship sounded like Rory's with her dad. Her mum had always complained how she'd wrapped him around her little finger. 'Did you never have contact with your father?'

'No. That's how I got to be so handy, fixing stuff. It was just me and Mum, so if something needed doing, we learned how to do it and we got on with it. She was pretty handy with a screwdriver.'

The way John spoke about his mother made it obvious how much he'd loved her. 'She sounds great. I love a strong woman.'

John picked up the sickly sweet hot chocolate and scrutinised the marshmallows floating on the top. 'Yes. Me too.'

Charlie came skidding into the room to get his hot chocolate. He looked from one mug to the other. 'Why has Belle got more marshmallows than me?'

Rory shook her head. Was this what it was like to have two kids? 'There's a bag of marshmallows in the kitchen. Go and take some more. Then you can take your drink up to bed with you.'

John drank his hot chocolate in three gulps, shivered like he'd just done a tequila slammer, and stood up. 'I'll go. Let you talk to her.' He paused. 'Go easy on her, Rory.'

It was all right for him to say that. He wasn't the one whose heart was breaking at the thought that her daughter had put herself into potential danger and Rory hadn't even known about it. She was grateful that he'd been there, though. She could have found Belle on her own, but she was glad she hadn't had to. 'Thanks for helping me to find her and for bringing us home.'

As they made their way to the hallway, they could see a trail of marshmallows leading upstairs. Charlie must have snuck the bag up to his bedroom.

John pointed to them. 'Just make sure they've both got a bag of marshmallows on them at all times from now on. Next time, we can follow the trail.'

*

Rory knocked softly on Belle's door, but there was no answer. She pushed the door open gently. Belle was in bed, asleep, or doing a very good impression of it. Freshly washed and in her pyjamas, she looked like a little girl again. Rory's little girl. But she wasn't a little girl any more. Rory put the mug of hot chocolate on Belle's bedside table and kissed the top of her head. The talk would have to wait till the morning. All she needed to do now was work out what she was going to say.

'I love you, little girl.' She whispered into Belle's hair.

She crept back to the door.

'I love you too, Mum.' Belle whispered.

CHAPTER THIRTY-SIX

The next day, Rory woke up before her alarm and lay in bed for a while, staring at the ceiling. She was going to have to talk to Belle this morning and she wanted to make sure that she got it right this time.

First, she called her mum back to talk about George and Olive and fill her in on the two search parties. As she'd expected, her mum was cross.

'Why didn't you call me, Aurora?'

'You couldn't have done anything Mum and, anyway, you had enough to worry about with Olive.'

'That's not the point; you should have told me. I could have come with you. The thought of you driving around on your own: panicking. You might have had an accident.'

'I wasn't on my own.' Might as well get it over with. 'John was with me.'

There was a pause at the other end of the line.

'John Prince?'

No. Rory wanted to say. *John McEnroe.* 'Yes. John Prince.'

If it was possible to hear a smile breaking, Rory could have sworn she heard it. 'Oh. Well. I'm glad. Glad that he was there to help you out.'

Rory had been glad, too. It had been such a tough day. She would never admit it to her mother, but maybe Sheila was right about this 'need' versus 'want' idea.

*

When Belle woke up, she was less hesitant than Rory had been in admitting that her mother was right.

'Before you say anything, I know. You were right.'

That wasn't how Rory had expected this conversation to begin. 'Right about what?'

'About men. About trusting them. About them all being after one thing.'

Rory felt winded. She hadn't meant to give Belle that message. She had only wanted to protect her. Prevent her from making a mistake. Ensure that she was ready for a world which might hold some disappointments.

'I never said that, Belle. I never told you not to trust men.'

'Well, you talked about life not being a fairy tale often enough. That there wasn't a perfect prince waiting for me. And you were right.'

This was too much to cope with at 7 a.m. Rory should be in the shower by now, but she couldn't expect Belle to go to school as if nothing had happened.

'Can we start with the events last night?'

Belle scrunched up her eyes and then opened them again. 'Nothing happened last night.'

Rory put her hand up to her head. She was exhausted. 'Belle, please.'

Belle jutted out her chin. And her hip. 'I mean it. Nothing happened. We didn't sleep together.'

Must not let the relief show on her face. Tread carefully. Teenagers are a volatile and unpredictable material. 'But you had planned to?'

Belle's face coloured. 'Maybe. I don't know. We'd talked about it but, I wasn't sure. I do… did… think I loved him. But when it got to it, I just wasn't ready.'

Slowly. Carefully. 'And he didn't try to… force you into anything?'

Belle shook her head. Then stopped. 'He did try to persuade me a little bit. But I just kept saying *not yet*. And then…' Her lip started to quiver.

Rory couldn't bear it when the edges of Belle's mouth turned down like that, but it was her fight to keep her voice from shaking that really churned Rory's insides. 'Then?'

Belle rubbed her nose. 'Then he started to get cross. Well, angry.'

Rory was trying to keep a lid on the anger herself. 'What did he say?'

'He said I was being pathetic. Childish. That we were supposed to be a proper couple and I was just ruining everything.'

Rory had to squeeze her hands together to stop her from banging them down on the table. 'And that's when you left?'

Belle nodded. 'That's when I started to' – she looked down at the floor – 'to put my clothes back on and he… he said… he said…' She started to cry.

Rory put her arms around Belle and pulled her in close. How could her baby girl be dealing with this already? Why hadn't the world moved on by now? 'Whatever he said will have been an absolute lie.'

Belle's face was scrunched up against Rory so her voice was muffled. 'He said that he was going to tell everyone that I had slept with him anyway and they would believe him. And he'd tell them that I was really rubbish and didn't know what I was doing.' She started to sob.

There was no way Rory could leave her and go into work. She would just have to be late for once. Let Nathan Finch call her into his office and complete one of his stupid 'why I was late to work' forms if she had to. Right now, she needed to be here with Belle. She laid her cheek on the top of her daughter's head. 'More hot chocolate?'

A soggy face nodded into Rory's chest.

*

Rory called St Anthony's to let them know she was delayed, packed Charlie off to school and then made hot chocolate for herself and Belle. Extra marshmallows.

'Before we start to talk about this...' Bastard? Demon? Excuse for humanity? '...*boy*, I think I need to apologise to you and clear up a few things.'

Belle nearly choked on a marshmallow. 'Apologise? What for?'

This wasn't going to be easy. 'I think I may have... *overdone* the whole "life is not a fairy tale" thing.'

Belle put her mug down. 'No, Mum. You were right. If I had been a bit more...'

Rory held up a hand. 'You do not need to be a bit more of anything. You are absolutely exactly as you should be. A little naïve, maybe. But no more than any girl of sixteen. I think that I kept on about the fairy tale thing because I didn't want you to be disappointed. To be hurt. To be...'

'Like this?' Belle gave a wry smile. 'Didn't really work out too well, did it, Mum?'

Rory put her hand onto Belle's cheek and stroked her face with her thumb. 'No, my lovely girl, it didn't.'

Belle covered Rory's hand with her own. 'I'll be okay, Mum.'

There was a lump the size of a fist in Rory's throat. 'Of course you will be, sweetheart. You will be absolutely fine. And I want you to know how proud I am that you stood up for what you wanted. Some girls are not that strong. They end up doing something they regret and that can make life complicated.'

'Is that how you feel about Dad?'

Rory was surprised. Where had that come from? 'Your dad? No. Definitely not. I loved your dad. And he loved me. I think. In his own "Scott" kind of way.'

'So why didn't it work out?'

'We were really young, Belle. We probably weren't ready to be parents. And we were both far too young to commit to one person.'

'You mean Dad went with other women. I'm not a baby, Mum. I know what he's like.'

'It wasn't just his fault. When your grandad died – my dad – I was pretty angry for a while.' Pretty angry was an understatement. There had been a large glass table and several items of crockery which hadn't survived that period of her life. Scott was definitely no saint, but he hadn't been the one throwing breakable items around.

'But you regret getting pregnant young and you were worried that I would be an air-head fairy tale princess who would end up doing the same.'

Rory sat back and looked at her daughter. When had she become so wise? Rory's mum was right, Belle wasn't a child any more. Perhaps that was part of the problem. Rory hadn't seen that. She took her time before answering.

'Maybe I did want to protect you. Make sure you were ready for the reality of life. But if you are asking me if I regret getting pregnant, the answer is no, Belle. Definitely not. How could I ever regret something that brought me someone as wonderful as you?'

Belle smiled. It took Rory's breath away. It was like looking at herself, twenty-two years ago. 'I am pretty wonderful, aren't I?'

Rory laughed and hugged her. She was going to be okay.

She held Belle out at arm's length. 'And I want to be clear about something. I don't think all men are the same. Your grandad is a good example. He was a very good man.'

'And John.'

If that fluttering feeling didn't go away soon, Rory was going to the doctor. 'John Prince?'

'Granny says John reminds her of Grandad. And John's a good man too, isn't he?'

Rory smelled a conspiracy. She was going to kill her mother. 'Yes. He has been very good to us.'

'So maybe you could stop telling yourself that life is not a fairy tale, too.'

Rory sighed. How was she going to get out of this one?

Last night had been truly awful. But John had been wonderful. Having someone to share some of the worry, to help to find a solution, to tell her she was doing all right – it had helped more than she could have imagined. When they had talked about his mum she had felt… a closeness? She shook her head. That was just his way. He was a helper. That's what he did. To read more into it was setting herself – and her mother and daughter – up for a disappointment.

'Belle, John isn't interested in me. He is a kind man and I am grateful, but there is nothing between us other than friendship.'

But Belle wasn't to be put off that easily. 'Do you honestly not like him, Mum? Do you promise me?'

Damn her clever daughter. She knew that Rory would not promise something she didn't mean. They had never promised anything to each other that they couldn't keep or that wasn't true. Rory couldn't promise Belle that she didn't have feelings for John. But she couldn't tell her how she did feel, because she didn't really know herself. *Just avoid answering. Change the subject.*

'Look, you don't need to go to college today if you don't want to.'

Belle groaned and leaned back on the sofa. You could always rely on the self-absorbed nature of teenagers if you wanted to distract them. 'What if he's told everyone we slept together? What am I going to do?'

'Actually…' Rory smiled; she had been thinking about this when she'd gone to sleep last night. In between fantasising about which part of Alfie she would like to dismember first. 'I might have an idea about that.'

But before she could explain, her mobile rang. It was Susie.

'Where the hell are you? We got *the call!*'

CHAPTER THIRTY-SEVEN

'The Call' is known to all teachers. The school inspectors are required to phone a school before midday on the day before they arrive. When that call comes, it sends a school into panic. Susie told Rory that the whispers had gone around during Period One: 'We got the call! We got the call!' When Rory arrived at school, the senior leadership team were congregated in the head's office – not to be disturbed. Occasionally, one of them would scuttle out and collect some folders or ask someone a question. Then they would scuttle back into the enclave. No one saw Derek Brown or Nathan Finch until lunchtime. Rory imagined them with a huge floor plan of the school laid out on the conference table, pushing miniature versions of the teaching staff around with a long stick.

When they did emerge, it was to make an announcement in the staffroom at lunchtime. The room was packed. You could smell fear. Derek had readjusted his tie about three times, but Nathan Finch was the picture of calm. He was the one who led the briefing.

'As you may have heard, we had a call this morning from the inspectors to let us know that they will be arriving at 8 a.m. tomorrow. Their visit will last either one or two days. On the first day, they will visit lessons and meet with myself, Mr Brown and the rest of the senior leadership team. The lead inspector would like me to underline to you that you are not to change anything that you were planning to do tomorrow; they would like to see your lessons delivered as planned.' He looked slowly round the room with a face which contradicted that last sentence in its entirety. 'But I would also like you to know that we are keeping the school open until ten o'clock tonight, in case you have any work you would like to get finished before you go home tonight.'

And it wouldn't have taken an MI5 codebreaker to read between the lines and work out what that meant, either.

*

Rory had pupils' books at home which she needed to collect and bring into school. The house was empty when she got there. Charlie and Belle had gone to Sheila's because Rory would be working into the night. A bit of spoiling by Granny would do Belle the world of good, and the two of them could comfort Sheila too. She'd practically adopted Charlie as her grandson.

Rory got a warm fuzz of contentment every time she walked into this hallway. John had done such a good job of it – and the rest of the house. There was no way she could have done all this on her own. The painting she'd done quite a bit of, and she had even given the wallpapering a go. But the plastering, the flooring, and the coving – that would have taken her years. She pushed an image of Sheila nodding knowingly at her from her mind.

Rory had got used to having John around the place. He'd helped her in so many other ways. Looking for Belle last night. Being so great with Charlie. Making her laugh when she was having a bad day.

She put her bag down in the sitting room and walked into the kitchen to get a glass of water. This was fast becoming her favourite room. When no one was there, she liked to lay out ingredients along the counter and pretend she was on a cooking show. The shiny cabinets. The granite worktops. She was so in love with it, she was even managing to keep it clean.

But there was something not quite right in here. She couldn't put her finger on it. The taps weren't on – she'd made that mistake before – and the cooker was off. Her eyes trailed around the room. What was it?

It was the same in the sitting room. A nagging feeling. Was something missing? Maybe it was just the lack of both Belle and Charlie. The house wasn't usually this quiet. Or was she just feeling unsettled by everything at school?

There was a knock at the door.

'Oh. Hi. I wasn't sure you'd be in.' John waved a set of keys as he followed her into the kitchen. Her keys. 'I just came to give you these back.'

Automatically, Rory started to fill the kettle. Strong tea, two sugars. She didn't need to ask. But she was confused about the keys.

'Why are you giving them back to me?'

He put the keys down onto the counter. 'I don't need them any more. You're all done. I came and cleared up this morning.'

John swept out a hand, encompassing the kitchen and the sitting room. That was it. That's what was missing. Tools. Boxes of tiles. Bags of plaster. There was nothing anywhere.

For the last two months, there had been a work in progress somewhere in the house at all times. Whether it had been a half-painted wall, a part-tiled floor or a bigger job like the boxes of kitchen cupboards they had all had to limbo around, something had always been awaiting completion. But not any longer.

Rory felt a fluttering in her chest. 'Are you sure? I mean. *Everything?*'

In her head, Rory visited every room in the house. The three bedrooms were painted. The upstairs bathroom was done. The kitchen. The sitting room. John was right; everything was done.

John smiled. 'Yep. Hard to take it in, isn't it? You finally got rid of me and my mess.'

This wasn't right. She needed time to take this in. To say the right thing. She hadn't even had time to think about what she might want to say. Whatever she had told Belle, Sheila or Susie, there was a small part of her which had… hoped? She had tried to trample it down. To remind herself that she was a customer and John Prince was just doing his job. But somewhere, at the back of her brain, the bottom of her stomach, the edges of her heart, she had wished that maybe, something might happen. She needed time to work this out. She needed to say something before it was too late.

But not now. She had to get back to school. The others were waiting for her. There wasn't a teacher in the land who wouldn't be squirreling away into the early hours the night before a school inspection.

John pulled a crumpled envelope from his back pocket. He didn't meet Rory's eye as he leaned over to slide it onto the kitchen counter. 'This is the embarrassing bit. My invoice. There's no rush at all.'

Rory swallowed. What had she been expecting? That he was going to work for free? Of course he had to give her an invoice for his time. Hadn't she been the one who had been so repeatedly insistent about paying him? *Life is not a fairy tale, Rory.*

'Of course. I'll… I'll get on to it straight away.' She picked up the envelope. Was he saying goodbye? Was this the last time she was going to see him? She needed to say something. Anything. Why was her mind completely blank? *Think, Rory, think!*

He took the envelope out of her hand and slid it back onto the counter, before turning to look at her. 'Don't look at it now.'

This was the moment. The moment when the hero took the princess in his arms and told her that he'd been in love with her all along. The moment when he'd proclaim that he'd been waiting for her all his life. The moment that…

Her mobile rang.

Susie sounded like she'd climbed to the top of the stress tree and couldn't get down. 'Rory! What are you doing? We need you back here. Penny is a mess.'

She had no choice. She couldn't let her friends down. 'I'll be right there.'

John raised his eyebrow. 'Everything all right?'

How many times had Rory seen that expression on his face lately? His 'ready to help' expression. She was really going to miss it. 'It's school. We've got an inspection tomorrow. I'm sorry. I have to go.'

John hopped off his stool. 'Of course. I'll… er… I'll see you around.'

Rory had no idea where she would see him 'around'. Apart from their initial meeting at B&Q and his random rescue the night she lost Belle's shoe, she had only ever met him at the house. And now the house was finished. When would she see him again? *Come on, brain.*

'I can drop the cheque round to you later in the week?'

John tapped the envelope on the kitchen counter. 'You can just pay it online. All the details are in there.'

Damn technology. 'Oh. Right. I'll do that, then.'

They stood there. Neither saying anything. Rory remembered telephone conversations with boyfriends in her younger days: '*You hang up. No, you hang up.*'

John took a deep breath…

Rory's phone rang again. Belle.

'Mum, I know you're busy, but can you drop Charlie's phone to Gran's because he's left it at home?'

John was getting his coat on.

Rory ended the call as quickly as she could. 'Yes. Got to go. Bye.'

John started to walk towards the door. 'I can see you're in a rush. I'll catch up with you later. I can see myself out.'

Unless she threw herself in his path, there was nothing that Rory could do to stop him. Had he been about to say something, or was she just inventing that in her own mind because she wanted him to? Damn Susie's panic call. Damn Charlie's forgotten phone and damn, damn, double damn the bloody school inspectors.

The front door banged closed. The same front door John had fixed for her all those weeks ago.

Rory shook her head to clear her mind and ran up the stairs to find Charlie's phone. Right now, she needed to forget about John and get herself into school.

CHAPTER THIRTY-EIGHT

Before she went to her classroom, Rory stuck her head in the door of Penny's.

'Thank goodness you're here,' Penny breathed out. 'I'm panicking about being observed tomorrow.'

Rory walked in and gave her a quick hug. 'Don't be. You are very unlikely to get a visit. Think of us poor English teachers; they're always all over us.'

Penny smiled. 'Looks like it's too late to give Nathan Finch a taste of his own medicine.'

'What do you mean?' Rory sat down behind one of the pupil desks and placed her splayed palms in front of her. 'Getting him to teach a lesson in front of the inspectors would be *perfect*.'

Penny's hand went to her neck. 'Surely not, Rory. We can't do that to him.'

Rory winked and then ran her eye over Penny. 'How's your stomach been today?'

Before Penny could answer, they were interrupted by a knock on the – open – door to Penny's classroom. 'Ah, there you are, Ms Wilson. Can I have a word?'

*

At Nathan's request, Rory followed him to his office, leaving her open-mouthed colleague behind her. How much had he heard? He motioned for her to precede him into his office and then closed the door firmly behind them. There was no offer of coffee.

Now seated behind his desk, he looked distinctly uncomfortable. 'I'm sure I don't need to tell you how important this inspection is to the school.'

He meant to *him*, but it was important for all of them. 'Of course.'

He tapped his fingers on the surface of the desk. 'And if anything should go... badly. It would not be good for any of us.'

This was ridiculous. If he had overheard her, Rory wanted to know. 'What are you trying to say?'

Nathan almost crumpled before her eyes. 'I heard what you were saying to Penny just now, Rory. And I know what's happened. I know you've rumbled me. And I wanted to say, it's fine. You win.'

This was a side to Nathan that she'd never seen before. A vulnerable one. 'Sorry. What do you...'

He held up a hand to stop her. 'I confess. I'm not a natural teacher. I'm better at the bigger picture. As soon as I could get out of the classroom into a management role, I did.'

But this didn't explain how he had got those management roles if he couldn't perform in the classroom. 'You still taught lessons before that. You must be able to teach?'

'The school I was in had a very prescriptive curriculum. We were given lesson plans to follow. Textbooks to work through.' He sighed. 'Rory, what you have, this teaching ability – not everyone has it. That's why we need strict rules that everyone can follow. Consistency makes for better teachers.'

He still didn't get it. 'That's just not true, Nathan. I agree that some teachers have an extra something. But anyone can improve. And making people teach like robots is not the way to do it.'

Nathan loosened his tie. He looked like it was choking him. 'My remit here is to improve teaching and learning. I can put new procedures and processes into place – I'm good at that. But the touchy, feely stuff... The coaching and cajoling of staff into doing things the right way...' He looked intently at Rory. 'That's where I was hoping you would come in. That's why I was in your classroom so frequently. I was checking you out.'

Rory choked back a laugh at his expression. Nathan flushed. 'Sorry, bad choice of words.'

'No, I'm sorry. It's just that 10-G thought you were checking me out for a different reason.' The atmosphere in here needed lightening. It felt like Nathan might cry. It was unsettling.

But Nathan didn't laugh. 'No, it wasn't you I…' He suddenly remembered himself. 'I mean, my interest in you was purely professional. I needed to work out if you could bring the skills that I was lacking. I was supposed to put together an action plan for improving teaching. But now the inspectors are coming in the morning and I haven't had time to…' His elbows thumped onto the desk and he planted his face into his palms. Was he trembling? 'I'm going to lose my job. No one will take me on this late in the year. Who'll take on a failed deputy head who only lasted two months?'

Rory shuffled in her seat. 'They're not going to fire you.'

A haunted face came out of Nathan's hands. 'How do you know? The governors were very specific. I gave them a whole raft of ideas about improving teaching practice and now…' He offered her his open hands. 'And now the inspectors are coming and I'm not ready. Nothing is ready.'

Rory may not have known how to install a kitchen or plumb in a bathroom, but when it came to teaching, she was confident. It was time for her to be the helper. On her terms. 'Well, it can be. I will help you. I can write a coaching programme for tomorrow. But only if I have your word that you will be more flexible on some of these new ideas. If you want teachers to be professional, you need to treat them like professionals. Let them decide what works with each of their classes.'

Nathan groaned and sat back in his chair. 'I don't know, Rory. How will I measure their progress?'

He *still* didn't get it. 'Not everything can be measured in numbers on spreadsheets. Sometimes you've got to use your own eyes and ears.'

Nathan ran his fingers through his hair, so that it was standing up in tufts. He looked like a young boy. 'But the inspectors are coming in the morning.'

Rory nodded and stood. 'If I have your word on this, I can spend tonight writing up a coaching programme which will knock their inspectorial socks off.'

Nathan stared at her for at least fifteen seconds. Then he nodded.

*

As the next day dawned, the school was unnaturally quiet. The caretakers had cleaned the place with a toothbrush; there wasn't a crisp packet or a piece of chewing gum to be found. Teachers stood in their doorways, ready to hook in any badly-behaved corridor clowns. The worst-offending pupils were being traded like the last day of the transfer window.

Rory had worked at school until 10 p.m. and then at home until the early hours, producing a coaching plan which would impress the most data-driven, hard-nosed school inspector. She had also knocked up a day of lesson plans which would secure her reputation as the model teacher to provide that coaching.

Annoyingly, no one came to observe any of these amazing lessons. However, an inspector *did* spend twenty minutes in Penny's lesson, which he later proclaimed to be 'innovative and exemplary'. Rory would enjoy reminding Nathan Finch of that for the rest of the year.

*

Susie and Penny came back to Rory's for a glass of wine. 'Do you think we did it?' Penny was still glowing from her positive feedback.

Susie chinked her glass against Penny's. 'Stop worrying. It was a good inspection. We'll get a decent rating and the parents and governors will be happy. Plus, the inspectors won't be back again for another couple of years at least.'

'I'm so grateful to you for your support these last few weeks. Both of you.' Penny's eyes filled. 'You are good friends.'

'Get away with you.' Rory nudged her. 'You're the one who is *innovative* and *exemplary*.'

Belle wandered into the sitting room. 'You lot seem happy.'

'We managed to turn the bad guy into a possible good guy for once.' Rory patted the seat beside her. 'Come and celebrate with us.'

Susie sat up straight. 'You're absolutely right. We need to celebrate. Properly, I mean. Not just with this Aldi bubbly. Why don't you have a party?'

Rory realised that Susie was looking at her. 'A party? Here? No.' Rory shook her head. 'Not my thing.'

But it *was* Belle's thing. 'That's a great idea! Oh Mum, please let us have a party. We need to have a housewarming anyway, to show everyone our new home now it's finished.'

Finished? Rory thought of the unopened envelope on the worktop. Her stomach flipped. It would be nice to show the place off, but she wasn't in the mood for a houseful.

'No, Belle, I don't think…'

But Belle and Susie were already making a list.

'I can bring Jim. Might get him off my sofa and out. Don't worry, I won't bring his awful mate.' Susie winked at Rory. 'Unless you need a date?'

Dragon Man? Did she really have to have him in her house? What other undesirables would she have to have trudging across her nice new floors? 'No thanks. I think I'll pass.'

'Can I bring someone?' Penny was hesitant.

Susie looked at her as if she was crazy. 'Of course! We want to meet this man of yours at long last.'

Penny smiled. 'And can I bring Colin? The librarian? He never gets invited to work parties.'

Susie winked at her. 'Is it because he's too much of a party animal? Rory has just painted these walls.'

Penny slapped her with the back of her hand. 'He's a very nice man. Clever and funny.'

'You lost Susie at clever.' Rory pretended to speak behind her hand. 'That's never been at the top of her list. What are his arms like?'

'I think she was talking to you, Rory; I have a boyfriend, remember?' Susie flicked the bottom of her hair with her hand and poked her tongue out at Rory.

'We'll invite John Prince, of course.' Belle was still making a list. 'We can't not invite him when he's the one who's done most of the work.'

Her over-exaggerated look of innocence made it clear that she hadn't given up on setting up Rory with John. On the one hand, Rory was pleased that Belle's unpleasant experience with The Nobhead – as Alfie was now unaffectionately known – hadn't robbed of her romantic notions entirely. On the other, she wished she'd direct them elsewhere. It was almost painful. She swallowed. 'He might not want to come, Belle.'

Susie frowned. 'Of course he will. Why wouldn't he? Has something happened between the two of you?'

'No. It's just that the work has finished now and he's probably busy starting a new job. I mean, it's not like we were friends or anything.'

The three of them studied her. Susie spoke first. 'Of course. Everyone's builder saves them from choking on an apple.'

'Or rescues them from their upstairs window.' Penny nodded slowly.

'Or helps to find their missing children.' Belle tapped the tip of her nose with the pen.

They managed to hold their faces straight for another ten seconds, then burst out laughing.

'Ha, ha. You are all so very funny.' Rory shook her head at them. Let them enjoy their joke. It was fine for them to assume that John liked her but, if he did, why had he never said anything? Why had he just left yesterday without even a backwards look?

Belle was still scribbling away on her notepad. 'What about Granny? She has to come. Maybe she might want to bring a friend.'

On that one, Rory was sure. Right now, after losing Olive, and with George not speaking to her, Sheila would be the one person less keen on coming to a party than Rory was.

CHAPTER THIRTY-NINE

Olive's funeral was on the following Monday.

Rory had offered to go with Sheila, although the chances of being allowed time off school to attend the funeral of her mother's neighbour were slim, but Sheila had told her that she would be fine with Barb and the others.

Rory didn't like to think about her mum having to go to that crematorium – the same one they'd used for Frank over fifteen years ago. She could still close her eyes and remember the neutral walls, neutral carpet, neutral chairs. The room had been full – her dad had had lots of friends – but she had only been aware of her mum beside her and the coffin in front of her. She shuddered.

On Wednesday, she popped in to see Sheila after school to see how she was. As always, they went straight to the kitchen so that Sheila could make tea.

Rory leaned against the door frame. There wasn't enough room for them both in Sheila's tiny kitchen. Particularly when she was in 'keep yourself busy' mode. 'So, the funeral went well?'

The ancient kettle was still getting itself in the mood for boiling, so Sheila busied herself with a dishcloth, wiping the sparkling surfaces. 'It was a lovely service. There were lots of people there and everyone sang.'

Rory smiled. Her mum had been so pleased with the strong voices at Dad's funeral. It was funny, the small things which brought you comfort. 'Did you speak to George?'

Sheila didn't look up, but shook her head and kept wiping. 'There were so many people there who wanted to talk to him, I just didn't get the chance. You know what funerals are like; long-lost relatives come out of the woodwork.'

Rory remembered. There had been people at her dad's funeral that she had never seen before and was not likely to again. They'd known their way around a free bar, though.

Sheila found a stubborn mark on the hob on which to focus her attention. 'The worst thing is, I know how much George must be suffering. If anyone knows what those first few weeks are like, it's me. After the funeral, people drift away. They "leave you to your grief" like it's an important visitor and you don't want to be disturbed. But you do. Because when you are alone, that's when the gaping hole opens and you don't know how you will ever get out.'

She stopped wiping and leaned forwards. Her shoulders started to shake.

'Oh, Mum.' Rory put her arms around Sheila as she cried. They stayed that way for a few minutes until the kettle clicked off.

*

Once they had their tea, they decamped to the small sitting room. It was always tidy and clean in here, but today everything had been polished to within an inch of its life. The rug looked as if every strand had been individually brushed and then the whole thing straightened using a set square.

Rory pushed a couple of the copious scatter cushions out of the way and sat down. 'So, is George staying with his daughter?'

Sheila picked up the displaced cushions and smoothed them down before putting them on another chair. 'He was, but he was at home yesterday. He came into the lounge in the evening when we were playing cards to thank everyone for the flowers that we sent to the funeral. Everyone got up to speak to him, even Sid, and he shook their hands and kissed the ladies on the cheek.'

Rory put her mug down on a coaster. These had also had the right-angle treatment. 'That's good. Did you get a chance to talk to him?'

Sheila picked up one of the cushions again and started to fiddle with the fringing. 'I couldn't. I couldn't move and he didn't even look at me. It must have been obvious to everyone and now they must definitely think that something happened between us.'

Rory reached over and took the cushion out of her mum's hand before she shredded it. 'I'm sure they don't, Mum. They probably didn't even notice.' And even if they had noticed, why would they think something was going on between them? George had lost his wife and Sheila had lost her friend – of course they would be quiet around each other. Almost everyone in Seymour House had been widowed: Olive's death must be bringing back memories for many of them.

In the absence of the cushion, Sheila had started to twist the edge of the throw in her fingers. 'But why are we being like this with each other? Absolutely *nothing* has happened between us. The only time we have even *touched* each other was that night we danced to the old music and Olive was there with us. It was her idea that we danced.'

Rory reached over and put her hand on Sheila's. 'I know, Mum. You've got nothing to feel guilty about; either of you. Like you said, these early days are so hard. He probably doesn't even realise that you haven't spoken. It's a bit of a bubble, isn't it?'

Sheila sighed. 'I know. You're right.' She patted Rory's hand and reached for her tea. 'Well, Karen is still calling me, so that is a comfort.'

Rory felt for Karen. You were never ready to lose a parent. 'How is she coping with it all?'

'She is really struggling, poor love. Now her mum has gone, she has been hit with a flood of old memories about her. Memories from a long time ago. How she was before her illness took hold.

She thinks it's because she hadn't allowed herself to think all those things whilst her mum was alive because it was too painful. She just focused on the mum who was in front of her. The mum who was vague and forgetful. Not the mum who had taught her to read and bake and kept every certificate she'd ever been awarded.'

Rory gulped her tea to push down the large lump in her throat. Grief was so unpredictable. It was the unguarded moments that got you. You weren't even thinking about the person and then something – a song, a scent – came into your consciousness and then – bam! It was like being winded. 'I know how she feels.'

'Of course you do. For us, it was a complete shock. For Karen, it's complicated. With Olive's Alzheimer's, she hasn't only just lost her mum; she's been losing her in pieces for the last eight years.'

The two of them sat there for a few moments, just sipping their tea. Lost in their own memories, recent and long ago.

Sheila took a deep breath and put down her mug. 'That's enough of that for now. How's my Belle?'

Rory had been surprised how quickly Belle had moved on from Alfie. If anything, she seemed relieved rather than upset by the end of their relationship. 'She's great, actually. She seems to have completely bounced back. Did she tell you about the speech?'

Sheila nodded and smiled for the first time. 'She brought it round to show me. Did you help her to write it?

Belle had to give a speech on a subject of her choice as practise for her extended project and Rory had suggested she use it to get her revenge on The Nobhead. 'I might have given her the idea.'

Sheila chuckled. 'It was very funny. So clever, how she compared consent to what you'd do if you were offered an ice cream. What was it? Oh yes! *"You can't tell someone that they have to eat the ice cream just because at some point it's going to melt."* Such a clever girl.'

Rory grinned. 'Her teacher was really pleased with her. They spent the rest of the lesson discussing the #MeToo movement. Even Alfie's best mate wasn't speaking to him by the end of it.'

She'd been so proud of Belle that day. She and Fiona had come home from college full of it. Giggling and laughing, like the old days. It had been lovely to see. Good friends were so important.

'Has she told you about this damn party she's organising?'

'Yes, I've heard all about it. She wants me to come, but I'll have to see, love. I'm a bit up and down at the moment.'

'Of course, see how you feel on the day. I wish I didn't have to go.'

Sheila patted her hand. 'Don't be like that. You've done a lot of work on that house; it'll be nice to show it off.'

'Belle is inviting everyone she can think of. Goodness knows how we're going to fit them all in.'

'I assume John Prince is coming? It would be unfair not to invite him when he's done so much of it.'

Rory knew full well that Belle had already spoken to Sheila about this. 'I think she's invited him, but we haven't had his reply.' They hadn't heard from him at all. Rory had paid his bill online – which had seemed almost ridiculously cheap – and had received an automatic email response from his accounting software thanking her for her payment. Nothing since.

Sheila's voice was gentle when she asked, 'Maybe he would be more likely to come if you invited him yourself?'

This had occurred to Rory, but Belle had already invited him. If she also contacted him, wouldn't that seem a little keen? A little desperate?

'I don't know, Mum. There was a time when I hoped there could be something there. But neither of us ever made a move. It's a bit late now.'

'Couldn't you just talk to him? What have you got to lose?'

Rory didn't want to think about this. 'I could say the same thing to you about George.'

Sheila looked at her intently for a few moments, then picked up their empty mugs. 'Come on, let's have another tea.'

Rory followed her out to the kitchen. 'Speaking of friends, how's Barb?'

After clicking the kettle switch, Sheila crossed her arms and raised an eyebrow. 'Very well indeed, actually. She wasn't as close to Olive as I was, but it shook her up; a death can do funny things to a person. She decided to move in with her bloke and left Seymour House two days later. She'd been waiting to see if he would ask her, but after Olive she just came out with it and asked him. I have to say I am glad. What is the point of waiting around for things to happen? You have to make them happen.'

Rory put her head on her mum's shoulder. Sometimes a death made you want to hide yourself away and never come out again. Sometimes it had the opposite effect: it made you want to live. 'Maybe you and I need to take a little bit of that advice, Mum.'

Sheila put her arm around Rory's shoulders and kissed the top of head. 'Do you know what, my lovely girl? I think you might be right.'

CHAPTER FORTY

Tiny fairy lights were strewn between the lights in the lounge. Music played from Belle's iPod – a strange mix which they had somehow agreed upon. Apart from birthday parties for Belle involving ice cream and jelly, this was the first party Rory had thrown in years. Maybe that's why she didn't know what to do with herself.

Sheila had been the first to arrive. 'Barb couldn't come, and I feel a little bit weird being at a party so soon after Olive. I might only stay a little while, but I didn't want to let Belle down.' She unbuttoned her cardigan and then started to button it up again.

Rory was hoping most of the guests would only stay a short while. 'That's fine, Mum. Go whenever you need to. Is everything okay?'

Sheila stopped buttoning, or unbuttoning, and looked at Rory. 'I spoke to George.'

'Well done.' Rory was impressed that Sheila had started to 'make things happen' to patch things up with George, but it did mean that Rory would have to uphold her side of the bargain and talk to John. If he turned up.

Sheila motioned for Rory to go back through to the sitting room and she followed her. 'I can't take the credit. I was fully prepared to knock on his door and talk to him, but he got there first.'

Rory turned around to look at her mother. Belle and Charlie were still upstairs, so it was just the two of them and Justin Bieber on the iPod. 'Oh?'

Sheila settled herself on the sofa. 'I was watching TV last night and there was a knock on my door. When I lived at the house I would have been worried about who might be the other side, but I don't have to worry about that now.'

'Mum. Cut to the chase.'

Sheila pulled a face. 'Well, I opened the door and there he was. He said that he was sorry to turn up so late – it was only 9 p.m. – but he had been meaning to come all day and had finally plucked up the courage.' She held up her hand to stop Rory rushing her again. 'I let him in and made him a cup of tea. We slipped into our old way of chatting, although it was a little different to be in my home rather than his.' She paused for a moment and looked thoughtful. 'Actually, he has probably only been to my flat a couple of times before and he never stayed for longer than a few moments because he always had to get back to Olive.'

'Mother, please!'

'Let me tell it my way, Aurora. No one else is here yet, anyway.'

Rory sighed. She had a point.

'We talked about the funeral and how good everyone has been, calling him and checking he's okay. I told him how much I'm missing Olive. One of the songs we listened to together came on the radio a few days ago and it really knocked me for six.'

Rory felt bad for rushing her mum.

'Then I talked about your dad and how I felt in the early days after we lost him. George thought he'd be prepared when Olive went, because he'd been losing her piece by piece for a long time. But he wasn't. He wasn't prepared at all. Well, you never are, are you?'

'No, Mum. You never are. I'm glad he's got you to talk to about it.'

Sheila smiled. 'We did talk and talk. It was almost eleven o'clock. I told him that he'd have to sneak out or we'd both be in trouble with Flo. We laughed about that and I told him what Barb had done when she moved out. She bought some slinky underwear for Flo and wrapped it up for her with a label saying, *"Some new knickers to replace the ones you always get into a twist"* or something like that. Flo almost blew a gasket. When she unwrapped them in the communal lounge in front of everyone, I think Sid nearly blew a gasket too.'

Rory grinned. 'I'm glad you can have a laugh. I'm sure that will do George good.' She stood up with the intention of going to the kitchen to rearrange the glasses again. Guests would start arriving soon.

But Sheila hadn't finished. 'That's when he said it. The thing that he'd come to say. The reason he has not been able to talk to me since Olive died. The reason he has been feeling guilty.'

Rory turned to look at her. 'Which was?'

Sheila fiddled with the locket around her neck. 'That he has feelings for me. More than just being a friend. And he feels terrible about it.'

The doorbell rang. Promising she would be straight back, Rory left Sheila in the sitting room to go and welcome her guests. Charlie was halfway down the stairs, but when he saw the group of teachers from St Anthony's, he pulled a face and disappeared back in the direction of his bedroom.

By the time Rory returned to her mum, Sheila was in the kitchen and had put the kettle on. Nothing said 'banging party' more than an old lady drinking tea.

Sheila smoothed her hair down. Then her dress. Then her hair again. 'We're just friends, though, me and George. There's nothing going on.'

'Really?' This was the perfect opportunity for revenge. 'Nothing going on? I've seen the way you look when you talk about him, young lady.'

Sheila held up a warning finger. 'Don't you dare.'

Rory was enjoying this. 'Maybe I should go and see him. Check what his intentions are?'

Sheila's face dropped. 'Oh, Rory. Please don't. Not even as a joke. It's too soon to be…'

'Mum. Really? Of course, I won't. Although it's for his sake, not yours. You deserve it after the ribbing you've given me these last couple of months.'

'Yes, where is John?' Sheila looked around. 'Is he coming later?' She screwed up her eyes. 'You *did* invite him, Aurora? We had a deal.'

Rory had needed to drink a large glass of wine to summon up the courage to call John and ask him if he'd got the party invite Belle had sent. But she had got his voicemail and chickened out. Sheila didn't need to know that.

'He's probably working, Mum. You know what he's like when he's on a job.' When he was working at Rory's he'd always been popping around. He was probably always like that. Rory hadn't been anything special. Just another single mother to help.

'I know what he was like when he was on *this* job.' Sheila looked keenly at Rory. 'Must be strange not having him around the place.'

Strange didn't come close. Charlie was still in and out all the time and Belle had stayed closer to home since The Nobhead incident. But it wasn't the same as having adult company. For someone who didn't speak much, it was surprising how big a space John left behind.

But Rory wasn't about to admit that. 'Oh, look. Susie's here. I'll speak to you later, Mum. Say goodbye before you go.'

Susie's face was strained. Dragon Man was with her. But he couldn't have looked less *with* her if he tried. Susie held up two bottles of Prosecco. 'Shall I put these in the kitchen?'

Rory followed her out. 'Everything okay?'

Susie shook her head. 'I think you were right about him. He's been downright horrible this evening. Almost scary. I nearly told him not to come but then he turned on the charm, said he's just had a bad day at work.'

Rory was pleased that Susie was beginning to see the light, but not that Jim was making her unhappy. 'What does he do when he's at work?'

Susie screwed up her face. 'I'm not really sure. He doesn't have a regular job. It all seems pretty casual.'

That was weird. They'd been dating for a few weeks now. Wasn't that one of the first questions you asked someone? 'What do you mean? Surely it's come up?'

'Sort of. I know he works on building sites. But I don't think he's like your John. Because, when I asked him to fix my shelf, he didn't have any tools for it.'

There was no point taking her up on the 'your John'.

Dragon Man appeared in the doorway. 'So, this is where you've disappeared to. Talking about me, are you?' His smile was almost a leer. What the hell had Susie ever seen in him?

Rory didn't want to hang around and play nicely, especially if Susie was going to give him the heave-ho. 'I'm just going to check on Belle.'

Belle was in the middle of her group of friends, telling them a story. Her hands were all over the place as she explained something in great detail. She looked radiant. Rory's heart squeezed. She was going to be just fine.

As soon as the story was finished, Rory put her hands on Belle's shoulders. 'I'm really sorry to interrupt, but do you know where Charlie is?'

'Sorry, Mum, I meant to tell you. He's gone to Harry's house. He was bored anyway and then when he realised there were going to be other teachers here, he couldn't face it. I think his exact words were: "It'll be like a detention but with rubbish music."'

Rory could see his point. She wasn't enjoying the party much herself. Maybe she should go to Harry's, too. At least there would be biscuits.

'Also, Mum, do you mind if I go back and stay at Fiona's tonight? The other girls are staying there and it'll be fun to have a sleepover.' Belle grinned at her girlfriends. 'It'll be like the old days.'

Rory did mind. There was a loneliness she hadn't been able to shrug off all evening. If Charlie was at Harry's and Belle was at Fiona's, the house would be empty. Her mum was planning on leaving soon and she didn't want to ask her to stay – she had a sneaky suspicion she might be planning on seeing George. But she couldn't stop Belle having fun. 'Of course not. I'm glad you want to get out again. You enjoy yourself.'

Maybe Susie would stay with her tonight. Rory turned to look for her. Dragon Man was in the corner of the sitting room, standing alone, slowly drinking beer from a can. He was staring straight at her. But, where was Susie?

Rory excused herself from Belle's friends, who were already cackling about some other boy in their year. She found Susie as soon as she walked into the kitchen, talking to a tall slim man. He turned as Rory came in. Was that… Colin the librarian?

CHAPTER FORTY-ONE

At house parties, kitchens are always busy places. Usually, it's where the drinks are kept, so people are in and out getting refills. But it is also a sanctuary for those who aren't quite full-on party people and who would rather lean against a cupboard and have a chat. The kind of place Rory would expect to find Colin the librarian. Not the place she would expect to find Susie. And definitely not the place she would expect to find the two of them together. Looking cosy.

'Rory. Thanks so much for inviting me.' Colin reached out and shook her hand. Bless him.

'Thank you for coming. I see Susie is looking after you?' Rory raised an inquisitive eyebrow in Susie's direction and got a wink in reply. Had someone slipped something into her drink?

Just then, Penny appeared with her boyfriend. Who bore a strong resemblance to Derek Brown. Their headteacher.

Derek smiled at Rory. 'Thanks for inviting me, Rory. I hope it's not too much of a shock?' He put an arm around Penny's shoulders and she giggled.

Had the world gone mad?

'Can I borrow you two ladies for a moment? I just want to ask you about something.' Rory practically pushed the two of them out into the hall. They had to go via the sitting room, where she tried to avoid the laser beam stare coming from the corner of the room. It was a good job that the tattoo on Jim's back couldn't breathe actual fire, or they would all be rather crispy by now.

As soon as they got to the hallway, Rory spun them both around by the shoulder. 'What's going on?'

'What do you mean?' Penny looked confused. 'Belle let us in ages ago, but you were busy talking so we've been mingling.'

Rory rolled her eyes. 'Derek Brown? When were you going to say something?'

Penny giggled again. 'Oh, that. Well, we had to keep it quiet at the beginning because it wasn't worth making waves if it didn't go anywhere. And then it was quite fun to keep it a secret, and then the inspectors were coming, and then you were going to have a party…'

Rory held up her hand. Drunk Penny talked way too much. 'And you.' She turned to Susie. 'Are you flirting with Colin?'

'I am!' Susie looked so proud of herself. She had clearly been flirting with most of one of the bottles of Prosecco she'd brought, too. 'You and Pen keep telling me I go for the wrong sort, so I've decided to take a walk on the nice-side for a change. And, actually, he is a very funny man!'

Rory was pleased that Susie was broadening her horizons partner-wise, but she was a little bit concerned about the smouldering pile of machismo currently in her lounge. Unless Colin was hiding a black belt in Ju-Jitsu under his library card, she didn't fancy his chances. 'But what about Drag… er… Jim?'

Susie brushed her off with the confidence of the very drunk. 'I've told him it's over. He's probably gone home.'

Penny was nodding along with her. Her flushed face suggested she had also been knocking back a few glasses of bubbly.

Rory slowed her voice down to the speed she used with newly arrived foreign students. 'But he's still here.'

'Is he?' Susie didn't look remotely concerned. 'I'm sure he'll go when he's finished his drink.'

'Oh, no.' Rory took her by the elbow and propelled her towards the sitting room door. 'You go in there and get rid of him. It's one man at a time under this roof, young lady.'

Susie zigzagged off in the direction of Dragon Man, muttering about it being, 'No men under this roof and that's the problem.'

First her mother and George, now Susie. And Rory had thought it was Belle who needed watching. She turned to Penny. 'I'm not being unreasonable, am I?'

Penny shook her head and then stopped when it almost made her fall over. She stuck out a teacher finger. 'Not at all. Your house; your rules.' She smiled. 'What do you think about me and Derek?'

'I'm really pleased for you. Honestly. He's a nice man.'

Penny beamed. 'He is.' She leaned in and whispered. 'And a little bird told me that the governors are very pleased with the coaching work you've started in the last couple of weeks. Apparently, they've been muttering about a possible place on the leadership team.'

Penny was looking at Rory expectantly.

'Leadership team? Me? No. I don't think so.'

'Why not? You've been at the school for years. You're a fantastic teacher. You'd be great. Plus,' Penny swept a hand around the room, 'this place is all done now, and Belle is almost all grown up. You'll have more time on your hands.'

Why did people keep reminding her of that?

'Anyway,' Penny had changed tack again. 'How do you think I should break it to Susie that Colin is gay?'

*

If Rory hadn't noticed Penny arrive, then there was a chance she had missed other people arriving. Or, more accurately, the one other person she was hoping would come. But John wasn't anywhere to be seen. It was still early though, and he would have gone home to shower if he'd been at work today. She shouldn't give up hope. Not yet.

Rory's sitting room was full of people. They were chatting, laughing and drinking; everyone was having a good time. Even the music that Belle had chosen had gone down well. The people in front of her were her friends; she liked them all. Loved some of them. So why did she feel so lonely?

The doorbell rang.

It was Nathan.

'Hi. I hope you meant it when you invited me?'

Rory smiled and took the bottle of wine he held out to her. 'I did. Come through to the kitchen.'

Either Susie's gaydar had started working or Penny had warned her that she might not be Colin's type, but her eyes lit up when she saw Nathan Finch. So did his.

'We like him now, right?' Susie whispered in Rory's ear. 'So, it's okay to…'

'Yes, it's okay.' Rory had a feeling that Nathan might be just the right mix of good and bad for Susie. And, in a short-sleeved casual shirt, he had surprisingly nice arms.

'I'm going to go home, love. I've rung for a cab.'

Rory turned to see Sheila with her coat on. 'Really? So soon?'

'I'm a bit tired, and this is for you youngsters really.' Sheila wasn't looking at Rory properly and she was fiddling with the collar of her good coat.

Rory narrowed her eyes. 'You're going to see George, aren't you?'

Sheila looked up. She'd been rumbled. 'He just sent a message to say that I was welcome to pop in for a cup of tea on my way home. I think he's feeling lonely. You don't mind, do you?'

Rory didn't want to say that she was feeling lonely too. 'No, of course not, Mum. You go. Maybe you and George could come over for dinner next week?'

Sheila looked horrified. 'We're not a couple, Rory. We're just friends and he has just lost his wife.'

From the look on her mother's face, you would have thought Rory was inviting them to an orgy. 'I wasn't suggesting anything, Mum. You've met Karen; maybe George might like to meet your daughter?'

Sheila blushed. 'I'm sorry, love. I'm just a bit worried about people's reaction to us being friends.'

'Well, the people who love you both know how much George loved Olive and how much you both miss her. Everyone else can take a running jump.'

Sheila held Rory's shoulders and kissed her on the cheek. 'He hasn't come yet, has he?'

Rory bit her lip and shook her head.

Sheila nodded decisively and then kissed her again. 'He will.'

*

The rest of the party went well. Fiona's mum came to pick up the girls and Rory managed to smile sweetly in her condescending presence. Even when Michelle repeated three times that she would ensure she kept a close eye on Belle *at all times*. Charlie rang to ask if he could stay at Harry's and, even though Rory didn't like it, he had already had the okay from his mum, so what could she say?

But John never came.

Susie and Nathan were the last to leave. Susie was hanging on his every word and he had a twinkle in his eye that hadn't come from a pile of lesson plans. As she left, Susie whispered drunkenly into Rory's ear. 'Just call him!'

Now that everyone had gone, the house was quiet. Very quiet. There were glasses everywhere and small bowls with the remnants of peanuts and crisps. She should be a grown up and clear things away, but she hadn't the energy. Instead, she slumped down onto the sofa and curled her legs up under her.

Everyone had complimented her on the house. Despite not wanting the party, she'd had a warm feeling watching her friends' surprise at what had been achieved in such a short time. It did look amazing; better than she had ever imagined it. The soft creams in this sitting room, the shiny white cupboards in the kitchen, the beautifully restored floor in the hall: there was nothing that needed doing. Even the bedrooms had been plastered and given a lick of paint before her mother's penchant for soft furnishings had turned them into something from an interiors magazine. Rory had wanted a beautiful home for herself and Belle and that was what she had. It was perfect.

So, why didn't she feel happy?

Everyone else in her life was doing just fine. Sheila might be grieving for Olive, but her friendship with George would bring them both comfort. Belle had bounced back from the episode with The Nobhead, and Penny was happy with Derek Brown. Even Susie was on a possible path to contentment with the new improved version of Nathan Finch. Charlie's mum was much better after her operation and he would probably be moving back in with her soon – which was surely a positive thing.

But Rory was sitting here alone.

It was all right for Susie to tell her to call John, but he hadn't turned up to the party. That was answer enough. Rory didn't need him to spell it out. Parties might not be his thing, they weren't really hers, but it would have been the perfect opportunity for him to call her – and he hadn't. He hadn't called since the day he'd left his invoice.

Rory swung her legs down from the couch. A good night's sleep would get rid of this melancholy. She turned out the light in the sitting room and walked through to the hall, stopping for a look in the large oval ornate mirror hanging beside the front door. The mirror was the only thing left from the house as she'd seen it on the first day, and it looked beautiful now that the mirror glass had been replaced. It would have been cheaper to buy a whole new mirror, but she'd had a rare moment of sentimentality and decided it belonged here as much as they did. She spoke to her reflection. 'Life is not a fairy tale, Aurora.'

She had her foot on the bottom stair when the doorbell rang.

CHAPTER FORTY-TWO

Hope bubbled in Rory's chest. *Stay calm. It might not be him.*

But it was. And he had Charlie with him.

Charlie darted straight past her. 'I need the toilet!'

Rory turned back to John. She hadn't seen him in over a week and he looked different. Was it his hair? Or just the fact he wasn't wearing paint-spattered jeans?

He shrugged. 'I was on the way round here and I saw him. He's had a bit of a falling out with Harry. Nothing serious, I don't think. But he'd left the house and was on his way back here. I picked him up.'

'Thanks. I'll have to talk to him about being out so late.'

John looked sheepish. 'I actually picked him up about two hours ago. He hadn't eaten, so I took him for a pizza. Look, Rory, I'm sorry I didn't come to the party. I'm just not very good at parties.'

She tried to look as if she didn't care. 'It's fine, there were tons of people here. It's been *crazy!*' She sounded like a teenager from an American sitcom. Seriously.

'Yeah, I guessed that.' He ran his fingers through his hair. 'That's kind of why I didn't come. Lots of people. Loud music. Not really my thing.'

Rory sighed and dropped the act. Who was she trying to kid? 'It's not really my thing either, to be honest. It was Belle's idea and I didn't have the heart – or strength – to say no.'

He had his hands in his hair again. 'I did want to talk to you, though.'

The butterflies in Rory's stomach cocked an ear. Or antenna? 'Yes?'

He took a deep breath, 'The thing is…'

The downstairs toilet door opened. It was Dragon Man. What the heck was he doing still here? He leered at her. 'There you are.'

John stood up straight. His face turned to stone. 'I'm so sorry. I didn't realise… Sorry. Look… Say goodbye to Charlie for me.'

Rory shook herself. 'What? No… I mean… I didn't…' How was Dragon Man still in the house? Hadn't he left before Susie? Why wasn't he saying anything? And why was he looking at John like that? John was backing out of the door. *Don't go. Please don't go.*

'Anyway, take care of yourself.'

And John was gone.

She turned back to Jim. 'I didn't realise you were still here. Susie left.' Keep stating the obvious, Rory.

'I know. It's you I wanted to talk to.' He smiled lazily. Rory felt a cold trickle down her spine. She needed to get him out of here as quickly as possible. Was it too late to go after John and get him back? He'd seemed like he was about to say something to her. She tried not to get her hopes up about what that might be.

She most definitely wasn't in the mood to rehash the details of someone else's break-up. 'I'm pretty tired, to be honest. It's been a long night. You really need to talk to Susie – I don't know what happened between you both. You should really speak to her.'

Dragon Man laughed. It wasn't a pleasant sound. 'I don't need to talk to Susie.' He took a step closer. 'I need to talk to you.'

That was when she started to feel frightened.

Rory wasn't weak and feeble. She'd done some self-defence. Could she remember it? The hallway started to feel very small. Especially when Dragon Man took a step towards her. 'Shall we?' He indicated the door to the sitting room.

Could she have this wrong? Was it the wine making her anxious? No, she felt sober right now. *Just stay calm.*

In the sitting room, she started to pick up the glasses and bottles that crowded every available surface. Act normal. Be firm. 'I really need to clear up from the party. Can we talk another time?'

Dragon Man sat down on her sofa and leaned back arrogantly, watching her. 'No. I've been trying to talk to you for a while. I'm not waiting any more.'

Rory squeezed an empty beer bottle. If he came at her, she could hit him around the head with that. Who the hell did he think he was, coming into her house – remaining in her house – and telling her what to do? 'Look, I'm not interested in you. Nothing personal, you're just not my type. So, if that is what you...'

She trailed off at the sound of his mocking laughter. 'Interested in you?' He sneered. 'Is that what you think?' He started to shake his head from side to side. 'Uptight teachers are not really my type either, I'm afraid.' He stopped laughing and stared at her. The kind of stare that made you feel vulnerable. Exposed. In danger.

'Then what do you want?'

Dragon Man leaned forward. His legs were far apart and he rested his elbows on either knee. His hands hung loosely between his legs and she could see how grazed and bruised his knuckles looked. According to Susie, he was some kind of builder. But John's hands weren't like that. Those were fighting scars.

'We'll get onto that in a minute. Firstly, I want to ask you a few things.' He was clearly enjoying controlling this situation. She'd known men like this before: everything on their terms.

She put the glass bottle down firmly – keeping it within reach – and folded her arms. 'Hurry up, then.'

He leaned back into the sofa again. 'How long have you been teaching?'

What was this? 'How long have I been... Why the hell do you want to know that? Fifteen years.'

'Always at the same school?'

This was ridiculous. But what else could she do but answer him? 'Yes.'

Dragon Man was nodding slowly. 'So, you haven't had a great deal of experience.'

Now he was attacking her professional pride. 'I wouldn't say that. I've done quite a lot of different roles. I've been a head of year and a strategy manager and…' She trailed off. Why was she trying to defend herself to this awful man? 'I like it there.'

'Send you on lots of these training courses, did they? Paid for out of taxpayers' money?'

'Of course I've been on training courses.'

'And in these training courses' – he was speaking slowly, almost as if he was enjoying every syllable – 'did they tell you that you needed to keep a professional distance from the kids you teach? And their parents?'

Maybe he was unhinged. Susie mentioned he'd been acting strangely. Rory glanced at the beer bottle.

He didn't wait for her to reply. He was leaning forward again. 'And did they tell you that your job was to teach the kids in front of you? Give them an education. You know. What you are actually paid to do.'

If he had such an issue with school and teachers, why had he dated Susie for so long? 'That is what I do.'

His lip curled, exposing a chipped front tooth. 'Oh no, *Ms* Wilson, you do *so* much more than that. I've been asking around about you. How the kids all love you. How you take a special interest in the pupils who are a bit thick. I could probably have done with a teacher like you when I was at school.'

Thank God she hadn't got any pupils like him. 'I do the best I can for all my pupils.'

He laughed. 'But some of your pupils are *special*, aren't they? Some of them get a lot of *extra* help. Some people might say that you go above and beyond. Others would say that you actually overstep the mark.' There was a hardness in his voice.

Rory heard movement upstairs. Charlie! She had forgotten that he was home. If he came downstairs, maybe that would be enough to make this vile man leave. Although she didn't really want him to see Dragon Man either. It was bad enough that John had got the wrong idea. John! She wished he was here right now. She didn't *need* him to sort this out for her, but she would very much have liked it. She would like to have him here full stop. Why hadn't she been braver and just asked him to stay?

Enough was enough. It was time to stop playing whatever game this man was trying to play and get him out of here. Right now.

She pulled herself taller. 'I have no idea what this is all about or what you are trying to achieve, but you need to leave now. If you don't, I'm going to call the police.'

He laughed again without any trace of humour. 'The police? Yeah, and they'd probably come out for someone like you, wouldn't they? You lot all stick together.' He grimaced. 'Don't worry, I'll go. But first I'm going to get what I came for.'

The blood drained from Rory's face and her feet felt like lead. Dragon Man looked very strong and she was a long way from the door.

But he wasn't talking about her. 'You have something that belongs to me.'

At that moment, Charlie appeared at the door to the sitting room. Rory turned to speak to him, but he wasn't looking at her. He was staring at Dragon Man. And the colour had completely disappeared from his face. He looked at Rory and his eyes were wide and frightened. Then he looked back at Dragon Man.

'What are you doing here? How did you find me?'

Dragon Man's face broke into a sinister grin.

'Hello, Charlie. Aren't you happy to see your old dad?'

CHAPTER FORTY-THREE

Dad?

Rory looked from Jim to Charlie and back again. Of course; that's why he had seemed familiar to her. He looked just like Charlie. His son.

Charlie hadn't taken his eyes from his father. His face was pale, and Rory had never seen so much fear in his eyes. She needed to do something.

'Look, Dra... er, Jim. It's late and your visit is a bit of a sho... surprise for Charlie. Why don't you leave your number and he can call you if he wants to see you?'

Jim slid his attention to Rory. 'And why don't you mind your own business? You've done quite enough already. Couldn't wait to move the boy into your house, eh? That's why it took me so long to find him. I came down here weeks ago, but he was never in the same place long enough for me to grab him. Foster carers, the hospital, his mother's place. Then he disappeared again. I even had to pick up some labouring work and find somewhere to stay. Mind you,' he winked, 'your mate has been pretty useful in that department lately.'

However unpleasant he was, Rory needed to stay calm. 'I have no idea what you are talking about, but this is my home. I do not want you here. You need to leave.'

Jim ignored her and carried on. 'She was pretty useful, actually, your Susie. When I bumped into her at the pub and found out she was a teacher, I realised that would be better route to Charlie – find out his school. Took a while to get the information out of her, though. Never mind, I'm here now.' He turned to Charlie. 'So, boy. Haven't you got anything to say to your old dad? Have you missed me?'

Charlie was frozen. But he moved his head slowly from side to side.

Jim laughed nastily. 'Well, I guess I asked for that. I wasn't the best dad around, was I? Still, I had a lot to worry about in those days. The little spell away gave me some time to think. Plus I met some interesting people. People that know how to find someone you're looking for.'

Away? Where had he been? Did he mean prison?

'But I'm out now. Fresh start and all that. Get your stuff and let's go. I've got a mate we can bunk with tonight and we'll get on the road back home tomorrow.'

Charlie didn't move.

The air was heavy. There was no way Rory was going to let Charlie go anywhere, and she knew from his expression he didn't want to go either. She moved closer to him. She just needed to get him back upstairs and then get this horrible man to leave. *Come on, Rory. Think!*

'Charlie, why don't you go back to your room? Let me speak to your dad about this.'

Charlie turned his attention to her. His eyes were haunted. She wanted to put her arms around him and carry him upstairs herself.

He shook his head. 'I'm not leaving you alone with him.'

Jim gave a hollow laugh. 'Don't worry, son. I'm not going to touch her.' He stretched his arms upwards, then put them behind his head and leaned back. 'I'm a changed man.'

Who the hell did he think he was? This was Rory's sofa, Rory's home, and she wanted him out of it right now. Her resolution to remain calm was wavering.

'You can't just waltz in here and whisk Charlie away. I am responsible for him and he's not going anywhere tonight. Just leave your contact details; I will speak to Charlie's mum and…'

'Charlie's *mum*?' He almost spat the words at her. 'Don't speak to me about that slag.'

Charlie snapped out of his stare. His fists clenched and unclenched at his sides. 'Don't you dare speak about my mum like that!'

Jim sneered as he laughed. 'Oh, we're quite the big man now, are we? Planning on landing one on me, are you?'

'Just go. I don't want you here. Just leave us alone.' Charlie's voice was trembling. Was that fear or anger, or both? Rory put a hand on his shoulder.

'Turned you against me, has she? Was it your mother or this one?' Jim nodded at Rory. 'Load of women around. No good for a boy. You don't want to listen to them. Come on, get your stuff.' He stood up.

Charlie took a deep breath. 'I don't need to listen to anyone. I remember.'

'Yeah, well. Like I said, I'm different now.' Jim stepped towards Charlie and stretched out a hand. 'Come on. I've had enough of this. Let's go. You can get your stuff later.'

Charlie was trembling all over now. Rory needed to do something. There was no way he was going anywhere with this man. But how to get Jim out of the house?

She stepped in front of Charlie and turned to face him. She held both of his arms and looked at him intently. She had to make him understand.

'Maybe you should go with your dad.' Charlie's eyebrows hit the ceiling. 'Go upstairs now and get some things for tonight. Don't forget your new toiletries I bought you.' Now his eyebrows knit in confusion. 'They are in my bedroom. On the side table. And while you're there, could you bring me my mobile phone which is there too?'

Finally, he looked as if he understood. 'Okay. I'll be right back.' He looked from his father to Rory. She gave him a short nod. *I'll be fine.*

Dragon Man took another step towards her as Charlie disappeared upstairs. 'Do you think I'm stupid? You're going to get the boy to do your dirty work and call the police?'

Rory moved so that she was between Dragon Man and the sitting room door. If he was going after Charlie, he would have to get through her first. And she wasn't going to roll over easily.

'Even if you get out the house with him, I am going to call the police straight away. How far will you get?'

'You forget an important fact. I'm the boy's father. I can take him anywhere I like.'

'And you forget that he is old enough to decide which parent he wants to live with. If you take him against his will, the courts will class that as abduction, which I'm assuming won't go down well with your probation officer?' Rory had just made the whole of that up. Including the possibility that he was still on probation. But she was banking on the fact that Dragon Man would not know that she didn't know what she was talking about. From the look on his face, she was right.

She had never seen a domestic abuser up close. Never experienced a man who would treat a woman the way this man had treated Charlie's mum. She got a brief insight into how it might feel to be on the receiving end of someone like him as she watched the range of emotions that played across his face now. Incomprehension. Anger. Pure hatred. 'You little bitch. I'm going to…'

The back door opened and John strode in. 'Move away from her, right now.'

Dragon Man held his hands up and moved a step backwards. 'What the hell are you doing back?'

'None of your business.' John walked up behind Rory and stood beside her. 'I think I heard you being asked to leave.'

Dragon Man pulled his shoulders backwards. He looked like a cockerel. Or maybe just the first four letters. 'I'm leaving. As soon as my son comes down, I'll be on my way.'

The stairs creaked as Charlie came down them. He came into the sitting room and stood on the other side of Rory. 'I'm not leaving.'

Dragon Man didn't even look at Charlie. He addressed himself to John. He put his fist into his other hand and started to rub it. Rory had thought people only did that in B movies. 'You're a bloke. What the hell are you doing, siding with her? I'm the boy's father.'

'And the boy – Charlie – says he doesn't want to come with you.'

Dragon Man lunged for Charlie and grabbed his arm. 'Who's going to stop me?'

In the next few seconds, everything seemed to go in slow motion. Charlie wrestled his arm free. John pushed Jim backwards so that he was standing on the rug. Rory dropped to the floor, grabbed the rug and pulled it hard. Dragon Man fell backwards, hitting his head on the coffee table. He was out cold.

For a moment, they were silent. Then John took Rory's hand and pulled her up so that she could put her arms around a trembling Charlie. He put a hand on her back. 'I knew you wouldn't get around to putting anti-slip tape under that rug.'

*

After the police and ambulance had been and gone and Charlie was in bed, Rory and John sat together in the kitchen. Rory had debated whether to call Charlie's mum at the hospital, but they'd decided it was better to go and see her in the morning so that she could see for herself that Charlie was safe. Rory had guessed rightly that Dragon Man was on probation – for GBH, the policeman had told her, off the record – and would be returning to detention at Her Majesty's pleasure after being checked out at the local hospital. She'd warned the police officers escorting Jim to A&E that Charlie's mum was also in that hospital, and they'd recommended Rory persuade her to get an injunction out against him before he left prison next time.

It was a relief to be sitting on her sofa next to John with a glass of wine in her hand.

'How did you get here so quickly?' Charlie had already told Rory that he had called John rather than the police. But that didn't explain how he had arrived almost as soon as Charlie had ended the call. His van was fast, but it wasn't a time machine.

'I was still parked outside when I got Charlie's call. I was angry with myself and I also didn't like the look of that man. It didn't seem like you were happy to have him there. So I hung around to see if he left.'

Rory took another gulp of wine. 'Well, I'm very glad you did. That was scary.'

John shrugged. 'Men like that are dangerous. And unpredictable.'

They sat for a while longer in companionable silence. Then Rory realised what he'd said.

'Why were you angry with yourself?'

John put his wine down on the table and shifted himself around in his chair. 'I was angry with myself because, yet again, I'd left without speaking to you.'

The butterflies were back. *Don't get your hopes up again, Rory.* 'Speaking to me? What about?'

John rubbed his nose. Then he rubbed his cheek with his knuckles. Then he cleared his throat. 'About your boiler. I know you think you don't need a new one but…' He shuffled closer and looked her in the eye. 'Are you really going to make me say it?'

Rory would have spoken, except the butterflies had somehow fluttered their way into her throat. She didn't move. Or breathe.

John looked down and used his thumb to rub an imaginary smudge from the back of his other hand. He took a deep breath. 'I know that you aren't looking to meet anyone, Rory. That you like it being just you and Belle. I was happy on my own, too, but… every time I see you… there is something…'

She hadn't imagined it. That feeling. And here it was again. 'I know. I feel it too.' She put her hand over his to stop him fidgeting. He looked up. Those eyes.

They sat in silence. Someone needed to make a move. It was her turn. 'So, you saved me from the Dragon Man?'

A smile began to flicker at the corners of John's mouth. 'Technically, you were the one who pulled the rug out and sent him flying.'

'So, I saved John Prince from the dragon?' Rory smiled as John leaned in to kiss her. 'I like the sound of that happy ending.'

A LETTER FROM EMMA

I want to say a huge thank you for choosing to read *Happily Never After*. If you enjoyed it, and want to be kept up-to-date with my future releases, just sign up at the following link. Your email address will never be shared and you can unsubscribe at any time.

www.bookouture.com/emma-robinson

I loved writing about Rory and the women in her life. Having been blessed with a wonderful mum and lots of great girlfriends, I value the importance of female relationships. The 'fairy tale' idea came about when my own daughter developed an obsession with princesses and I was forced to ad-lib her bedtime stories to make the female characters less pathetic.

Please help me to tell others about *Happily Never After* by writing a quick review. This is only my second book, so I'd love to hear what you thought of it and which parts you enjoyed. Reviews make a huge difference in helping other people find my book and I am grateful for every single one.

I also love hearing from my readers. Come and join the fun on my Facebook page, Motherhood for Slackers. They are a friendly bunch and we even let boys in. You can also find me on Twitter or on my website. Chatting to you will make a lovely change from persuading teenagers that Shakespeare isn't boring, listening to my son talk about Minecraft or being bossed around by my six-year-old daughter.

Stay in touch!

Emma

motherhoodforslackers

@emmarobinsonuk

www.motherhoodforslackers.com

ACKNOWLEDGEMENTS

I'd like to say another hugely grateful thank you to my brilliant publisher Isobel Akenhead for her enthusiasm, support and fantastic editing skills. Big kisses go to Kim Nash for her wonderful PR and round-the-clock emotional support (thanks Twinny!) and to the whole Bookouture family for their help, humour and online hijinks.

Thanks again to my fantastic beta readers Kate Machon, Elizabeth Symonds, Martin Ross and Marie Dentan who read and annotated my first draft within a week of asking. You have helped above and beyond.

Grateful thanks to all my friends and family who have shared my books online and encouraged/pressured/threatened their friends into ordering them. I hope I haven't let you down.

Thank you to Stephen Bonnington for answering my questions about Crohn's disease and to the friends who shared their dating horror stories. Thanks also to the residents of my nan's sheltered accommodation thirty years ago who unwittingly provided my sister and I with so much suppressed laughter it physically hurt.

To my wonderful mum for all the Nana sleepovers, Nana pasta and Nana soup (and for unofficial PR activity to random strangers on the bus). And to the inventor of Minecraft for keeping my two favourite small people occupied during final edits.

To my husband Dan who listens to my writing highs and woes and treats those two imposters just the same. Thank you for everything you do.

And lastly, an immense thank you to everyone who read *The Undercover Mother* and took the time to write a review. Putting your first novel out there is terrifying and your lovely words were like unexpected Prosecco after a long week at work. I hope you like this one too.

xxx

Lightning Source UK Ltd.
Milton Keynes UK
UKHW02f0705251018
331179UK00011B/209/P